Finding Peace

Finding Peace

A Novel
Andrew Barriger

iUniverse, Inc.
New York Lincoln Shanghai

Finding Peace
A Novel

All Rights Reserved © 2003 by Andrew Barriger

No part of this book may be reproduced or transmitted in any form or by any means, graphic, electronic, or mechanical, including photocopying, recording, taping, or by any information storage retrieval system, without the written permission of the publisher.

iUniverse, Inc.

For information address:
iUniverse
2021 Pine Lake Road, Suite 100
Lincoln, NE 68512
www.iuniverse.com

ISBN: 0-595-28823-5 (Pbk)
ISBN: 0-595-65881-4 (Cloth)

Printed in the United States of America

Dedication

This book is dedicated
to everyone who feels different
and goes on anyway.

Table of Contents

Summer's End 1
The Winds of Change 13
Trick or Treat 26
The Next Generation 39
Psycho Pie-Baking Week 51
Fallout 63
The Night Before the Day Before 76
The Day Before 89
Thanksgiving Day 101
The Aftermath 114
A Better Choice 127
Disaster 138
The Meaning of Family 150
Easter 163
Prom 176
Endings 188
Epilogue 199
Afterword 203

Acknowledgment

The reception of my first book, *Finding Faith*, has been incredible. I want to thank each and every person who has taken the time to write to me and share the experiences in his or her life. Ultimately, communication is what it's all about.

As for *Finding Peace*, I have to thank Ron Donaghe and Betty Conley, whose tireless friendship, dedication, and support made this book possible (also, they did a little editing), and Cathy H., for offering advice on how to "keep it real."

Lastly, I thank my family for their continued love and support.

All the best,

Andrew Barriger
June 2003

Chapter One

Summer's End

Sunlight streamed through the window blinds, alternately warming and blinding the two sleeping beauties. With a sigh and a groan, one moved his legs to disentangle himself from the other. Feeling the pressure of the other body, he opened his eyes against the bright rays.

"Felix, it's too warm for you to sleep on my legs," he muttered.

At the other end of the bed, the gray striped tabby stared back at him, green eyes heavy, showing not the slightest hint of compassion. At least he was lighter than Molly.

Taylor wiped the sleep from his eyes, slow as ever to wake up. As expected, the other side of the bed was already empty, Tom having left for work hours before. He had adjusted to Taylor's very light sleep habits early on, opting to use the bathroom down the hall to get ready, rather than wake his sleeping friend.

Throwing his legs over the side, Taylor rose, making a quick circuit of the room to pick up the clothes discarded from the night before. Tom was usually very tidy, but had worked into a routine of leaving the room "as-is" as part of his attempt to not wake Taylor. Taylor saw a little clean up as a small price to pay to not have to wake up at three or four in the morning when Tom went off to work in the bakery.

Replacing Tom as the town baker had proven unusually difficult. Though they had been together for two years, Tom had wound up working most of the last two summers. Taylor took it in stride, though secretly wanting to have Tom only to himself. To make matters worse, Taylor frequently got pulled into helping out while the young girl who generally worked there was away. She had returned several weeks before, getting him off the hook.

Now if only they could find a permanent baker who was not his...what? Taylor still struggled to define what he should call Tom. Boyfriend? Too weak. Husband? Then who was the wife? It sure as hell was *not* Taylor. Lover? Trendy, but a little gothic. His Tom, that's what he was. And he was Tom's Taylor. Maybe that's all they really needed. That and to not have his Tom be the baker—it would be nice to wake up and have his Tom in the bed next to him.

Room restored, he grabbed a fresh set of clothes for himself and made his way to the bathroom. Minutes later, he emerged refreshed and ready to face the day. Of course, it was only Sunday, so there wasn't a whole lot to do.

On the bed, Felix had long since gone back to sleep and paid Taylor little attention. Tom thought it was a good idea for them to have a pet and had returned home one day with Felix. According to the animal shelter, he was about a year old, left there when his owner had to move away to a place that didn't allow animals. He had been declawed, so he was a house cat, and his calm temperament was something Tom thought Taylor would appreciate. For his part, Taylor didn't really care whether they had a pet or not—he had grown up around animals, but his last pet, a golden retriever named Molly, had chosen to continue to live with his best friend and next door neighbor, Gen. Felix, of course, followed Tom everywhere, but spent just enough time with Taylor for them to keep a grudging friendship—usually with each keeping one eye on the other.

Taylor made his way downstairs, pausing at the front door to pick up a pair of sandals. It was late September, which would normally have meant it would be quite warm, but they had been experiencing an unusual cold spell. He had opted for a long sleeve T-shirt and shorts to ward off the morning chill.

He bounded down the back stairs, not bothering to lock the door behind him. It was a sensation that he still found unusual, having grown up in an area where it was considered a good idea to keep things secured.

"Mornin', Mr. Mayor," a voice called from over the fence to the left.

"Hi, Mr. Olsen," Taylor replied automatically. He passed the end of the fence and found the older man watering his golden yellow rose bushes that separated their two yards. "How did you know it was me?"

"Already been to the bakery," he gruffed, stooped over, letting the spray dance over the leaves. "He's the only one there this morning. Couldn't get your tuckus out of bed?"

"Emmy's supposed to be working," Taylor defended. Though they had never discussed it, he knew Mr. Olsen found his and Tom's relationship to be amusing. "I didn't know."

Mr. Olsen squinted up at Taylor, his wrinkled face and large nose reminding Taylor of the late Walter Matthau. His thinning sweater matched the roses. "You're darned lucky he's so nice to you. I'd have hauled your butt down there myself, but he wouldn't let me."

"I'll go right away, sir," Taylor said, feeling like he was twelve all over again.

"Well? Don't let the door hit you in the butt."

"Yes, sir," Taylor said, then headed down the street. He could have driven, but it was only four blocks, so it seemed kind of a waste. He felt a shot of water hit his legs as he walked out of the driveway and heard Olsen mutter something about missing. It occurred to Taylor the only thing he missed was hitting him higher.

As he passed Gen's house, he noticed the front door was still closed. Usually she was an early riser, but having Miguel living with her had calmed her down a bit. Taylor smiled as he remembered the day they'd moved him in. It was actually Tom who made the first comment, but as usual, Gen let him get away with it. As long as he kept slipping her chocolate croissants, he could get away with murder.

Farther down the street, several other people were already up and in their yards, watering plants, washing cars and the like. All greeted him by his appointed title. He'd tried for the first year to convince people to just call him Taylor, but it hardly ever took. Ever since the Fall Dance two years before, when he'd let the elected Mayor appoint him to take over when he retired, he'd been "Mr. Mayor."

The election was due to take place in November, but to his knowledge, no one was planning to run against him. In fact, he'd not been planning to run, but Rob Grady had nominated him and Tom had promptly seconded the nomination. Taylor didn't really mind—after all, the position was almost purely a figurehead and took very little of his time away from his real job, that of owning a small law firm with his longtime friend and business partner, Pete Madson.

As he neared the downtown area, he saw a familiar face coming toward him and waved. The woman waved back, shuffling a bag as she held her daughter's hand in the other.

"Hey, Taylor, how are you?"

"I'm good, Mel. Hi, Amanda," he greeted.

"Hi, Mayor Connolly," the little girl responded politely. He could hardly believe she was the same little girl he'd first met on a very similar walk a little over two years ago.

"How come you're not working?" Mel asked.

Taylor rolled his eyes. "I didn't know he was flying solo this morning," he defended. "I just found out when I came out and Mr. Olsen went after me."

"Well, good thing you're heading in. It's pretty busy."

"He's not mad, is he?"

Mel laughed. "Tom? Does he ever get mad?"

Taylor sighed. "Not usually," he admitted. "Okay, I'd better keep going."

"Have a good one," Mel said. Amanda said goodbye and they continued on their way back home.

Taylor rounded the corner and saw that there were indeed several cars parked outside the bakery. He jogged across the street at its center, confident that he wouldn't get a ticket for J-walking at this time of the morning. Also, he was the Mayor.

As he approached Downey's Bakery, he was surprised to see a golden yellow dog tied to the lamppost outside as though she was meant to be there.

"Molly?" he said.

She glanced one eye in his direction, but otherwise paid him no attention, having long since decided she was Gen's dog. If Molly was outside…

"Connolly!" he heard from inside the antique screen door.

He pulled open the door and found a line of people patiently waiting at the counter. Tom turned, surprised to see his…Taylor…come through the door. Gen stood to one side, leaning against one of the display cases, a croissant in her hand.

"Hi," Tom greeted, a bright smile—his Taylor Smile—crossing his face. "I was just calling you. We've had kind of a rush and I'm still baking. Would you mind helping out?" His voice was calm and soft, just like it always was when he talked to Taylor.

"I got the word as I walked up," Taylor explained, rounding the counter and grabbing an apron. "I see Gen has been helping," he observed, shooting a look at his friend as he stopped to wash his hands.

"I would have if you didn't get yourself down here," she said between bites.

With Taylor to help him, Tom made short work of the crowd and in minutes everyone had their orders and the bakery was once again quiet. Gen had taken a seat at one of the small tables, neatly licking the last of the chocolate from her fingers. As the last of the patrons left, Tom turned and gave Taylor a quick kiss.

"Thanks, hon," he said. "I thought I could do it without Emmy, but it got too crazy."

"You should have just said something. You know I'd have come in."

"Better to keep you rested for later," Tom answered with a devilish wink. He disappeared into the back to pull more of the fresh baked goods and replenish the cases.

"Where is Emmy?" Gen asked, walking behind the cases and washing her own hands. She donned an apron and started loading trays of bagels into baskets.

"College entrance tests," Tom said.

"Hard to believe it's already that time," Taylor said. He gently bagged loaves of bread that had been allowed to cool.

"Time flies when you're having fun," Gen said. She adeptly dropped the tray of bagels into the basket like a pro. Taylor remembered the first time he had met Tom, watching him execute the maneuver. He was very impressed at the time. Two years later, they had all done their stint at helping out in the bakery and it was almost second nature.

"It'll be strange to have her gone next year," Tom admitted.

"I just hope Mrs. Caillan remembers to staff *her* job," Taylor said.

"Actually…" Tom began.

Taylor stopped, turning to look at him. "What?"

Tom looked at his shoes, moving his feet a bit nervously. Taylor walked over, leaning down to make eye contact. "Tommy?"

"Mrs. Caillan offered to sell us the bakery," Tom said, wincing in anticipation of Taylor's response, his gray eyes taking on a slightly violet shade as they often did when he was under pressure.

Taylor merely stared at him, his own bright blue eyes never wavering from Tom's. "Sell it to us?" he repeated.

"Mmm-hmm," Tom nodded.

Gen had moved a discrete distance away, taking donuts from a tray to replenish the cabinets. She studiously looked away, having no idea how Taylor would react. Though he was generally even tempered, every now and then, the Irish came out in him.

"Sell it to us," Taylor said again, leaning back against the counter. "Tommy, what will we do with a bakery?"

"The same thing we do with it now?" he ventured.

Taylor shook his head. "We do it now to help Mrs. Caillan. You're a teacher, I'm a lawyer. We have *jobs*. What are we supposed to do?"

"I don't know," Tom said. "She basically wants to just give it to us because we've worked here for so long. I hate to let it go."

Taylor nodded. "Yeah, I've figured that out," he said.

"What is that supposed to mean?"

He met Tom's gaze. "It means you were supposed to be done when you graduated, yet here we are, two years later, still working."

Tom's cheeks flushed. "Hey, I didn't *make* you come down here."

"You were about to!" Taylor exclaimed.

"Don't do me any favors," Tom said, pushing past Taylor to go into the back room.

Taylor watched him go, dumbfounded. What had just happened? Had they had a fight? They never fought—neither of them felt fighting was a way to accomplish anything. In fact, Tom never even got mad…well, almost never.

"Well?" Gen said, interrupting his thoughts.

"Well what?" Taylor asked, turning to her.

"Well, get back there and talk to him," she prompted. "I'll cover things out here."

Taylor grimaced in spite of himself, but dusted his hands on his apron and headed toward the baking room.

Tom banged several pans on a rolling rack, pushing it back into a wall. Grabbing a padded mitt, he pulled several sheets of bread from the oven, adding them to another cart. It nearly tipped as Taylor jumped to grab it.

"I've got it," Tom said. "You can go."

"I'm not leaving," Taylor said.

"I've got it, Taylor. I've run this place on my own before," he said, turning his back.

"You're not alone now," Taylor said. "Remember?"

"Look, I know you don't want to be here," Tom said, still facing away. "Just go home. I'll be home this afternoon."

Taylor walked up behind him, gently wrapping his arms around him. Tom tried to pull away, but Taylor held him with just enough force to keep him close. "I'm not leaving," he repeated.

Tom laid his arms over Taylor's and he relaxed back, taking a deep, quivering breath. He turned and Taylor realized his eyes were red.

"You're crying?" he said.

Tom flushed again and tried to push him back, but Taylor held fast. "Hey, I'm sorry," he said, holding Tom to him. "Tom! I'm sorry—I didn't realize this place meant that much to you."

Tom met his eyes and Taylor gently wiped the damp streaks from his cheeks. He smiled softly, never letting Tom go. "I didn't mean to accuse," he said.

"I know you hate that I still work here."

Taylor shook his head. "I don't hate it at all. I would just like for *us* to have more time together."

Tom sighed. "So would I."

Taylor met his eyes, which were still dark with tears. "You know I would never say no to anything you want."

"I want you to want it, too."

Taylor laughed. "If it's what you want, I *do* want it, too. We're one, remember?"

Tom looked away, clearly lost in his own thoughts. Taylor said nothing for a moment, just holding him close and letting him think.

"Do you think we can do it?" Tom asked.

This time, Taylor thought before he spoke, considering what might be involved in actually owning the business. Downey's was a fixture of the town and very busy, but he had no idea what was actually involved in running it. In the years he'd been with Tom, all he'd ever done was stock the shelves and sell the baked goods.

"I honestly don't know," Taylor said.

Tom met his gaze evenly. "Will you try?"

Taylor laughed. "You know I will," he said. "You knew I would before you even asked."

"Taylor," he sighed, relaxing against him. Tom was a good three or four inches shorter than Taylor's six-foot height, leaving him just the right height to lay his head on Taylor's shoulder. "Thank you."

"Don't thank me yet. This means you're really going to have to work your butt off."

"Promise?" Tom said, looking up.

Taylor smiled, realizing he'd been had. He planted a kiss squarely on Tom's soft, red lips, pausing for the briefest of seconds before he pulled back and looked around.

"All right, Mr. McEwan, no more banging the equipment around when you're mad, either. I'm sure we're going to find out this stuff is expensive."

Tom puffed up, meeting Taylor's stern expression. "Oh, no you don't. I'm in charge of this bakery, Mr. Connolly. I'll bang stuff whenever I like."

Taylor raised a bemused eyebrow and Tom blushed a bit as he realized what he said, but he quickly turned back to the oven. "Now, quit distracting me before I burn all this bread."

"Yes, sir, Mr. McEwan, sir," Taylor said. He turned to go.

"Tay?" Tom called. He walked over and kissed Taylor again. "Thanks."

Taylor smiled, wiping streaks from his Tom's face again. "We're a team," he repeated. He gave Tom a quick hug, then went back out front.

Gen handed the bag across the case, smiling broadly as she did.

"You're all set, Mrs. Jensen. Thanks for coming in."

"Always a pleasure, dear," the venerable Mrs. Jensen said. "I just never know which of you kids I'm going to get to see." She smiled as Taylor came up behind Gen. "Taylor! Now there's an unexpected pleasure. How are you, dear? How's Tommy?"

Taylor smiled warmly at the old lady he'd come to know from working at the bakery over the last few years. "I'm good, Mrs. Jensen, and Tommy's great. He's just pulling fresh loaves of bread from the oven now."

"Wonderful," she smiled. "I'm always so glad to see you boys here. I wish you could still be here all the time."

Gen turned to Taylor, a question on her face.

"Actually, Mrs. Jensen," Taylor said, glancing between the lady and Gen, "you'll be seeing a lot more of us."

"Oh?"

Taylor nodded, taking a breath. "Tom and I have just decided to buy the bakery."

Gen smiled broadly, nodding to herself. Mrs. Jensen's face brightened and she clapped her hands together.

"Really? Oh, that's wonderful! Taylor, I'm so happy for you boys! I can't wait to tell everyone in town."

Taylor held up a hand. "Oh, uh, no, Mrs. Jensen, not just yet."

"Oh, dear, news like this simply can't be kept secret!" she exclaimed, heading for the door. "Everyone is going to be so happy to have you both back here. Bye!"

"Bye…" Taylor waved behind her, feeling as though he'd let the genie from the bottle. The door closed and Gen turned to him.

"Good work," she said. She laughed as she realized Taylor's expression had become one of near shock. She hugged him. "It'll be okay, honey. He knows what he's doing."

"How are we both going to work and run a successful bakery?"

"It'll work out," she said. "Life just does."

"Mrs. Caillan, I'm going on record, one last time, to advise you that you should have your attorney review these documents," Taylor said.

Across the table, Margaret Caillan, the woman who had owned Downey's Bakery the entire time Tom had worked there, stared passively back at him. She was every bit the little old lady—short, about as big around as tall, wearing a blue flowered print dress and sweater, glasses and white hair. Her eyes crinkled at the corners as she spoke.

"Taylor, you boys could have taken advantage of my trust a dozen times over. If I had the slightest doubt about your honesty, we wouldn't be here right now." She looked at Tom, to Taylor's left. "When my father started the bakery thirty years ago, we all thought he was crazy. How could he make a living at it? Within a year, we could barely keep up. People drive a half hour to buy my father's bread. When I couldn't run things anymore, I found Tom. He's been there for me for almost six years. None of my own children want anything to do with it. The least I can do is give it to someone who cares."

Tom smiled, embarrassed at the attention. Taylor cleared his throat. "Yes, ma'am," he said. "My business partner, Pete, prepared all of these documents. I want to go over them in detail with you to be sure everything is exactly as you want it."

Mrs. Caillan waved a hand. "What's to discuss? You will pay me half the profits for the next year, I transfer everything to you, including the right to the name. I'm going to live in Florida with my sister—I just need enough to get me there and get me situated."

"And you understand that profits—" Taylor started.

"I know what profits are, Mr. Connolly," she said. "And I know that you could conceivably cook the books to show no profit. But I know you won't and that's all I need." She stared at Taylor and he stared back, each silently regarding the other. Finally, he nodded.

"Okay, Pete," he said, turning to the man at the end of the table. "I guess we're set."

Pete went through the various documents, legally transferring all property and debt of the business to Tom and Taylor. Tom had insisted that Taylor be a part of the business, even as Taylor tried to point out that he already had his own business. Tom said the firm was between him and Pete, but the bakery would be theirs, together. Taylor ultimately relented, seeing no point in arguing when it was clearly what Tom wanted. Most of their property was shared jointly anyway, so what difference would one more thing make?

After what seemed an endless series of documents, Pete finally passed the last page between them, then straightened the stack of documents and stood.

"That's it. It's done," he proclaimed.

Mrs. Caillan reached into her pocket and pulled out an old, worn key, which she handed across the table to Tom. "This is the original key to the store," she explained. "It's all yours now." Though she smiled, the sadness was still evident on her face.

"You know you'll always be welcome whenever you want to visit," Tom said.

She nodded. "That's kind, Tommy," she said. "But, I'm not going to be back this way, I think. I've done enough traveling for one lifetime. It's time to retire." She pushed herself up from her chair, using the table to steady herself. "Well, it's time for me to go. You boys have lots of work to do and I have to finish packing."

Tom and Taylor led her to the door, opening it to the cool autumn breeze and bright sun. She hugged both of them, smiling as they stood together before the door.

"You take good care of each other," she admonished. "You're both very lucky. I'm just glad you were able to find each other."

"Thanks, Mrs. Caillan," Tom said. He leaned back ever so gently against Taylor.

She waved again, then got in her car and drove off. Taylor casually draped one arm around Tom, listening to the rustle of the leaves as the wind touched them. "Well," he said, "Now you've done it."

"Now *we've* done it," Tom said, holding Taylor's hand where it rested on his stomach.

"Yep."

"I'm happy, Tay," Tom said, his head just leaning against Taylor's cheek.

"So am I," Taylor admitted, feeling a peace he'd so often sought, but rarely found.

*   *   *

The basket of rolls made its circuit around the table as each hand reached in to take one. Tom sat to Taylor's right, with Gen beside him, then Miguel, Anita, Pete, Sandy, and finally, John to Taylor's left. John returned the basket to the center of the table, turning his attention to Tom.

"So, are these the first official Downey McEwan's rolls?"

Tom smiled proudly. "You bet they are! I even saved the first bag for us this morning."

"Quite an honor," Sandy observed, spreading a generous portion of butter on hers.

"Speaking of buns in the oven," Gen said, "How much longer?"

Sandy patted her plump belly, smiling. "About two more weeks. The doctors say mid-October."

"Do you know what the sex is yet?" Pete asked.

She glanced to John, then turned back to Pete. "I do, but John wants it to be a surprise."

"Oooh," Pete whined. "Just whisper it in my ear."

"No way," Sandy said. "I know how you keep a secret."

Pete gave her his best "who me?" look, but Anita patted his hand.

"She's right, honey. Secrets just aren't one of your strong suits."

"But I keep good secrets," Pete argued. "I never told Taylor what you said about his pants."

Taylor eyed Pete from the other end of the table, but didn't take the bait. Sandy turned to him hurriedly. "Taylor, I didn't say anything about your pants."

He smiled. "Don't worry, I believe you. Remember, I have to work with this guy all the time."

"And a lucky guy you are," Pete confirmed.

"I'm only lucky when I'm working with this guy," Taylor said, patting Tom's arm.

"Aaawww," Pete mocked.

"You should hear what he says about me when you're not here," Tom complained, meeting Taylor's gaze. Taylor pulled his hand away, realizing he would have no quarter that meal.

"So, Miguel, you're quiet tonight," John observed.

He nodded, his fork half-way to his mouth. "Just trying to stay out of the line of fire."

"Good luck," Sandy said.

"Really," Anita seconded. "I used to try to do that, then realized it's everyone for herself."

"Besides, you're able to live with Gen," John said.

Gen held her spoon as though to flip mashed potatoes at him.

"Don't you dare," Tom warned. "I have a hard enough time keeping this place clean just with Taylor."

Taylor looked affronted. "Speak for yourself, mister. Who picks up the dirty clothes every morning?"

"Oh, now it's getting good," Pete said.

"Careful, Petey. You've got your fair share of dirty little secrets," Anita said.

Miguel stepped in to the fray to ward off further escalation. "So, Anita, how long until you're on Sandy's plan?"

Anita let go a quick laugh. "Are you kidding? I already have one more kid than I'm ready for."

"Hey!" Pete complained.

"Everyone for herself," Sandy reminded, patting his arm.

Pete shook his head, laughing. "It's not fair that I got stuck between them," he said, looking to Taylor.

"Look who I got," Taylor retorted, gesturing to Tom and John.

John held up a loaded spoon. "I'll help you clean it up," he offered to Tom.

Tom closed the door behind Gen and Miguel, leaning up against it as he flipped the lock on the handle. "I'm exhausted."

"Hear, hear," Taylor seconded, reaching down to free his feet from his socks. He usually wasn't one to dress up in his own home, but Tom convinced him people would be dressed up a bit for a sit-down dinner. Of course, he was right, but people were gone, so toes could be free.

Tom moved to the couch and Taylor stretched out next to him, resting his head on Tom's leg. Tom slipped his hand under the partially unbuttoned collar of Taylor's shirt, gently massaging his chest.

"What time do we have to get up?"

"I have to be there at four," Tom said. "You don't need to come down until seven."

Taylor shook his head, his eyes, already closed. "No, we're a team. I'm not going to sleep in while you're working."

"I need you to run the store, Tay. I usually do the baking myself, you know that."

"I still feel guilty," Taylor said, his speech becoming slurred.

Tom laid his head back on the ample cushion of the couch. "That's okay, I'll let you close up," he said.

Taylor sighed. "Tommy, I'm thirty-two."

"Yeah?"

"Why do I feel like I'm a hundred?"

"Because your…uh…" he stumbled, unsure of what to call his relationship to Taylor. Recovering, he said, "Because I talked you into buying a bakery."

"Maybe I shouldn't like you anymore."

Tom smiled. "I don't care if you like me or not, as long as you love me." He moved his hand to softly caress Taylor's cheek.

Taylor laughed. "Not much chance of undoing that one."

"Good, then take me to bed and ravage me with…sleep."

Taylor laughed harder, picking himself up off the couch, then pulled Tom up with him. "How could I say no to that?"

They made their way upstairs, not even bothering with the lights—after all, Tom would be up in a matter of hours anyway. Taylor shook his head, wondering what fate had planned for him next…and instantly wished he knew how to keep his mental mouth shut.

Chapter Two

The Winds of Change

    A cool breeze brushed Taylor's face as he made the trek up the sidewalk toward home. He felt his hair rustle, reaching up to push his bangs back. He'd let his blonde locks grow back out a bit since being with Tom, feeling less like he had to fit any particular appearance mold. His hair parted just off to the right, gently flowing down with a light, natural appearance. In the early weeks of fall, his tan was rapidly disappearing, but he felt little care for that, either. Concern for one's appearance was more about concern for acceptance, and he'd never felt more accepted in his life.

    Or more tired. The day had started off cool but sunny, and the weather guy said it was going to stay that way. So, Taylor decided a little exercise would do him some good and walked to the office. It wasn't until he was halfway there that he realized how tired he really was from working the night before with Tom. He'd somehow managed to drag himself through the day, but was really looking forward to getting home and relaxing on the couch.

    As he'd feared, finding a qualified baker was proving difficult. Heck, finding any baker seemed to be beyond their reach. He'd have been happy just to have someone who wanted to work whom they could train. That was the problem with a small town—people already had jobs or only wanted to work in the higher paying confines of the city. But Taylor held his tongue. He didn't want Tom to get upset again—he really didn't mind the bakery, except that having more or less two full time jobs was proving a bit of a strain. Luckily, they'd found a lady to run the place during the day—Tom had to teach and Taylor wasn't really qualified to bake anyway. He mainly tried to provide two extra arms and hands to keep Tom from having to do all the work himself.

For his part, Tom seemed like an endless fountain of energy. Taylor wished he could have even half the energy of his...of Tom. He sighed. He wanted so much to have a formal name to call this man with whom he shared everything, but society just hadn't caught up to them. The list streamed by in his head, the way it always did, but he just couldn't be happy. "Partner" sounded too professional—they were business partners, true, but that wasn't the foundation of their relationship. "Significant other" was just a PC leftover from the nineties. Or was it the eighties? Whatever the case, it was a whole millennium ago, so it was not useful for the current day. "Honey baby sweetheart poochikens," he thought. Nah, too hard to say.

My Tom, he thought—the same solution that always seemed to present itself.

"Taylor! Aren't you even going to say hello?"

Taylor looked up. Without even realizing it, he'd been walking along staring at the sidewalk, lost in thought. He was already home and Gen sat on her swing seat with her feet up on the porch rail.

"Hi," he said, turning to walk up the path to her steps. "How are you?"

"I'm good," she said. "You look like you're pondering again. Big case?"

Taylor laughed, setting his bag down and joining her on the swing. Molly sat to one side, ignoring him.

"Yeah, the Case of the Invisible Baker." He chose to ignore the other train of thought he'd really been on. He wasn't sure what to do about it...yet.

"Still can't find anybody?"

"Not yet. I think we're going to try advertising in a couple of the city papers to see if we can find someone who might want to drive a bit."

"You'll find someone."

"I know. I mean, I'm sure we will. But I might be dead by then."

Gen turned sharply. "What's with all this pessimism? Everything okay with Tom?"

Dammit! Sometimes having an intuitive person for a best friend wasn't such a good plan. "Yeah, everything's great."

"Except?"

Taylor shook his head. "Everything is fine, Gen. We're okay. I'll admit, the stress of running two businesses while he's still trying to teach is stretching us a little thin, but love will conquer all, after all."

"Love still needs to get rest every now and then, honey."

"Speaking of love," Taylor began, deftly changing the topic. "How is Mr. Miguel lately?"

Gen broke into a grin as she looked away with a hint of embarrassment. "Things are going really well," she confirmed. "Is it too much to hope they'll stay that way?"

Taylor shook his head. "Not at all. No one deserves a little happiness more than you. You're there for everyone else and it's time someone was there for you."

She smiled. "You're always there."

Taylor laughed. "Someone who can be there in ways I can't."

She nodded. "Okay, yeah, that's nice too."

Taylor continued to watch her. "So what are you thinking?"

She shrugged. "It's going well."

"Any talk of a more…permanent arrangement?"

"Maybe."

"You're holding out on me."

"Maybe."

He was about to say something else when Miguel's car appeared in front of the house. He pulled up, waving as he passed on his way to the garage. Seconds later, he appeared from around the side of the house and bounded up the stairs.

"Hi, Taylor," he greeted, shaking hands. He turned and gave Gen a quick kiss. He stood back, facing them both. "So, what are you two up to?"

"I just shanghaied Taylor on his way home," Gen said, circumventing the discussion they'd been having.

"Can't walk through this town and get a moment's peace, can you?" Miguel observed.

"Not usually," Taylor agreed.

Miguel held up his briefcase. "Actually, I'm glad you're here. Could you take a look at something for me? Won't take a minute."

"Sure," Taylor said, moving to get up. Gen followed him as they went into the house.

"Anything special you'd like for dinner?" she asked.

"I was thinking it would be nice to go out," Miguel said. "We haven't been to Alberto's in a while."

Gen nodded. "Cool, I can do with not cooking. Taylor, would you and Tom like to come along?"

Taylor caught the look of disappointment in the microsecond it was on Miguel's face, but he recovered and nodded an invitation. However, it was enough for Taylor.

"Thanks, but I think Tommy and I will be staying in tonight. He's probably already asleep."

"Bakery's still killing you, huh?" Miguel said, clearly relieved.

"Yeah."

Gen shrugged. "Well, your loss, then. I'll go change while you guys go over your stuff."

She jogged up the stairs and Miguel led the way to the couch, dropping his briefcase on the coffee table. Instead of opening it, he shifted his sport coat around and withdrew a box from a pocket.

"I need your opinion," Miguel explained. "You know Gen better than anyone."

Taylor saw the box and suspected immediately what it was. As he slowly opened it, his expectation was confirmed.

"Jesus, Miguel!" he whispered. Inside was one of the most stunning rings Taylor had ever seen. The band was bright yellow gold, covered in diamonds, topped with a marquis cut stone that had to be at least two carets.

"She'll like it?"

"Are you kidding?"

He smiled. "It's not too much?"

Taylor laughed. "I don't think anything is too much for Gen."

Miguel looked uncertain for one of the first times Taylor could ever remember. "It's not too soon?"

Taylor shook his head, wrinkling his face. "Are you kidding? You've been together for two years. Tom and I only knew each other for a few months before we were shacking up."

Miguel nodded. "Yeah, but you're not married," he said.

Taylor felt an oppressive weight on his shoulders with that statement. He knew Miguel meant nothing by it, merely observing that they were still both "single," too, but Taylor still felt like he'd been punched in the gut. It was as though all the passing thoughts he'd had in the last few months coalesced into that one statement. He felt sick to his stomach.

"Yeah, we're not married," he managed, trying not to show his hurt to Miguel. Miguel had struggled with his and Tom's relationship when they first met. Though he was always pleasant and cognizant of the relationship they both shared with Gen, he had finally admitted one night that he'd never known any gay men personally before and he had a lot of questions. It had led to one of the more productive discussions Taylor had ever shared, and Miguel had been far more comfortable since that time, but there was still a sort of distance.

For his part, Miguel was too wrapped up in his own concerns to realize what he had said or how Taylor had taken it. He pocketed the ring and it occurred to Taylor why he wanted to take Gen to dinner. He was doubly glad he had turned down the invitation so as not to ruin Miguel's plan. Even if he couldn't be married, he sure would be glad when Gen was.

"You think she'll say yes?" Miguel was still following his original line of questioning, so Taylor set his thoughts aside and caught up.

"Yeah. Definitely. In fact, I'd say it's something she'll be happy to hear."

"What will I be happy to hear?" Gen asked as she made her way down the stairs.

Taylor was nothing if not fast on the draw. Years in the closet had made it a requisite skill. "Miguel was just discussing plans to fix the deck in the back," he covered, having just actually had that very discussion a few days before.

"New ideas?" Gen asked, turning to Miguel.

"No, I was just confirming which permits we would need. Our Mayor is always glad to help," Miguel said, offering Taylor a silent nod for pulling the discussion in the right direction.

"Nothing like having officials in your pocket, huh?" she said, smiling to Taylor.

"Don't start rumors!" Taylor said, heading for the door. For once, it seemed her truth radar was off and he wanted to get out of the way. "I'd better be getting home. My...Tom will be hungry, too."

Gen and Miguel bid him goodbye and he grabbed his bag from the porch as he made his way across the lawn and through the hedge to his house. *Our house*, he thought. *The house we share.* The house that Tom is deeded onto as "joint tenants with full rights of survivorship." Not "husband and...husband."

Taylor frowned. "Hi, this is Tom McEwan, my joint tenant with full rights of survivorship," he thought.

They had separate medical policies. The school district didn't have same-sex partner benefits and Taylor's law firm was too small to offer them. They had life insurance, naming each other as beneficiary, but they could name the man on the moon if they wanted to, so that meant nothing. Taylor and Pete had done the legal research to sign a ream of documents granting wills, living wills, patient advocates, powers of attorney, et cetera, et cetera, et cetera. Miguel and Gen would have a marriage certificate and that would be that. Clean and simple.

Yeah, but you're not married. Hundreds of pages and Tom was still McEwan and Taylor was still Connolly. They could even petition to have their names changed, but it would be a sort of flim-flam, just a change of names.

He tried to remind himself not to be upset about it. He was, after all, a discrimination lawyer. The laws were changing—slowly—to give more and more rights. Certainly, they were in a better position than they had been before. The trend to pass "defense of marriage" acts had slowed and a number of states were considering civil union laws. Of course, a civil union was expressly designed *not* to be marriage, so the ever-present question of title would still be out there.

He closed the door behind him harder than he meant to. Tom peeked around from the kitchen, immediately smiling brightly as his eyes landed on Taylor. If there was anything Taylor most loved about Tom, it was the way his face brightened when he looked at him.

"Hey, you," he greeted, making his way over to pull Taylor into a hug and plant a warm kiss on his lips. He leaned back, holding Taylor's shoulders in his hands. "Honey, you look spent."

Taylor nodded, letting go a long sigh. He didn't want Tom worrying about the things on his mind. Tom was happy and that was all Taylor cared about. He'd deal with the legal crap later, when his mind was clear. "Long day," he said simply, dismissing any further consideration.

Tom accepted the explanation, pulling him close again. "Maybe we should slow down," he said. "I feel bad because I know you're doing this for me."

Taylor shook his head. "I'm doing this for us. It's okay. Things have been a little slow anyway, so Pete's taking a lot of the load while I'm tied up. He's okay with it."

Tom still looked uncomfortable, but he managed a smile anyway. "I took out an ad when I got home. It'll start on Thursday."

Taylor smiled, genuinely relieved. "I'll keep my fingers crossed."

Tom laughed. "Well, you'd better wait until after dinner. Spaghetti with meat sauce—my mom's recipe."

Taylor dropped his bag by the door. "Sounds perfect."

"Go change," Tom said. "I'll have it ready when you come down."

Taylor nodded. "Thanks, Tommy," he said, heading for the stairs. Just before starting up, he turned back to Tom. "I really love you."

Tom's face beamed. "I really love you, too."

Taylor went up the stairs and headed to their bedroom. Felix was in his usual spot at the foot of the bed, curled into a little cat-ball, sound asleep. Taylor wondered what stroke of luck gave him such lethargic pets.

He pulled off his clothes and dropped them at the foot of the bed, separating dry cleaning from washables. Planning on an evening in, he pulled on a light T-shirt and shorts. The late October weather was a little cool, but Tom and an afghan would fix that. Happily barefoot, he made his way down the back stairs to the kitchen.

To his surprise, the lights were dimmed and Tom had two candlesticks on the table. He'd served two settings on their better china, a gift from Taylor's mom.

"What's the occasion?"

Tom smiled, holding out his chair. "You are."

"Me?" Taylor asked, sitting. Tom joined him, his warm eyes watching Taylor closely.

"You," he repeated.

"Why?"

Tom reached out and took his hand. "Taylor, you have no idea how important you are to me. I've spent so much time on my own, and now I have you to share my life with me. I know that no matter what, you'll be there, supporting me all the way. You not only let me take on this bakery, but took it on with me, even as it takes everything you have to keep up. You never complain, never get mad. I think it's important to take the time to show how much you mean to me."

Taylor was speechless. He felt the weight Miguel's unintended comment had placed on him lift in that one instant as he stared into Tom's warm, loving eyes. In his life, he had never known anyone like Tom—*his* Tom—and he knew he was the luckiest man on Earth.

"Thank you," he finally managed. "I don't know what to say."

Tom smiled. "You don't have to say anything. This is me saying something to you."

Taylor rolled his hand over, meeting Tom's soft grip. "I love you."

"I love you, too," Tom said, never looking away.

Taylor took a deep, shaky breath, not used to feeling so emotional. He looked at the meal Tom had prepared. "Well, we shouldn't let this get cold."

"Dig in," Tom said. He continued to watch Taylor. Taylor glanced over to where their hands were intertwined, but wouldn't let go. Tom didn't let go either. With a small shrug of acceptance, he reached over and picked up his fork with his left hand, spinning it in the spaghetti.

Tom laughed as he managed to work enough onto the fork and got it to his mouth. With a last tight squeeze, he let Taylor's hand go. "I guess you should be able to have your dinner," he said.

"I'm doin' okay," Taylor said.

Tom nodded. "There'll be plenty of time to hold on to each other later."

"Oh?" Taylor said.

"Emmy has the day off from school tomorrow."

"Really," Taylor said.

"She's gotten real good at taking care of the baking."

"Is that so?" Taylor said, doing some math.

"She mentioned having a friend who could help her get things done around the store. We wouldn't need to come in until later."

"Uh-huh," Taylor said.

"Think you might like to sleep in?"

Taylor regarded Tom closely, feeling a contagious grin work its way across his face. "After a fashion."

Tom nodded, both to Taylor and himself. "Then the sooner you finish that dinner, the better."

He had his plate emptied in record time.

Taylor awoke with a start, the light of the sun already in his eyes. Why hadn't his alarm gone off? He moved to roll over and realized he couldn't—Tom was curled tightly into his back, his arm over Taylor's right side. Slowly, the memory of the previous night flooded in…and Taylor smiled in spite of himself. He reached a hand up to take Tom's, running his fingers gently over its smooth surface.

"Good morning," Tom whispered behind him.

Taylor rested against him, enjoying the warmth and comfortable intimacy he'd needed so badly the last few weeks. "Hi," he said simply.

"Sleep well?"

"Like a baby," Taylor said. "How long have you been awake?"

Tom shrugged, pulling Taylor tighter to him. "A little while. I was just letting you sleep. It's not very often I get to see the sun come up."

"What did you do about school?" Taylor asked.

"I'm sick."

Taylor snickered. "Oh, that's too bad. I shouldn't get too close to you, then."

"Too late," Tom said and rolled onto his back, pulling Taylor next to him. "We need more mornings like this."

Taylor sighed, still half asleep. "I'm not going to argue that point."

"Maybe we should close on Mondays and Tuesdays," Tom suggested. "At least until we can find a few people to help run the place."

"Can we afford it?"

Tom took Taylor's hand in his. "I'm not sure we can afford not to."

"It's okay, Tommy," Taylor said. He rolled onto his stomach so they could talk face to face. "You don't have to worry."

Tom smiled. "It's not just me worrying, Tay. I'd like to get to wake up *with* you once in a while, too. I know we'll find someone, but in the meantime, we deserve some time, too. For cryin' out loud—you're trying to be a lawyer, the Mayor, and help me run the bakery, all while I'm trying to teach."

"In that case, we need Sunday and Monday," Taylor said.

"Sunday?"

"Yep. We need to have a day fully off, not just a day off from the bakery. We need a day when we can go to bed, sleep in as late as we want, and have no responsibilities."

Tom smiled, nodding. "You know, that doesn't sound bad at all."

Taylor pulled a pillow—his pillow—up under his head, resting it on Tom's arm and laying his arm across Tom's chest. They lay together in silence for a while, enjoying just being together and the complete lack of demands, even if only for a couple hours.

"Hey," Taylor said, breaking the silence. "In all the, uh, excitement last night, I forgot to tell you what happened."

"What's that?" Tom asked.

"Miguel bought a ring."

"For Gen?"

"Uh-huh."

Tom looked over to meet Taylor's eyes. "No kidding? Good for him!"

Taylor pressed on. "They were going to dinner last night."

"Huh. Maybe that was the phone call."

"Phone call?"

Tom nodded. "Yeah. Just before I fell asleep, I heard the phone ring and it sounded like Gen's voice. I figured it could probably wait."

"Let's find out," Taylor said. He reached over Tom for the cordless phone next to the bed and pressed the button to retrieve messages from the answering machine.

"One—new—message," the voice said. A female voice replaced the machine. "Hey, guys, it's Anita. John just called—Sandy's in labor. Thought you'd want to know. She's at Valley General. It's about eleven thirty now. Feel free to call my cell phone. Pete and I are going over now. See ya."

Taylor turned off the phone, looking at Tom. "Gen, huh?"

Tom shrugged. "I was *very* tired."

Taylor smiled and gave him a kiss. "Good. We should probably get over there, though."

Tom set the phone on the table, pulling Taylor down to him. "I'm sure Sandy can handle a delivery without us," he said simply, running his hand slowly down Taylor's bare back...

The doors parted and Taylor strode into the hospital like a man with a purpose. Tom trailed along behind, trying to look inconspicuous. Taylor saw one of the security guards eye them, but he headed directly for the elevators like he knew exactly what he was doing. The doors to the elevator opened and they disappeared inside.

"Aren't we supposed to check in?" Tom asked.

"Meh," Taylor said with a shrug. He hit the button for the maternity floor and they went up.

"Anita never answered my call," Tom commented.

Taylor nodded, pointing to the obviously amateur "No Cellular Phones in the Hospital!" sign.

"Oh, yeah," Tom said. Taylor slipped his arm around him for a quick hug right before the doors opened.

The nurses' station faced them as they exited.

"Can I help you?" a nurse asked as she took in the newcomers.

"We're here to see the Atkins family."

"Friends or family?"

Taylor hated that question. What difference did it make? What constituted a friend versus a family member?

"Friends," he answered honestly.

The nurse nodded, gesturing to their right. "There is a waiting room just down the hall. They already have the maximum visitors, but I'll let them know you're here."

"Thanks," Taylor said, trying to appear casual. "What's the room number?"

The nurse hesitated, guessing that they might not wait in the waiting room, but answered anyway. "Four twenty-five."

As they turned to walk away, he noticed the tiniest hint of a smirk on her face and that she didn't get up to go tell John and Sandy they were there. He also noticed the sign indicating the room was in the same direction as the waiting room. Wordlessly, he passed the empty waiting room and headed for the sign that read, "425."

"You're gonna get us kicked out," Tom whispered.

Taylor shot him a sidelong glance. "When have I ever gotten us kicked out of a place?"

"There's always a first time," Tom said. Taylor quietly opened the door and heard the sound of voices within.

"It's about time!" Gen said as Taylor rounded the privacy curtain. "Where have you two been? Anita called *last night*."

Tom looked her straight in the eye. "We were already in bed. We didn't get the message until this morning because we didn't have to run the store today."

"Oh?" John asked, a question on his face.

"Oh," Taylor said, giving him a sour look.

"You just missed Pete and Anita," Gen commented.

Taylor's eyes were on Sandy, who held a small bundle in her arms. She smiled at him, beckoning him over. "There's someone here who wants to meet you," she said.

Taylor leaned over to see the baby's face, buried in a pile of blankets. The first thing he saw was a tiny pink nose and deep blue eyes. Tom leaned in behind him, eager to get his first look at the newest member of their "family."

"Meet Taylor Thomas Atkins," Sandy said.

Taylor felt his jaw drop as he looked her in the eye. Tom rested his head on Taylor's shoulder, pulling him into a hug.

"Really?" Taylor asked.

"Yep," Sandy confirmed. "Chad is already named after John, and we named Wendy after Gen, so we thought it would be only fitting to name the new one after you guys."

"Conveniently, he's a boy," John pointed out. "'Thomas' would have been a funny name for a girl."

"True," Tom agreed.

"Want to hold him?" Sandy asked.

"Yeah," Taylor said. He gently took his namesake from her arms, careful to support his head, and held him close. "God, look at him, Tommy!"

"He looks just like you," Tom whispered.

"He'd better *not*," John chided from across the bed. With similar complexions and coloring, Taylor and John were often mistaken for brothers.

"I'll be back in a minute," Gen said. "I'm going to get something to drink. Anybody want anything?"

A chorus of "no thanks" passed around and she excused herself. Taylor turned to Tom and gently held the new baby to him.

"Is it okay?" Tom asked Sandy.

"Of course."

Tom took the baby and Taylor watched as he broke into a broad smile—the Taylor Smile—only for a new generation of Taylor.

"We want to ask you something," John said, looking to both Tom and Taylor from the other side of the bed.

"Okay," Taylor said. Tom nodded, still watching Taylor Thomas in his arms.

"We want you to be his godparents," Sandy said.

"Both of us?" Tom asked.

"Yes," John confirmed. "We want the two of you to be his godparents."

"I, uh," Taylor said, looking to Tom. "Of course."

"We're honored," Tom said.

Sandy took John's hand and smiled. "Thank you. We knew we could count on you."

"Well then," Tom said, "to commemorate the occasion, let's get pictures!" Sandy looked less than thrilled at the prospect of being photographed so soon after labor, but put on her best smile anyway.

"Do you think we could do that?" Tom asked. They were on their way home, and Taylor sat in the passenger seat, lost in his own thoughts. Taylor said nothing, deflated in the seat, staring out the window.

"Tay? Hello? Earth to Taylor…"

"Huh? Sorry, I was just thinking. Could we do what?"

"Could we be parents?"

Taylor looked over at Tom. "Of course we could."

"Why don't we?"

"Did you take Biology?"

Tom shot him a look. "That's not what I mean. Why don't we think about adopting?"

Taylor sighed. "It's hard. The cards are stacked against same-sex couples adopting children. Besides, we're not around enough to look after children."

Tom considered Taylor's words, watching the road stream past them in the light misting rain of the afternoon. "We could be around enough."

"I know," Taylor said. "But we're not at that point right now. There's no hurry."

Tom was silent again, and Taylor looked at him. "You okay?"

He kept his attention on the road. "I always thought I'd have kids."

"Because you thought you'd be with a woman?"

Tom nodded slowly.

"Why didn't you ever say anything?"

Tom shrugged. "I didn't want to upset you or have you think…I don't know…that I wasn't sure or something." He looked over, worry in his eyes. "I mean, I am sure, Taylor. I love you. I've loved you as long as I've known you."

"It's okay, Tommy, I believe you."

Tom looked back at the road. "I just always sort of figured I'd get over it or something; that I'd find someone I could stand to be with so I could have a normal life." Taylor nodded, silently prompting him. "Then I met you and realized what it felt like to *want* to be with someone." He looked upon Taylor again. "I *want* to be with you," he said pointedly, looking back at the road. "So, I thought it was okay—at least I could be happy myself, even if it meant not having kids."

"But you're not happy?"

Tom turned sharply. "God, no, Taylor, that's not it at all. I *am* happy. That's my point—I am happy, I love you, but part of me still wishes *we* could have kids. I mean, I wouldn't even consider them without you in my life, but now that you *are* in my life, there's still a void for their sake. I want to have a family with you, Taylor. You and me and our children, together."

Taylor put his hand on Tom's, at a loss for words after the intensity of his feelings on a topic they'd never discussed before. He found it ironic to consider how closely Tom's words echoed his own recent thoughts. They both wanted to be able to be committed to each other, to a family, to a concept—they wanted to be able to live the American Dream, with one little twist.

"Tommy, if you want it that bad, we'll find a way," Taylor committed.

Tom glanced at him, still watching the road. "What do you want, Tay? Do you want all those things?"

Taylor chuckled, a small laugh at the irony of their shared inner turmoil. "Oh yes," he confirmed. "Yes, being able to live a normal life is something I've wanted for a long time. I've just never been able to figure out what normal really means. So, I decided to be happy with a good life. That's what I've had with you, and that's what I intend to continue to have with you. If you want to share that good life with some kids who need loving parents, that seems like a pretty darned good idea to me." He looked at Tom, holding his hand a little tighter. "You know, it's amazing: just when I think I can't love you any more, you say something like this and I fall in love with you all over again."

Tom smiled, meshing his fingers with Taylor's and they both retreated into their own thoughts. Inside, Taylor shook his head, ever amazed by the heart of the man who had pledged his life to him and to whom he had pledged his life. Somehow, some way, he would make this right for Tom—he would give Tom the life he wanted. It was his promise.

Chapter Three

Trick or Treat

Taylor pulled into the driveway, moving quickly to the garage, trying to beat the storm. Thunderstorms were uncommon in October, but the weather had been ominous all day. In the early evening, dark clouds rolled in and he knew it would only be a short time before the lightening would be starting.

Careful to leave enough room next to Tom's car, he hopped out of the Jeep and pulled open the back hatch. Occasionally, he missed his Jag, but he had to admit the Grand Cherokee was more practical and Tom truly loved getting to drive the Jag to work. He may not be able to marry Tom, but he could be sure he had a nice car.

Taylor gathered up the plastic grocery bags, managing to get all of them in one load. With his free hand, he slammed the hatch, then hit the button to close the garage behind him. Tom met him at the side door.

"I was just coming out to help you," he said, reaching for some of the bags.

"It's okay," Taylor said. "I'm just trying to beat the weather."

They walked into the kitchen, dropping the bags on the table. "Good thing," Tom said. "The weather guy was just on saying we're going to get severe thunderstorms. There's even a tornado watch."

"Great," Taylor said. He reached for the bags with cold items first, stocking the refrigerator.

Tom went through the other bags, loading everything else into various cupboards and the pantry. He stopped as he reached into one and came out with several bags of candy.

"Hungry?"

Taylor glanced over, then gave him a look. "It's for Halloween."

"How many cities are you expecting to send their kids?"

"I don't want to be stingy. I always liked the houses that gave more than one candy bar when I was a kid."

Tom nodded. "So you're bribing the children."

"I am not bribing the children," Taylor defended.

Tom stuffed the bags into a cupboard. "Their parents, then?"

"I'm not bribing anybody," Taylor grumped.

"Awfully defensive, for someone on the up and up, Mister Mayor," Tom said with a smile.

"Who pulled your chain tonight?" Taylor griped, closing the refrigerator door.

"I've got some good news."

"Okay," Taylor said, prompting him to go on.

"I found a morning baker."

Taylor's eyebrows went up. "Really? Who?"

"A student answered the ad in the paper. No experience, but a smart kid."

"From the college?" Taylor asked, putting the empty bags in the trash.

"From the high school," Tom said.

Taylor froze, then slowly turned, closing the door under the sink behind him. "He's in high school?"

"He's a senior," Tom explained. "Already eighteen, so we don't have to worry about hiring laws," he defended, knowing how his favorite lawyer would think.

"Tom, he's still too young. He needs to focus on finishing his education."

Tom met Taylor's stare. "I worked while I got my degree."

Taylor shook his head. "You were in your mid-twenties. This guy's just a kid. What about when he wants to go out with his buddies at night, but he has to get up at three or four in the morning to go bake bread and make donuts?"

"I don't think that's a top priority for him," Tom said.

Taylor's eyes narrowed. "What do you mean?"

"Taylor, he's gay. I mean, he's not out, but...well, you can just tell."

Taylor sighed, leaning back against the counter, rubbing his eyes in disbelief. "So you've got an eighteen year old kid who *might* be gay who wants to come work for the two most infamous people in town? Well, if people don't think he's gay before, they sure as hell will when he's working for us."

"They don't think Mrs. Johnson is gay," Tom said.

Taylor looked at him deadpan. "I'm sure the fact that she's married to a man helps keep up the image for her."

Tom pulled out a chair and sat at the table. "He applied on his own, Tay. I didn't ask him—I don't even know him, though Emmy said she does. She says he's kind of a quiet kid, which is no great surprise if he's gay. If he needs a job and wants a job, I'd like to help him out."

Taylor pulled out the chair across from him, lowering himself into it with a sigh. "So would I, Tommy. But here's the thing—you're a teacher at that school and eighteen or not, he's a student. What are his parents going to think? Are they going to like him getting up at three a.m. to go to work?"

"He said he lives with his dad who doesn't pay a whole lot of attention to what he does. He likes this job because it's near the college and will help him pay tuition. He's basically in the same boat I was in, Taylor. Mrs. Caillan helped me out—how can I turn my back on someone else who needs help?"

"I'm not asking you to turn your back. I'm pointing out the possible dangers in undertaking this course. The last thing you and I need is to give this town any cause to change its mind about us."

Tom's face darkened a bit. "Taylor, I don't think anyone in this town will think less of us—or even be surprised—if they find out we're helping a kid."

"By having him work in the bakery starting in the wee hours of the morning," Taylor finished.

Tom stood up. "You know, I thought *you* would be happy about this."

"Tom, I *am* happy at the thought of having someone to help. And I'm not trying to second-guess your decision. I only want to point out the potential pitfalls for both of us."

"I told him he could start tomorrow."

Taylor said nothing, merely looking at him.

"I thought you'd agree with my decision. I guess I was wrong." He turned and walked into the living room. Taylor followed him, taking a seat on the couch next to him.

"I didn't say you were wrong. I said it's a decision that may cause us problems. Don't get upset."

Tom laid his head back on the sofa, eyes closed. "Taylor, I'm exhausted. I'm worn out. And the worst part is, it's my own fault—I bit off too much. Now I have a kid who needs a job, wants to work, and needs help. I think it's worth taking a little risk."

Taylor pulled Tom into his arms. "Then you've made your decision. Part of being the owner is having to make the big choices."

"I want you to agree with me."

Taylor smiled, resting his head against Tom's. "I agree that you have the best of intentions and that the idea is sound. My only caution was that others might not share our opinion. If they don't, then we'll deal with it. It's okay, Tom."

Outside, as dusk approached, the sky was finally lit with lightening. Thunder shook the floor. The storm Taylor had sensed approaching was upon them and he did not appreciate the none-to-subtle metaphor for recent events in his life.

The next morning, he rolled over in any empty bed to see the light of overcast skies through the blinds. A glance at the clock said Tom and his new charge would already have gone to school. He wouldn't be able to get the run-down until later, when Tom would no doubt stop by the office as he usually did on his way home.

He considered their discussion from the night before. He knew neither of them had been at their best in recent weeks, constantly on edge to try to keep the carefully timed details of their life in balance—and not always succeeding.

Tom had gone on to tell Taylor more about the new guy—Wayne McInerney—and his background. He lived with his father, his mother having married and moved out of state the year before. His father was less than a model citizen, working as a laborer in one of the factories in town—at least until his next medical leave, which he took as often as possible. Wayne's twenty-three year old brother Teddy also lived with them, though his primary occupation involved keeping local liquor establishments in business or trafficking various substances.

For all the cards stacked against him, Wayne was remarkably well adjusted, merely keeping to himself for the most part. Tom couldn't even particularly quantify why he thought Wayne was gay, it was "just a feeling." Taylor decided he would reserve judgment until he met the kid. Tom was one of the smartest people he knew, but he'd only been out for a couple years, so his "feelings" might not always be on the money.

Taylor thought about Tom. What was going on with him lately? For the almost three years they'd been together, Tom had been virtually unflappable. Taylor, usually mild mannered, would occasionally go into a rant about some happening in the world and it would always be Tom who pulled him back to Earth. Yet, in the last few weeks, they'd had a couple almost-fights and Tom had actually had tears in his eyes a couple times.

He shook his head—one thing he couldn't stand was seeing Tom cry. Most of the time, his even-temper also meant he could take a lot. The first time he'd ever seen him cry was when he thought Taylor was having a relationship with someone else. Tom and Gen had driven to New York so Tom could finally tell Taylor how he felt about him, once and for all. A misunderstanding sent him running for the stairwell, with Taylor chasing after him, still in his bare feet. They'd talked and the reconciliation started the relationship they'd both waited a lifetime to share.

Though the possibility for trouble existed because of Wayne, Taylor had to admit he wouldn't mind the first morning that Tom didn't have to leave in the middle of the night. Realistically, he expected that to still be a couple weeks away, but at least someone had finally turned on the light at the end of the tunnel.

He continued to wonder what to do about the other issues that existed in their relationship. He felt tremendously fortunate—their issues were *because* they loved each other so much, rather than because they were losing interest. Tom wanted kids, Taylor wanted to be "married," and society didn't think much of either idea. Taylor fought discrimination cases all the time, yet knew of very little precedent to help them. It would come down to people who thought like they did being in the positions necessary to make their wishes happen. It was possible, but it would take a lot of work.

Beside him, the phone rang and he reached over to pick up the handset. The display read "UNAVAILABLE". He nearly put it back, but then decided it was unlikely a solicitor would be calling so early.

"Hello?" he said, making no effort to conceal he'd just awakened.

"Taylor, is that you?"

"Yes, it's me," he said, frowning.

"Oh good. It's Donna, Tom's mom. How are you? Did I wake you?"

Taylor shook his head, realizing it was pointless in a phone conversation. "No, it's okay. I just woke up a couple minutes ago."

"Oh, good. I never know what time to call you boys."

Taylor chuckled. "Well, these days it's a pretty good bet somebody will be up most of the time."

"Still no baker?" Donna asked.

"Actually, he hired someone who started today. Thing is, the guy is pretty young and has no experience, so we'll have to see how he works out."

"It's always something for you guys, isn't it?"

Taylor yawned. "Tell me about it!"

He could hear Donna take a breath on the other end of the phone. "Well, here's the reason I'm calling. The holidays are coming up and Don and I are trying to plan what we're doing. We were wondering if you boys have given any thought to where you plan to spend the holidays?"

He sighed. "No, we haven't gotten that far yet. I just finally bought Halloween candy last night for trick or treat tomorrow."

"I know. You boys are so busy. I understand. Will you do me a favor and talk to Tommy and let us know as soon as you can?"

Again, Taylor nodded. "Yeah, I'll try to remember to ask him tonight and one of us will get back with you. If not tonight, then soon. Do you have any particular ideas in mind?"

"No, no," Donna said. "Don is taking off the whole week this year and Mandy thinks she'll be home from school on Tuesday. She said most of her professors are just giving up on the week."

Taylor smiled. "Yeah, I remember mine used to do the same thing."

"She mentioned bringing a friend home for the holiday. I guess he doesn't have anywhere to go and his family is in California."

"That sounds like a good plan," Taylor agreed. "I used to bring people home now and then when they didn't have a place to go."

"Well, check with Tom and see what you guys want to do and let me know, will you, Taylor?"

"You bet," Taylor confirmed.

"Okay. I won't keep you any longer—I know you have a million things to do."

"Today's a light day. I only have a half million," Taylor countered.

"Lucky you. Take care, honey," she said, sounding very motherly. Taylor was thankful that Tom's parents had, by and large, been accepting of his announcement. They hadn't been particularly surprised—a twenty-five year old kid who doesn't date raises a few eyebrows. As was often the case, his Mom had handled it better than his Dad, but both continued to support and love him. After the first year or so, they had even started to warm up to Taylor, Tom's dad often referring to him as "son."

"Thanks, mom," Taylor said. "Have a good morning, okay?"

"Will do. Bye now," Donna said and hung up.

Taylor turned the phone off and set it down on the bed beside him. He was stretched out across the bed, his head on Tom's pillow. He could smell Tom's scent intermingled with his cologne and he missed him again. What would they do for the holidays? He wasn't sure, but he knew one thing—they weren't making donuts!

"Pies?" Taylor queried.

"Yeah, don't you remember?" Tom asked.

He shook his head. "No, I guess I don't. Was I there?"

Tom laughed. "I guess you were in spirit. I thought for sure you'd remember."

"It all runs together," Taylor admitted.

Tom nodded understandingly. "It's okay. But, back to your original question, I just don't see how we can plan to be away that week. Wayne will be doing well by then, but he can't handle that volume of orders, even with Emmy and Mrs. Johnson to help."

"When do you start taking orders?" Taylor asked.

"September."

"Oh. How many so far?"

Tom didn't even speak, his silence an answer unto itself.

"Oh," Taylor said again.

Tom picked up his and Taylor's plates and carried them to the sink. As he scooped the remainders of dinner into the disposal, he said, "I think we should just have them here."

"Your family?"

"*Our* family," Tom said. "Why not invite your parents and Bryce and his family, too? Our parents can take the guest rooms, Bryce and Ellie can make do in the office and Mandy and her friend can use the sofa bed."

"That's eight adults and Dylan. How will we entertain them?" He rose to clear the rest of the dishes and help Tom load the dishwasher.

"It's only a couple days. We can always take them into the city and see a show, go to the movies, go shopping, drive around...there are lots of things to do."

Taylor pondered the idea. "What about transportation?"

"My parents don't fly. They'll drive over—it's only about five hours anyway. Between the Jeep and the Jag, we should be able to get everybody else."

"It'll be like the frickin' Brady Bunch thanksgiving."

Tom smiled. "You can decide who has to play Alice."

"Do you think they'll get along?"

"Would they dare not?" Tom asked. He took Taylor's hand and led him in to relax on the couch.

"My parents can be a little maddening," Taylor said. "They're very...cultural."

"Snobs," Tom clarified.

"Exactly."

"Your parents are wonderful people," Tom said. "They'll be fine. My parents could use a little culture."

"My parents could use a little reality," Taylor admitted.

"See? It's perfect." Taylor didn't look convinced. "Okay, how about if we invite Gen and Miguel? Gen just said the other day that they don't have anywhere to go."

"You're asking for trouble," Taylor said.

"It'll be fun," Tom said, putting a reassuring hand on Taylor's shoulder. "Come on, let's do it. If nothing else, it'll go down in history."

"That's the exact feeling I've been getting," Taylor said.

Taylor stood at the back door, and lightly tapped the frame. He heard the rustling of people moving inside and Gen's face appeared in front of him. She pushed the door open, a perplexed expression on her face.

"Since when do you knock?" she asked.

He shrugged, walking in. "I guess since you got engaged. It doesn't feel right to go walking into someone's home, you know?"

"I walk into your house," Gen said, leading him into the living room.

"I suppose that's true," Taylor agreed.

Miguel looked up, then held out a hand in greeting. "Hi, Taylor."

"Hey, Miguel," Taylor said. He took one of the chairs opposite their position on the couch. "How are things going?"

He gave a dismissive shrug. "Can't complain. Gen's still going to marry me."

"Must be doing something right," Taylor agreed.

"So far…" Gen said. She turned to Taylor. "So, what's up, T?"

Taylor cleared his throat. "On behalf of Mr. McEwan and myself, you are cordially invited to spend Thanksgiving with the McEwan-Connolly's. We're sure it will be a truly memorable experience," he finished.

Gen's face brightened and Miguel nodded appreciatively—a virtual cheer from him. "That sounds great!" Gen exclaimed, looking to Miguel. Again, he nodded quietly, offering silent agreement. "How many people do you have? What do you need us to bring?"

Taylor explained what had happened and how they'd reached their plan. Gen laughed at the idea of trying to keep the two families entertained. She'd had occasion to meet both of them and understood the complexities.

She turned to Miguel. "Do you care if they…?" she asked, not even bothering to finish her question as he shook his head. Smiling, she said to Taylor, "Why don't you have your brother's family and Tom's sister and her friend stay here? We have plenty of room and it will create less of a disturbance in your house."

"Really?" Taylor asked. "Are you sure?"

"Definitely," Gen confirmed. "Don't even think twice about it. It'll be fun. Miguel's family is too far away and God only knows what my parents will be doing. We'll get the benefit of a family for the holidays and you'll get the benefit of outsiders to buffer your families for the holidays."

Taylor looked visibly relieved. "You guys are a godsend. Tom is going to be thrilled."

"And you're surprised?" Miguel asked with uncharacteristic humor. Taylor often forgot that just because he was quiet didn't mean he wasn't interested.

"I know, I know," Taylor said. "So, how are the wedding plans coming?"

"Ugh," Miguel said, shaking his head. "Be glad you don't have to deal with it. It's endless—churches, reception halls, guest lists, meal choices, cakes, dresses, tuxes, table toppers, invitations…just when I think we're almost done, Gen brings home the next bridal magazine."

"Are you complaining?" Gen asked.

"No, ma'am," Miguel answered smartly.

Gen turned to Taylor. "The plans are coming very well," she confirmed. "We're looking at late May for a date."

"Outdoors?"

She nodded. "We're looking at using the Pavilion. Of course, the city people don't want to rent it out this far in advance. You wouldn't know who we might talk to to get an exception, would you?"

Taylor smiled, the message clear. "I'll see what I can do. With the election coming up, I don't want to bend too many noses. You never know who might run against me as a write-in candidate."

"Trust me, no one wants to be Mayor," Gen said. "That's why the last mayor was there for over twenty years."

Taylor nodded. "I know. They made one guy stay mayor even after he died."

"He almost got elected to another term," Gen agreed.

Taylor rose. "Well, I'm glad you're coming, but I need to get home."

Gen walked him to the front door. "How's the new guy?"

"Not bad, I guess. Tom says he's trying really hard and picking it up quick. I'll just be glad to get a few days' break sometime soon, you know?"

Gen laughed. "Yeah, then pie baking week will kick in."

Taylor turned. "You know about that?"

She nodded. "Yeah, Tom has already enlisted our help. Didn't he tell you?"

"He may have," Taylor admitted. "Apparently, I agreed to it and never knew either. I keep losing track of things."

"Honey, you're entitled," she said, patting his shoulder.

Taylor walked out, quickly crossing back to his own yard. The lights were on inside, which meant Tom was home. Trick or treat was the following night and he had mentioned to Taylor that they should have everything ready so they didn't have to worry about it when they got home.

He entered through the front door, which was unlocked in what had become the customary fashion. The TV was on and a light shone through the darkened dining room from the kitchen. Taylor passed through the two rooms to find Tom seated at the kitchen table, eating a Snickers bar.

"Those are supposed to be for the kids," Taylor reminded him.

"I only had one," Tom said between bites, then quickly dropped his hand over the incriminating wrappers—several more than one.

"Gen and Miguel are in," Taylor said, pulling a Mounds from one of the bowls. "They offered to have Bryce and Mandy and company stay at their place so we only have to deal with our parents."

"Cool," Tom said. "Have you called your family yet?"

Taylor shook his head. "I figured I'd make sure the buffers would be in place first."

Tom frowned. "It's not going to be that bad, Tay. Where's your usual optimism?"

"Squashed under the jealous foot of reality." He pulled the cordless phone from its cradle and selected one of the speed dials.

"Hi, Mom, it's Taylor," he said. "I'm fine. Yeah, he's good, too." He looked to Tom. "Mom says hello."

"Hi, Mom!" Tom called out, reaching for a Milky Way.

"You're gonna be sick," Taylor whispered, then said, "No, Mom. Tom's just eating all the Halloween candy before trick or treat tomorrow." He laughed. "Mom says they'll egg your car."

"I'll deadbolt the garage door," Tom said, straight faced. Nobody messes with *his* Jag!

Taylor continued his conversation. "Yeah, everything's great. Actually, I was calling to talk to you about Thanksgiving. We've been trying to plan what to do this year—Tom's mom called and needed to know. We were thinking it would be fun to have everyone here." There was a pause while his Mom said something. "Yeah, we have plenty of room. You remember my friend Gen? She invited Bryce, Ellie and Dylan to stay with her. She's got room for Tom's sister and her friend, too."

Tom watched the interchange with passing interest, reaching for another candy bar. Taylor reached out and slapped his hand away without missing a beat.

"Yes, I know you like to get together with Aunt Esther, but we'd like to have people here. No one has seen our new house yet and it will be a great opportunity for you and Dad to get to know Tom's family." More talking passed on the other end and Tom slipped another candy bar. Taylor glared at him, but he stayed out of range. "No, Mom, I don't expect you to cook. Tom and I can more than handle a turkey and some side dishes. And God knows we will have plenty of baked goods." At that, Tom rolled his eyes and sat back in the chair. "Yes, we've mentioned it to the McEwans and they like the idea." Taylor was bending the truth—they already knew Tom's parents were ready to come to their place. They could finalize the details later.

Taylor smiled, leaning on the table. "Great! Yes, just let us know when the flight is coming in and we'll arrange transportation. No problem, the airport isn't that far. Have Bryce give me a call and we'll work out the details. Wonderful! Yes, I'm looking forward to seeing you, too. I will. Okay. Love you, too. Bye." He hit the disconnect button.

"Mom sends her love," Taylor said, facing Tom.

"They're coming?"

"They're coming," Taylor confirmed. "Now we just have to convince your Mom."

Tom looked at the clock. "They'll already be in bed. I'll call her tomorrow night. She won't care—she'll just be glad to see us. It'll be fun to have them all here at once."

"So you say," Taylor said.

Tom reached across the table and took his hand. "Worst case scenario, they can't get along and fight all day. We still get to go lock ourselves in our room and forget about them at night."

Taylor gave a reluctant smile. "I like that plan."

"Want to practice now?"

Taylor looked up, then nodded. "I'll get the lights."

"Trick or Treat!"

"Dracula and a mummy," Taylor observed, dropping candy into the outstretched bags. "Very scary!"

"Thanks, Mayor Connolly," the monsters said. Their mom waved from the sidewalk, watching as they ran next door to Mr. Olsen's house.

Next door, Gen and Miguel waved.

"They get cuter every year, don't they?" Gen called over from the porch swing where they waited to hand out candy.

"Sure do," Taylor agreed.

"What kind of candy do you have this year?"

Taylor shrugged. "Whatever Tom didn't eat last night."

More costumed figures were coming their way as Taylor heard Tom on the phone inside the house.

"No, it's not a problem," he said, exasperated. "You can stay with us. Gen *volunteered* to have Mandy and her friend stay over there. Taylor's brother and his family are staying there, too. No, I don't know what Gen's family is doing, but apparently it doesn't involve coming here."

"Trick or treat!"

Three more hobgoblins had appeared at the steps and Taylor refocused his attention on the kids, dropping candy bars into their plastic pumpkins.

"Hi, Taylor."

He looked up to see their friend Rob from down the street standing there.

"Hi, Rob," he greeted, looking more closely at the kids. "Is that you, Amanda?" he asked.

"Yeah, it's me. Dad wouldn't let me trick or treat unless I dressed up, so I decided to be a witch."

"That's one way to get even with him," Taylor said, laughing.

Rob nodded. "Then Mel said I had to come along."

"At least it's a nice night."

"True," Rob agreed. "Where's Tom?"

"On the phone," Taylor said. "His Mom wanted to know what we're doing for Thanksgiving."

"They can never let one holiday finish, you know?"

"It's a mom thing," Taylor said. "We're trying to have everyone here this year."

"Both families?" Rob asked.

"Yeah."

He shook his head. "Now *that's* asking for trouble."

Amanda took Rob's hand. "Come on, Dad, let's keep moving."

"I guess I have to go," Rob said as she pulled him in the direction of Mr. Olsen's. He heard Amanda holler a thanks over her shoulder as she disappeared in the darkness.

"…No, you don't have to bring anything," he heard Tom say as he walked up to the door. "No, just you and Dad and Mandy. Sure, come on whatever day you like. There are always things to do in the city. What? Well, if he doesn't want to go, he can always just stay here. Yeah. Okay. No, Taylor is out handing out candy right now," he said, appearing at Taylor's side. He lowered himself to sit right up next to Taylor, offering a comforting warmth in the cool night air. "Okay, I'll tell him. Love you, too. Bye, Mom." He pressed the button to turn off the phone and laid his head on Taylor's shoulder, releasing a sigh.

"I thought she wanted to get together with us," Taylor commented.

"She does, but they get funny when they have to leave their home. You know, comfort zones and all," Tom said. He sat up, taking a candy bar from the bowl.

"Hey, those are for the kids," Taylor complained.

"I'm helping them learn sharing," Tom said, taking a bite. "Anyway, it's all settled. They're going to come a day or two early."

"What about pie baking?" Taylor asked.

"We'll get it done," Tom said. He leaned into Taylor and Taylor enjoyed the closeness in the relative privacy of darkness.

"Ever the optimist," Taylor commented.

"Is there a better way to be?"

"Nah," he said. More kids were coming their way, similarly outfitted as whatever monster was popular for the year. "How long do we have?"

"Three weeks," Tom said, dipping his hand in the bowl to retrieve enough candy bars to hand to each of the kids. They all thanked them and their parents waved a hello. Taylor remained ever impressed at the friendly treatment they received in the town.

The rest of the evening proceeded without incident and as quickly as it had come, October was gone and November was upon them. Unfortunately, the following morning was one where Tom had to get up early, so they were already asleep by the time the clock struck twelve. Taylor's last thought was to wonder what they'd have to deal with next and he regretted it as soon as it passed through his head…

Chapter Four

The Next Generation

Taylor lowered himself into the chair, groaning like an old man. Gen handed him a steaming cup of tea, seating herself on the couch beside him. Outside, a cold wind blew the remaining leaves from the trees, a reminder that another summer was gone and the icy winds of winter had replaced it.

"So, what brings you over in the middle of the afternoon?" she asked, dark eyes watching Taylor intently.

"Pete had to go to the city to argue a case today and the office was quiet, so I decided to treat myself to an afternoon off. I saw you were home, so I dropped in."

Gen nodded. "Seems like I'm hardly ever home anymore," she said. "All of a sudden, business is pouring in and I'm struggling to keep up. Miguel says it's starting to be like you and Tom."

Taylor shook his head. "Don't let that happen," he said. "At least, wait until you're married. The stress is almost more than I can take sometimes."

"How's the new guy working out?"

"So far, so good," Taylor said. "I wasn't too thrilled with the idea at first, but he's been really doing a good job and Tom has even gotten to take a little time off. He slept in for the first time in weeks the other morning—and was almost late to work!"

"It'll all work out," Gen consoled.

Taylor waved his hand dismissively. "Oh, I never had any fear about that. It's just getting to the point of it working out. I'm amazed at his stamina, though. I was whipped in the first week, but he still goes at it day in and day out."

"And being closed on Sunday and Monday?"

"It's working out okay. There was some initial grumbling around town, but we promised to make it temporary—just until we can get enough help."

Gen nodded, sipping her tea. "Do you think it will be temporary?"

Taylor took a sip from his own cup, gently setting it back in the saucer. "As long as Wayne works out. Tom is still working on staffing up some more—we'd rather have too many people than too few right now, you know?"

"It's a delicate balance," Gen agreed. Her ring glinted on her finger, even in the overcast light coming in from outside. Taylor gestured to the ring.

"So, have you set a date yet?"

She smiled. "Trust me, you'll be the first to know. We're still thinking about May, but neither of us can make up our mind. Of course, in typical male fashion, Miguel doesn't really care, so it's mainly been Anita, Sandy, and me trying to figure out the details. One of the biggest problems has been to figure out who to have for my Maid of Honor."

"What's the problem?" Taylor asked, taking a sip.

"My best friend is a man."

He coughed, catching the cup in the saucer as he set it on the table. Gen rested a hand on his back, but didn't pat it, knowing he just needed to cough it out.

"Sorry!" she said. "You okay?"

"Yeah, okay," Taylor said, taking a couple deep breaths. "Gay or not, I am *not* wearing a dress."

"I know, I know," Gen said. "You're a guy, a big studly man, got it."

"Just so we're clear," Taylor said, resting his elbows on his knees.

"We were thinking about breaking with tradition," Gen went on, unfazed. "Miguel has two sisters, I have you and Tom. We were thinking we'd have men in black tuxes, with vests either navy blue on my side or maroon on Miguel's side. Then the girls on either side would have dresses to match."

"Will the guy—girl ratios match up?"

Gen shrugged. "We'll just have each person walk up separately. We figured we'd skip the wedding party dances, then it wouldn't matter. That way, you don't have to dance with Miguel's Best Man, Alex."

"Is he cute?"

Gen glared at him. "I'm going to pretend for Tom's sake that I didn't hear that."

Taylor sat back, again sipping his tea, thinking. Finally, he looked up. "So, you're planning to have *me* stand up with you?"

"Who else would I have?" she asked. "I mean, I could pick one of the girls just to keep up appearances, but why? Miguel was the first one to suggest it, and he was sincere. I know he was more conservative at first, but his attitude has really come around."

"I guess so," Taylor agreed.

"So, what do you think?"

Taylor smiled. "You know I'll do whatever you want. Except wear a dress."

Gen laughed. "I know, but what do you *think*? Does it sound like a good idea, or will it come off looking silly?"

"It will only look silly if we act like it's silly," Taylor said, parroting a phrase Tom often used. "If we all treat it as perfectly normal, everyone else will have to do so as well. Besides, I think anyone you're going to invite already knows you well enough to know you'll do what you think is right, not just what tradition demands."

Gen nodded, appreciating the implied compliment. "In that case, I'm asking you to be my..." she paused, clearly uncertain of what to call the position. In a moment of inspiration, she said, "I'm asking you to be my Gentleman of Honor."

Taylor nodded gravely. "The honor will be mine," he said.

"Do you think Tom will be willing?"

"I think he'd be hurt if he wasn't included," Taylor admitted.

Gen nodded, her decision made. "Don't say anything. I'll come by in the next day or so and talk to him."

"Okay," Taylor agreed. "In that case, I'm not going to say anything about my participation, either. I don't want him to think you asked me and he was an afterthought."

"Sounds good," Gen said.

Taylor stood. "Speaking of Tom, I should run over to the bakery and see how he's doing. He'll be out of school now and he usually stops by there on the way home."

Gen showed him to the door. "Thanks for stopping by," she said. "I'll come see you guys tonight or tomorrow to talk to Tom."

"Sounds good," Taylor said. He leaned over to give her a kiss on the cheek, then headed home to get his car.

Less than two minutes later, he parked in front of the bakery and hopped out. The November winds were as cold as the October winds had been warm and he hoped it didn't bode for a snowy winter. The last few years they'd managed to avoid significant snowfall and that was just fine by Taylor. He was more of a water sports guy than a snow sports guy.

Tom had taken down the screen door and stored it, commenting there was no point to have it in the way when they had to keep the main door closed anyway. Taylor pushed the old wooden door closed behind him, struggling against the wind. If the temperature dropped too much more, they'd wind up dealing with snow.

"Hi, Taylor."

Emmy was stooped over in one of the display cases, cleaning the inside of the glass. Most of the cases were empty in the late day, Mrs. Johnson having gone home for the day, leaving the clean up work for Emmy and Wayne to prepare for the next day.

"Hi, Em," Taylor greeted back. "Is Tom here?"

"He's in the back," she said. Even with Wayne learning very quickly, Tom still tried to come in and help him get everything ready for the morning baking. Taylor still wondered where he found the energy, but he could never accuse Tom of slacking off.

He made his way around the counter and edged past Emmy as she did contortions to reach the various angles of the glass. Rounding the corner, he walked down the hall to the baking room, walking in like he owned the place...which, of course, he did.

The visage at the center of the room stopped him cold. Tom and Wayne knelt in the center of the floor, holding each other tightly. Wayne had his shirt off, which he held in one of his tightly balled fists where his arms encircled Tom. His head was turned away from Taylor, buried in Tom's shoulder. Tom had his back to Taylor, not realizing he was standing there.

"Uh, hi guys?" Taylor said hesitantly, unsure of what he'd walked in on.

Tom's head turned sharply and Wayne jumped, clearly surprised and embarrassed. Tom didn't really let him go, but turned enough so he could see Taylor.

"Tay, I'm glad you're here," he said, his voice quiet and a little sad.

As Taylor saw Wayne's face, he realized the young man was crying. He still wasn't sure why he wasn't wearing his shirt, but figured he'd give Tom a little leeway on that one.

"What's going on?" Taylor asked, trying to keep the edge from his voice.

"You'd better have a look at this," Tom said, his voice urgent.

Taylor walked closer, looking at both of the men as they still held each other on the floor. Slowly, he circled Tom. Wayne watched him peripherally, expression still embarrassed and hurt. He buried his face in Tom's shoulder again.

As Taylor came around them, he was again stopped cold. This time, he realized something very different was going on and he felt the first tendrils of fear work their way up his back. There, in Tom's arms, he saw Wayne's bare back, black and blue, purple, brown and green, bruised and rebruised from repeated attacks. In an instant, his concern for what was going on between Wayne and Tom was replaced with concern for what was going on in Wayne's life to cause such marks to be on his body.

"My God," Taylor breathed. He knelt beside Wayne, his hand gently touching his back. Wayne flinched at the slightest touch and Taylor drew his hand back, not wanting to hurt the boy. "How did this happen?" he asked.

Wayne sat mute, eyes squeezed shut, face red, head tight against Tom's shoulder. Taylor gently rested his hand on Wayne's shoulder, picking an area that appeared to be devoid of marks.

"Wayne, you need to tell me what happened. I can see from the marks that this isn't the first time. I need to know what happened so Tom and I can help you."

He sniffed back tears, slowly opening his eyes. They were an almost hunter green, but very bloodshot from tears. He sat up a bit, his brown hair mussed from resting against Tom's chin. Taylor realized Tom's own eyes were damp, more from frustration at seeing someone mistreated. Absently, he reached back to run his hand over Tom's back, too.

"It's nothing," Wayne said.

Softly, Taylor shook his head. "I know you feel like you need to protect someone, Wayne," he said, "but this time, you need to talk to us. We're your friends and we're on your side. I want to make sure this doesn't happen to you again."

"They say I'm a faggot," he spat. "That I'm queer. They say I'm nothing but a useless fairy." Wayne's face contorted in pain, not from his physical wounds, but from the emotional conflict within himself.

"Who says that?" Taylor asked, his voice more gentle than he could ever remember it. He hated to see anyone in pain, but this poor lost kid was more than he could bear.

Wayne froze, some inner turmoil wreaking havoc on him as he fought with himself over wanting to protect his tormentor and wanting to be free of the burden. Taylor continued to gently rub his shoulders, trying to offer reassurance and comfort in the face of the enormous burden the young man carried. He shook his head, jaw tight.

"You need to release this burden," Taylor said. "We're going to be here for you. I promise."

"Tell him," Tom whispered, never letting go.

Wayne turned to look at Tom and Taylor saw the trust between them. Tom nodded, reconfirming his words. Wayne looked down, unable to face Taylor.

"My dad," he said softly. "My dad and my brother. They just keep shoving me around, telling me I'm a fag."

"Since you've worked here?" Taylor asked.

"No, before that. It's been a while. I've never had a girlfriend or gone to a dance," Wayne admitted. "They keep saying if I wasn't queer, I'd have a girlfriend."

Taylor felt at once relieved and horrified. He was relieved that it wasn't association with them that had brought on this treatment. He was horrified that Wayne's own "family" would treat him this way.

"Are you?" Taylor asked, voice a virtual whisper in the warm room.

Wayne's eyes snapped up, terrified. Taylor didn't know whether he would—or could—answer the question honestly, but he thought it would be better for all of them to try to get the truth on the table. He knew from his own experience that telling this first person was the hardest and it would never seem as daunting once it was out there. He could also see that Wayne both wanted to tell him, but had been so abused physically and emotionally that he was nearly scared to death over what might happen. His gaze was locked on Taylor's. Taylor said nothing, trying to keep the fire he felt toward Wayne's family from expressing itself in his eyes. He wanted Wayne to feel comfortable telling him the truth. He could see the truth there, in Wayne's eyes, but he needed it to come to the surface, where they could all deal with it together.

Wayne took a couple of deep breaths, then slowly nodded. Taylor smiled thinly, both to reassure him and from the relief the answer brought to him. He would help this boy, but he could only do it if he was willing to accept help. Admitting his sexuality to himself was the first step—everything else would come from that one step.

Taylor nodded, pulling him over to give him a reassuring hug himself. He didn't know Wayne that well, as he worked with Tom most of the time, but he felt a new found protectiveness toward him.

"It's going to be okay," Taylor said. "Tom and I will be here for you, all the way."

Wayne nodded and Taylor looked over his shoulder to Tom, who silently mouthed the words, "thank you." Taylor gently pushed Wayne back, realizing he had a couple good bruises on his chest, too. He gently held him, hands on his shoulders, catching his gaze.

"Here's what we're going to do," Taylor said. "We're going to take you to a doctor and have you checked out. The bakery is going to be closed tomorrow."

"No," Wayne said. "I don't want anyone else to know."

"No one else will know for now," Taylor promised. "We have a friend who is a doctor. I'll call him and make sure everything is handled discretely."

"Okay," Wayne said. He looked defeated, but also relieved, probably feeling like he had someone on his side for the first time.

"You're eighteen, right?" Taylor asked.

"Yeah," Wayne said.

"Good. That will get us around pretty much everything as far as custody and rights goes. You can stay with us tonight. Tomorrow, I'm going to make a couple calls to find out what we need to do to protect you and keep this from ever happening again."

"Tay?" Tom said. Taylor looked up. "I told Wayne he can have the apartment upstairs."

Taylor looked ready to argue, but bit back his comments. In front of Wayne, he nodded. "We'll work out the details as we go," he said. "First step is to make sure you're okay physically. Next step is to keep you that way. Then we'll move on to the long term stuff."

He stood, helping Wayne up. Tom stood behind them, watching Taylor.

"Go ahead and get yourself cleaned up," Taylor said. "We'll let Emmy know she can go and bring the car around back. Come on out when you hear the horn beep."

"Okay," Wayne said, staring at the floor. Taylor hugged him again, feeling the strength of his arms as Wayne held him tight.

"You're going to be okay," Taylor said. "You're not alone now."

"Okay," Wayne said, a sob in his voice. He let go and pulled on his shirt, dusting the flour from his clothes. Taylor led Tom out and they walked into the store.

Tom told Emmy they weren't going to be open and that they had to go. He told her they'd lock up and he'd see her in school the next day. She gave him a quizzical look, but hung her apron on the door and headed out the front door with them.

As they pulled their doors closed, Taylor started the car and headed down to the cross street that would take them to the back of the building.

"How did you find out?" he asked.

Tom shook his head, his own expression taking on a look of shock. "Completely by accident. I bumped into him and he winced like I'd punched him. I kind of jokingly said 'don't be a baby' and hit him on the back. His face looked like I'd hit him with a lead pipe. He tried to cover it up, but I could see from his face it was more than just a small thing. I pulled up the back of his shirt and saw the first of the bruises. He tried to avoid it, but I told him I wanted to see what had happened. He took off his shirt, then broke down. That's when you walked in."

"I don't know what to do next," Taylor said. "Legally, he's an adult, so he doesn't have to go back there. But abuse doesn't always stop at the door to the house. If I say anything to the police, they'll have to press charges. The school is probably the same way. I wouldn't mind putting those guys in jail, but I don't know if he's ready for that."

"He's definitely not ready," Tom agreed. They pulled up to the door and Taylor tapped the horn lightly. Wayne appeared, quickly locking the door behind him. He pulled open the back door to the Grand Cherokee and Taylor found himself thankful for the deeply tinted glass.

Taylor looked at Wayne, who had pulled on a warm coat over his T-shirt. His eyes were still red, his face was streaked where tears had run, and his hair was messed with white flour. Wayne watched him in return, still uncertain about what was going to happen next.

"You okay?" Taylor asked.

"Been better," Wayne admitted.

"You're gonna be okay," Taylor affirmed.

Wayne nodded and Taylor offered a reassuring smile. He put the car in drive and pulled away.

"You're going to Rick's?" Tom asked.

"Yeah. Would you call him and tell him we're going to pull up around back? Tell him we'll explain when we get there."

"Okay," Tom said, taking his phone from his pocket.

Taylor navigated them to the office of their friend, a local chiropractor, using back roads where he thought they would attract the least attention. Wayne looked both scared and empowered, as though his long nightmare was finally coming to an end. Taylor could only imagine how his life had been, especially as he got older and was expected to behave in a way he didn't understand and couldn't bring himself to act.

Taylor had come out in his early twenties, while a student in college. Coming from a fairly cultural family, his revelation had been met with virtual indifference. His parents admitted the thought had crossed their minds and said it made no difference to them. His brother said he "knew" and promptly offered to introduce him to some of his gay friends. Few of Taylor's friends had given it a second thought and those who did weren't friends anymore.

Tom's coming out was much more recent and had been a function of meeting Taylor. After breaking up with a long-term boyfriend, Taylor had moved to live with Gen for a few months. The first Saturday he was in town, he'd taken his dog for her morning walk. A neighbor, Rob, recommended he stop at the bakery when he got to town. Taylor often wondered if Rob, who claimed he'd immediately recognized Taylor as gay, sent him to the bakery as a setup. Whatever the case, he'd met Tom and there was an instant attraction, try as Taylor might to ignore it. Tom finally came out after a disastrous incident at a town dance when one of the attendees "outed" Taylor in front of much of the town. Tom finally told Gen he was interested in Taylor and they drove to New York to get him when he fled with a friend. Tom admitted he was more concerned with having Taylor in his life than how people might judge him based on his sexuality. To their delight, the town had been almost endlessly supportive, ultimately making Taylor mayor.

Wayne's situation clearly wasn't so supportive. Taylor knew a number of people who had negative experiences with family or friends and it had always bothered him. He'd never been directly involved in any of them though, and he couldn't remember any of them involving such blatant abuse. He could somewhat understand how the shock might result in people needing to distance themselves, but he could not and would not accept abuse of any kind.

He didn't know much about Wayne, but from what he did know, he was a very nice kid. Tom had hired him at the end of October, about two and a half weeks before. Since that time, Tom had spent as much time as he could educating him on how to run the bakery and had been very happy with his progress. Taylor had been around him a few times and found him to be a friendly young man, though a bit shy. Taylor knew he tended to have a more dominant personality, so it didn't surprise him when some people felt shy around him. But, from what he knew of Wayne, he was someone who deserved a little help.

They pulled up to the back door and Taylor stopped the car. As they got out, Rick met them at the door and hustled them into a waiting exam room.

"Hi, guys," he said hesitantly, wondering what was going on.

"Hi, Rick," Taylor greeted in return. Wayne sat on the table and Tom stood next to him, resting against the table.

"What's the story?" Rick asked.

Taylor and Tom gave him the quick run-down, trying to fill in as many of the details as possible to avoid making Wayne repeat them to a stranger. Rick glanced at him from time to time as his attention was drawn back and forth by the two men. Finally, as Taylor finished with their discussion in the baking room, Rick nodded and turned to Wayne.

"Let's get you checked out," he said. "I can see if there's anything major. If there is, you'll need to see a medical doctor. If not, we'll just let you go."

"Okay," Wayne said.

"You guys can wait in the hall," Rick said. "There is no one else here right now."

"They can stay," Wayne said.

"They'll be right outside," Rick said. "Don't worry. We can even leave the door ajar."

"Okay," he said again, still looking scared.

"We'll be right out there," Tom said, giving him a reassuring pat on the shoulder. He followed Taylor out, leaving the door not quite closed behind him. He heard Rick tell Wayne to go ahead and take off his shirt as Taylor led him a little farther down the hall.

"What do you know about his parents?" Taylor whispered.

"His mom's gone. She got married again and moved away. He lives with his dad and his older brother, neither of whom are real winners. It's like I said before, he's trying to earn enough money to put himself through school."

"What's going to happen if we let him use the apartment?"

Tom shrugged. "I don't know. He's an adult legally. You tell me."

Taylor shook his head. "I don't know, either. I'm going to have to do some research. How's your school? Is there anyone there we can get to help us without causing a scene?"

"Maybe," Tom said. "I'll do a little asking discretely."

"Try to avoid telling them who the student is. The last thing we want to do is cause him more trouble."

The door to the exam room opened and Rick led Wayne out. He was clad only in his socks and a paper exam smock. As they walked by Tom and Taylor, Rick said, "No peeking, boys." Wayne blushed, but kept the smock closed behind him. Tom gave him a little whistle anyway and he glanced back with a hint of a smile.

As they went into the X-ray room, Taylor nodded.

"He'll be okay."

Tom took his hand. "Thanks for being so great today," he said.

"Would you expect any less of me?" Taylor asked.

"Absolutely not. I'm just thankful you were there to help. I honestly didn't know what to do."

Taylor laughed nervously. "I *don't* know what to do. I'm just winging it, too. I'm glad you're here to help with the winging it. He seems to really trust you."

Tom nodded. "I think I'm the first person to ever believe in him."

"Is he a good student?"

Again, Tom nodded. "Yes, but he avoids anything that will bring attention to him. When I had him in class, I realized he would deliberately throw a grade if it meant he'd have to read in class. I started not making him read and he got straight A's."

Taylor shook his head. "How can anyone take a great kid and treat him that way?"

"I have no idea."

The door opened and Wayne came back down the hall, passing between them and back into the exam room. Rick came out and placed the X-ray films on a light box. He gestured for Tom and Taylor to join him.

Speaking softly, he said, "He's got a couple minor fractures in his ribs and some bruising of a couple organs. Nothing life threatening, but he definitely needs to be pulled from that environment so it doesn't keep happening."

"We're already on that," Tom said. "He's staying with us tonight and I told him he can take the apartment above the bakery."

Rick nodded. "I don't know what your situation is," he said, "but if you can do it, I'd say it might be a good idea for him to stay with you for a while."

"Oh?" Taylor asked.

"He's going to need support, stability, and security. He needs to know there are people around him who care about him and will look out for him. Giving him a place to live where he won't be abused is a good idea, but he shouldn't be alone just yet."

"Right," Taylor agreed.

"Is he gay?" Rick asked.

"Yeah," Tom said.

"Then being around you two will also help him start to accept himself, too. The fact that he was willing to let you see what has happened to him is really a way of asking you for help. He never would have put himself in that position otherwise. You both seem willing to help, so I'm telling you it's a good idea. You should probably also see if he'll talk to Steve a little bit. I shouldn't speak for him, but I'll bet he'd be willing to help out for free for a while, just to give this kid a leg up."

"He's going to be okay?" Tom asked.

"Physically, his wounds will heal. Emotionally, it's going to be a longer road," Rick said. "He's lucky to have you guys to help him out."

"Thanks, Rick," Taylor said, shaking his hand.

"What do we owe you?" Tom asked.

Rick shook his head. "I'll just take a couple of those artery blocking chocolate croissants the next time I'm in, okay?"

"Are you sure?" Taylor asked.

Rick nodded. "Just make sure he's okay, okay? Bring him back in a week and let me have another look. I want to make sure all the bruising and swelling goes down as it should."

Wayne appeared at the door, once again dressed.

"Sounds good," Taylor agreed.

Rick let them back out and they took the back roads back to town.

"Is your family home now?" Taylor asked.

Wayne shook his head. "My dad works nights and my brother will already be at the bar."

"Would you like to stop and pick up some things?"

Wayne looked at him. "Are you sure you want me to stay with you? I don't want to be any trouble. You've already done so much."

"Wayne, we will not put you back where you can get hurt again," Tom insisted. "We can either let you pick up your stuff or we can just take you back. It's up to you."

"Okay, I'll get some stuff, then," he said.

He guided Taylor to his house and they pulled up. Taylor agreed they'd wait in the car and Wayne would flash the light twice if the coast was clear. If he didn't flash the light, Tom and Taylor would follow him in less than a minute. Taylor told him to go ahead and grab whatever he could carry so he could be gone for a few days, if necessary.

The light flashed and they relaxed. Taylor kept an eye on the darkened street, watching for any lights that might be oncoming cars. The house was in a worn out part of town, several miles from where Taylor and Tom lived. He could just imagine what Wayne's family must look like if the status of their house was anything to go on.

"Never rains but it pours, huh?" Tom said.

"I'm just glad we can help him," Taylor said.

"Do you think this is a good idea?"

Taylor chuckled. "Who knows anymore? I think it's the right thing to do, so that's good enough for me."

Wayne returned, pulling the door closed behind him. He flew down the stairs, winded and beads of sweat on his brow. He slammed the door of the car behind him, tossing two bags on the seat.

"I tried to go as fast as I could," he managed between breaths.

Taylor backed out. "It's okay," he said. "You're safe now."

"What are you going to do?" Wayne asked, watching Taylor in the rear-view mirror.

"I don't know," Taylor admitted. "I'm going to start by getting information."

"Will your dad notice if you're not there?" Tom asked.

"Probably not. He works nights and I'm gone by the time he gets home most of the time," Wayne said.

"Good. In that case, we will all sleep easier tonight," Taylor said.

He weaved his way through the streets to finally bring them to their driveway. Parking the car, he hopped out and helped Wayne with the bags. He was surprised by the weight and realized the young man had packed not to return.

Smiling to himself, he followed Tom and his charge into the house. He'd wanted kids and realized this was a form of a test. Wayne may not be theirs, but his fate was in their hands now. It was up to them to help this poor kid rise above his circumstances and Taylor promised himself that was exactly what he would do. He could never predict what hand fate would deal him next, but he would make the best of what he had. Wayne McInerney needed friends to care about him and caring was something Tom and Taylor had in abundance.

Chapter Five

Psycho Pie-Baking Week

"So how does this work again?" Pete asked.

To say that the bakery was a mess was an understatement of near monumental proportions. In nearly every available space, pie boxes had been assembled and stacked. The walls were covered, the floor had just enough space to walk through the sea of maroon boxes. Everywhere, "Downey McEwan's Oven Fresh Pies" boxes were in sight. Gen and Emmy sat behind a makeshift counter that was really nothing more than a folding table near the door. Behind them, people rushed to fill orders and track receipts while still others bustled in the baking room, pulling cooked pies from the oven and replacing them as fast as the physics of baking would allow. Taylor had never seen such madness in his entire life.

"It's really simple," Taylor said, moving a stack of empty boxes so he and Pete could fill them with freshly cooled French Apple pies. "First in, last out. Obviously, people want to get their pies as close to Thanksgiving as possible. So, the sooner they placed their order in the fall, the later their delivery date. People taking delivery today only ordered a couple weeks ago. People taking delivery by Wednesday ordered back in August."

"I'll admit Tom bakes a mean pie," Pete said, "But I definitely wasn't thinking about Thanksgiving back in August."

"Me either," Taylor agreed. "But you can bet I will be next year."

Pete and Anita were among the hapless victims who had been called upon—begged, really—to come help deal with the throngs. People came from as far as forty-five minutes away to get their hands on a fresh baked pie. Some were lucky enough to get some of the "over baking" Tom had figured in for those people who didn't know they needed a reservation. As the week progressed, there would be fewer extras and more reservations only.

Wayne pulled the sheets of pies from the cart, leaving them on the display cases for Taylor and Pete while he took the mobile rack to the back to restock. Taylor had long since lost count of how many pies they'd baked and made up his mind he wouldn't ask until it was all said and done. Some things weren't worth knowing while he was stuck in the middle.

"Speaking of Tom, where is he?" Pete asked. Anita had pulled baking duty with Wayne while Emmy got a break out front with Gen. Rob and Mel had agreed to be the relief team, expecting to show up in a couple hours.

"Had to meet with the principal tonight," Wayne said, rolling the cart away.

"Got sent to the principal's office, huh?" Pete said, eyeing Taylor.

Taylor frowned. "That's funny. He didn't tell me he'd be late."

"Anything important?" Pete asked.

"Hope not," Taylor said. His hands were a virtual blur. Grab a pie. Set it in the box. Fold in the lock tabs. Add a sticker for the flavor. Next.

"How's he doing?" Pete asked, lowering his voice and nodding in Wayne's direction.

"So far, so good. He hasn't been home in almost a week. We took him to get more of his stuff the other night and he left his dad a note. So far, nothing."

Pete shook his head. "You've gotta be kidding. This guy torments the kid and then ignores the fact that he's gone?"

Taylor shrugged. "Maybe that's what he wanted. Maybe he's too drunk to care. I don't know—I've never understood people like that."

"But the whole point of the abuse was that his son was gay. Now he's living with two guys—you'd think that would be enough to incite a riot."

Taylor stopped moving, giving his friend and business partner a look. "Pete, I would just as soon *not* incite a riot if it's all the same to you."

"I didn't mean that you would do it on purpose," Pete said.

Gen came around the island of boxes, eyeing their progress. "All right, you two. Less talking, more boxing."

"Hey, we've nearly got all of the pies caught up," Taylor defended.

Gen nodded, acknowledging their work. "Good, then you can start moving them over by Emmy and me. We're going through them almost faster than we can grab them."

"Is everything on schedule?" Taylor asked.

"So far," Gen said, picking up some of the completed pies. "I just need more French Silk right now."

Taylor felt the phone on his hip vibrate and he reached down to take it from the clip. A glance at the colorful display showed him it was Tom.

"Hi there," Taylor greeted warmly. "You gonna join us?"

"I'm still at school," Tom said, his voice anything but happy. Taylor was immediately serious.

"What's wrong?"

"Wayne's dad called the school today. He's trying to make a scene. I think you might want to come over here."

"I'm on my way," he said. He turned to Pete, who already knew there was a problem from the look on his face. "I've gotta go. There's a problem at the school."

"Wayne's dad?" Pete asked.

"Yeah. Don't say anything to him. I'll be back as soon as I can."

"Okay."

Taylor made his way through the hallway to the back, glancing into the baking room to see Wayne and Anita busily preparing the next trays of pies while the rest baked in the oven. There were pies and pie parts everywhere. Taylor realized he may never eat pie again. One good way to keep off the pounds—work in a bakery.

He burst through the back door, heading directly for the car. Tom had taken the Jeep the last few mornings, saying he didn't want to tempt anyone to do something to the Jag. Though the school had, by and large, been quiet, he'd heard some mutterings from some of the students who knew something was up with "that quiet kid."

It incensed Taylor to think that the kid who kept to himself and bothered no one was a target of derision. Of course, it was hardly a new experience, but it still made his blood boil. There was no acceptable reason or excuse and he certainly had no intention of standing for it.

He sped through the streets, a man on a mission. He'd already done a lot of the research on what, if any, laws pertained to their situation. Given that Wayne had already reached the age of majority, there really wasn't anything his father could do. Wayne was legally an adult and if he didn't want to live with his family—or even have any contact with his family—no one could force him to do so.

That said, Taylor had also pointed out that the school would no doubt be unhappy with a teacher interjecting himself in the affairs of a student. No matter how well intentioned, school districts did not like to have the appearance of telling a family how to conduct itself. While Wayne's family could certainly use some guidance, Tom would not be the first choice to provide it.

Of course, the fact that he was the…guy…with the mayor of the town would further complicate the situation. They weren't just a couple of gay guys trying to help some kid—they were a schoolteacher and the town mayor. For once, Taylor liked the idea of using his power and position to an advantage. Wayne needed them and he was going to be there for him.

In less than a week, Taylor had already seen a perceptible difference in the young man. His confidence was growing and he smiled more often. He was positively running the baking area, keeping the flow of pies moving with the help of whomever of their friends got wrangled next. No matter how inexperienced the baker, he guided the process and made the person feel like he or she could do it. Though Taylor had occasionally helped Tom, he'd never done the volume they were doing now and had even done his tour in the baking room. At this job, Wayne was all business, showing Taylor the most efficient way to do each of the necessary tasks.

At night, when they got home, he was more subdued, often choosing to just sit in a chair and watch TV quietly. He would often ask if there was anything he could do for Tom or Taylor, as though he felt he needed to earn his keep. Slowly, they were getting him to relax and trying to get him to feel a little less like the weight of the world was on his shoulders.

The night before, they'd checked his wounds and found they were healing well. Rick did a couple more x-rays and said the worst was done and he would fully recover. Wayne had broken down when they got home, holding on to both his newfound friends as though he would never let go.

Taylor had talked to Steve, Rick's…partner…and asked for information on how best to help him. Steve was one of two psychiatrists in the town and had gotten the low-down on the situation from Rick. Taylor wanted to be sure they did everything they could to help Wayne and did nothing to worsen his situation. Steve said that simply being his friend would be a good start as they helped him to meet new people and come out of the shell he'd built around himself.

Taylor pulled into the nearly empty parking lot, taking a spot at the front. He hopped out of the car, only then noticing he'd left his coat at the bakery as the cold air bit through his thin sleeves. He and Pete had gone there directly from their office, still wearing the dress shirts their jobs demanded.

He entered the building, headed for the main office. Tom met him at the door.

"Thanks for coming," he said. Taylor had rarely been around Tom at the school, but he saw someone other than the man he was used to seeing. Tom wore a pressed navy blue shirt and beige slacks with cordovan tasseled loafers—quite a bit more formal than the casual attire he usually chose.

Pulling Tom back into the corridor, Taylor spoke softly. "What's going on?"

"Wayne's dad had somebody call the school district. He's threatening to sue."

Taylor frowned. "On what grounds?"

"Violation of the school's fiduciary responsibility to see to the safety of his son," Tom quoted.

"You're kidding, right?" Taylor asked.

"'Fraid not," Tom sighed.

Taylor shook his head. "Okay, let's go," he said, opening the door.

Tom followed quietly, already sensing Taylor's mood. Though Taylor was a pussycat to the people he cared about, he was a lion to anyone who crossed them.

The principal rose and introduced himself. "Mayor Connolly? I'm Dr. Hargreaves," he said. Turning to the other people at the table, he said, "This is Joel Weiss, District Counsel, and Ellen Caffery, Superintendent."

Taylor's face bore none of its usual good humor as he realized these people had grilled Tom for the last several hours without the privilege of counsel. He decided they were probably unused to dealing with matters such as this and fired the first shot.

"The school is violating its responsibility by failing to restore Wayne McInerney to his father's home where he has been repeatedly abused?" Taylor's voice rang with both a question and a statement as he stared down the three faces on the opposite side of the table. He didn't mention Tom, keeping his attention focused on the people before him. Slowly, Hargreaves lowered himself into his chair and Taylor followed suit.

"Mr. McInerney believes it's his right as a father to determine the best place for his son," the superintendent said. "It is the policy of this school district not to interject itself into the private affairs of families."

"The school district has a responsibility to see to the safety and well-being of its students," Taylor countered.

"A privilege that has been denied to us by Mr. McEwan's failure to notify the school of this problem."

"Mr. McInerney's rights have already been abrogated by the fact that his son has reached the age of majority," Taylor asserted.

"Mr. McInerney does not deny that his son has a right to choose," the school district attorney said. "He is simply arguing that the district has a responsibility to see to the safety of its students, whatever their age."

"Then the school district should be commending Mr. McEwan for taking the initiative to help a troubled student remove himself from a harmful, potentially deadly situation." Taylor's voice was sharp and cutting. Tom glanced at him, but quickly looked away when he saw the intensity of Taylor's gaze. Like Taylor to him, he had rarely seen Taylor operating in his professional capacity and he was surprised by the power he commanded.

"It remains our position that no one in our faculty should take matters into his own hands. If the school is to adequately protect itself from liability, we must have all the facts," the superintendent said, watching Taylor.

"Mr. McEwan did not seek to deliberately deceive the school district. On the advice of counsel and at the request of Wayne McInerney, he did not reveal the existence of the problem pending research into Wayne McInerney's rights."

"Which rights?" the attorney asked.

"Primarily, his right to determine for himself where and how he wanted to live."

"So you assert you planned to inform the district?"

Taylor nodded. "Of course. However, that would be done at a time and in a manner of Wayne McInerney's choosing. As an adult, he is entitled to the same right to privacy as the rest of us."

"Regardless, it is the policy of this school and this school district that the proper authorities be brought in whenever a student is in trouble. Mr. McEwan lacks the experience and training to adequately handle a situation of this magnitude," Hargreaves said.

"Really?" Taylor asked.

"We have trained counselors and support staff ready to handle problems exactly like this," Hargreaves continued.

"Do you?" Taylor asked. "Which problem, exactly, will they be handling?"

Hargreaves faltered, unsure of where Taylor was taking the conversation. "The, uh, problem we're discussing. The abuse Wayne McInerney has suffered."

"The abuse your trained, experienced staff has been unable to recognize for the duration of Wayne's education in this district?" Taylor asked. His voice never faltered as he sat with his hands clasped before him on the table.

"We can't be expected to find each and every case on our own," Caffery said.

"But that's exactly what you've argued on behalf of Mr. McInerney," Taylor said. "You said the district has a fiduciary responsibility to see to the safety of the students in its charge. Based upon that, you should have known about the abuse a long time ago."

"One of the best methods to acquire that information if from our staff," Hargreaves said.

"What is the cause of Wayne's abuse?" Taylor asked.

"The cause?" Weiss queried.

"Yes, why is he being abused?"

"That's something we would have to ask Mr. McInerney," the superintendent said.

"Your trained staff of experts hasn't already figured it out?"

The three of them glanced at each other and the attorney spoke. "We're not at liberty to discuss a case involving a student."

"That student is my client," Taylor said. The truth of the statement might be arguable, but he'd come back to that later.

"It's not uncommon for teenage sons and their fathers to have physically confrontational relationships," Hargreaves said. "That is one of the reasons it's important for us to be able to interject."

"The district's policy is to avoid involving itself in a family's affairs," Taylor reminded.

"So long as it doesn't involve harm to the student," the superintendent pointed out.

"Wayne has been harmed."

Hargreaves' face reddened. "The point of this meeting is not Wayne McInerney. The point of this meeting is the failure of Mr. McEwan to properly handle the situation according to district guidelines."

"The point of this meeting," Taylor clarified, "Is that a young man at this school was being brutally beaten by his own father and brother because he is homosexual. The point is that he confided in someone he felt he could trust because he didn't know where else to go. That person, Mr. McEwan, has in turn taken responsibility for helping him, as a friend. Because he is of the age of majority, policy or not, Mr. McEwan is *not* required to share this man's private struggles with you or anyone else. If he were underage, the situation would be different. He is not underage and, therefore, is capable of deciding for himself who he chooses to tell what and when. You have chosen to have a virtual witch hunt in defense of a man who has repeatedly attacked his own child because of a part of himself that is beyond his control. It is *not* this school district's place to interject itself in Wayne's life, so long as Wayne is satisfied with the situation as it is. As for Mr. McInerney's rights, Mr. McInerney can go to hell. If he wants to sue this district, Mr. McEwan, or me, just let me know what the court date is and I'll show up. Mr. McInerney is a vicious, ruthless man who ought to be in jail, except that his son still cares too much for him to put him there. Your only responsibility is to respect Wayne's wishes and do your level best to make sure no other students under your *fiduciary* charge are forced to endure what he has gone through."

The three district representatives were wide-eyed, clearly not expecting a tirade of such magnitude. Without further adieu, Taylor stood, leaning over to face them.

"And let me make one other thing perfectly clear: there will be no repercussions on Tom with regard to this incident. What he did he did on the advice of his lawyer, me, and at the request of Wayne McInerney. Wayne's father's rights and school district policy have no place here. If you choose to take action against Tom, I promise you, we will meet again in front of a judge. Be advised that I represent Tom McEwan and Wayne McInerney in this matter and any correspondence with regard to it will be directed to me."

The three faces before him were visages in stone. The two academic personnel turned to the attorney, clearly out of their league. He nodded. "We understand, Mr. Connolly. I will consult with my clients and advise you on our next course of action."

Taylor nodded, finally looking at Tom. Tom read his body language and rose to join him. Taylor turned to the people across the table. "Thank you, lady and gentlemen. Have a good evening."

He turned and held open the door for Tom, following him out. They said nothing as they exited the school, Taylor quietly following Tom to his car. He was a couple spaces down from the Jag in the teachers' lot.

"Christ, Taylor, it'll be a miracle if I don't get fired," Tom whispered, hopping into the Jeep.

"You won't get fired," Taylor promised. "Trust me, they don't want this thing to escalate. It's too complicated for them. Wayne's dad may put more pressure on them, but if he does, I'll put a little pressure on him and he'll go away."

"What can you do?" Tom asked.

"Threaten to expose his behavior publicly. Threaten to press criminal assault charges against him. I already talked to the chief of police and have that base covered. Right now, they're not pressing charges because they don't want to traumatize Wayne any more and there aren't any other children in the house who may need protection. All it would take is one phone call, though, and Mr. McInerney will find himself in jail. The district really doesn't want to be involved, but they have to protect themselves in case word gets out."

"I hope you're right," Tom worried.

Taylor smiled reassuringly. "Relax, it'll be okay. Just remember we're doing the right thing—and we're doing it together."

Tom smiled reluctantly.

"Okay, now get a move on. We have pies to bake and Wayne's been pulling oven duty since school let out. I'm sure he could use a break."

"Yes, sir," Tom said, putting the car in drive. He backed out and pulled away, headed toward town.

Taylor walked back toward the Jag just as the attorney for the district, Weiss, came out of the building. They regarded each other for a moment and Taylor waited while he walked up.

"You're the one who argues all the employment law cases, aren't you?" he asked.

"That's me," Taylor said, taking it a little easier on him away from the table.

"You've done some good work," Weiss said, a subtle compliment.

"Thank you."

He sighed, glancing down at the car. "We don't want to have to make an issue out of this, but I'm afraid Wayne's father may back us into a corner. Like it or not, Wayne is a student at the school and Tom is a teacher. There are certain boundaries there that shouldn't be crossed."

Taylor nodded. "In principle, I agree," he said, "But there also has to be an understanding that each situation is different. You know and I know that this district is not geared to handle something like Wayne's situation. It's not that it would be impossible; merely that Tom and Wayne have been able to handle it better on their own. Wayne needs a mentor, someone to look up to. That's what Tom is doing for him. By giving him a safe place to stay, we're able to make sure he can begin to heal, both physically and emotionally. The school might try to do that, but it's something friends can do better."

"You're Wayne's friends?" Weiss asked.

Taylor nodded. "I think we are. From what Tom has told me, he doesn't have a lot of friends. I'm sure the facts of his life combined with the abuse from his home have only exacerbated the situation. We've had Steve Hayes involved and he's volunteered to talk to Wayne when he's ready."

Weiss nodded. "Tom mentioned that earlier. We aren't trying to conduct a witch hunt, Mr. Connolly. We want what's best for Wayne, too. Our job is also to help protect the integrity of the system, though."

Taylor nodded. "Let's hope none of us has to go through this again."

"Agreed."

"What are you going to do about Wayne's dad?"

Weiss smiled thinly. "I'm going to tell him the truth. We investigated the situation and learned that Wayne has left his home willingly and of his own accord because of the abuse he was receiving there. I'll tell him that, as a legal adult, Wayne has that right and the school district is powerless to intercede. I'll advise him that his best course of action will be to let the matter drop so as to avoid the district having to bring in the authorities and press criminal charges. With any luck, it will make the whole thing go away."

"And Tom?"

Weiss shook his head. "That's for the administration to decide. Off the record, I'll tell you that I'm advising them to verbally remind Tom of his obligations to report incidents related to students, but to otherwise let the matter drop. It really is in no one's best interests to further escalate this into a scandal."

Taylor nodded. "I hope they follow your advice. It's the same thing I would tell them."

Weiss smiled. "Frankly, I don't want to have to stand across a courtroom from you."

Taylor accepted the compliment quietly, opening the door to the car. "Have a good evening," he said.

"You, too," Weiss said, heading off toward his own car.

Taylor made his way back to the bakery in the darkness of night. It continued to amaze him how quickly summer had passed. Already, dusk was shortly after five and it was dark by six. He promised himself he would one day move to an area where it stayed light longer…but he knew he was really lying to himself at the same time.

Entering from the back of the bakery, he walked down the warm hallway outside the baking room. Inside, Tom and Wayne were both covered in flour, keeping the giant mixers running at full tilt. Rob and Mel had spared Anita, who was out front working boxing duty with Pete. Miguel had joined Gen at the front, freeing Emmy to sort the stacks into something more manageable. At the door, traffic had died down around the dinner hour, but the schedule still had a large number of people due to arrive before they finally closed the doors at nine.

"How many more days?" Pete asked. Anita smacked him, reminding him that they were there to support their friends.

As Taylor joined them, Pete checked to make sure no one else was within earshot. Gen had brought a radio earlier in the day, giving them something to listen to other than each other.

"How did it go?" he asked.

Taylor gave a non-committal shrug, taking off his tie and dress shirt in the warmth of the space, leaving on just a white T-shirt over which he pulled on a white apron.

"It went okay. We had a confrontation of a meeting, then left. I talked to the attorney for the district before I came back and his position basically echoes ours, though he couldn't say so in the meeting. Wayne's an adult, he can do what he wants. Tom's obligation to report his discussions to the school is much more murky given the extenuating circumstances. He's advising the school to let it drop and Wayne's dad to get lost before he lands in jail."

Pete nodded. "Sounds like good advice to me. You think they'll go for it?"

"I think so. The only unknown is Wayne's father. Hopefully, he'll know to leave well enough alone."

The words had no sooner passed his lips than the door opened with a bang and a man stumbled in from the street. Taylor looked over the piles of boxes and immediately knew they were in trouble. Miguel rose to face the man while Gen backed away. Taylor turned to Anita.

"Get Rob," he said quickly. "Be ready to call the police."

He rounded the counter from the end nearer the windows, Pete right behind him. Miguel stood in front of the man, an impassible barrier.

"Get outta mah way…damn Spic," the man slurred. "Ah'm here to get mah boy."

"Sir, I think you need to go," Miguel said, never raising his voice. Rob appeared from the baking room, Anita and Mel standing near the phone. Tom and Wayne appeared and Taylor saw the fear on the young man's face.

"Ah said get outta mah way, boy," the man yelled at Miguel, trying to push his way past. Miguel stood firm, neither shoving him, nor letting him through. "Wayne! Wayne get your butt out here! It's time to go home!"

Tom pushed Wayne back, trying to keep him from being visible to his father. Taylor saw the tears pass down his face, though he was sure Wayne didn't even realize it. Tom stood in front of him, acting as a shield from the visage before him.

"Ah said move your *ass*," the senior McInerney insisted, shoving Miguel. Rob, Pete, and Taylor moved as one, rounding the table and standing with Miguel.

"You need to leave now," Taylor said, voice firm. Though he was thin, he was strong and he would not back down to a bully, no matter who he was.

"Ah'm not goin' without mah son!"

"Your son is staying here," Taylor said. "You're not going to touch him ever again."

"Get your faggotty ass outta mah way or I'll knock you on it," he said, holding up a fist.

"That would not be a good idea," Rob said. "Now leave before we have you arrested."

"Wayne!" he hollered. "Get out here and face me, boy! Now!"

Wayne pushed past Tom, eyes never leaving his father. Tom reached for him, but he shook him off. He rounded the counter, walking up behind the four imposing men in front of his father.

"I'm not going with you," he said through a clenched jaw. "I'm not going to let you hurt me anymore."

McInerney shook his head. "Stop your yappin' boy and get in the car. I put up with your shit long enough. Get your ass home and get to workin'. You played with these faggots long enough."

"No!" Wayne spat, slicing the air with his hand. His face was a deep red and tears flowed freely from his eyes, but he paid them no notice. "No! These people are my friends! They *care* about me. They believe in me. They don't hit me with a baseball bat for burning a piece of chicken. And they don't care that I'm gay!"

McInerney's face went beet red. "No son'a'mine is no fairy. You stop talkin' that way, boy. Hear me? Now you get your ass home and we'll take care this on our own."

"No," Wayne said, shaking. "No, I'm never going to speak to you again. I don't ever want to see or hear from you again. Go away and never come back!"

McInerney shook with rage. "You will not talk to me that way, you hear me? You ain't no faggot. Now you get home!"

Wayne laughed, a painful, sorrowful expression devoid of humor. "That's just it, Dad. I am gay, a fairy, a faggot, a queer, whatever else you might like to say. So you'd better get used to it because there is nothing you can do to change it."

In his alcohol induced rage, McInerney suddenly stopped. For one brief second, he looked at Wayne and saw him for who he really was, for the man he really was. But the second passed, leaving only his hatred in his wake.

"Then you're dead to me. Don't ever come 'round me again, you hear? I don't ever want to see you again. You leave your brother and me alone. You ain't got no family no more. Jus' you and your fairies."

McInerney shoved open the door and stumbled back out onto the street, heading off in whatever direction he'd come. The four men all let go the breaths they had been holding and everyone went back to work to give Wayne some space. Taylor put an arm on his shoulders and Wayne fell into his arms, tears flowing down his face, his body still shaking and wracked with sobs. Taylor led him into the back, followed by Tom, while everyone else made themselves busy out front, mainly standing around as far from the hallway as possible.

Chapter Six

Fallout

A few short hours later, Taylor called off the baking for the night and sent everyone home. Tom worried over their ability to meet their orders, but Taylor held fast, pointing out that they were all exhausted and had been through a lot that day. Gen and Mel volunteered to take the early shift, as they had the most flexible schedules, to allow Tom and Wayne time to sleep in for once. Both bakers thankfully accepted and minutes later, they were on their way home.

Taylor could see Wayne was as emotionally whipped as his poor body had been the week before. Confronting his father would be a good thing for him in the long run, but it had drained him in the near term. After he pulled himself together, he bravely pressed on, ever a part of the team, continuing to run the baking room as though nothing was wrong. To their credit, everyone else tried to honor his bravado, continuing the breakneck pace and cracking jokes and telling stories. But his heart wasn't in it and even Tom agreed he needed to rest.

So Taylor got them home and they got Wayne to bed. Tom said he thought he'd call in for both of them tomorrow. He planned to go meet with Steve and probably have Steve join him in meeting with the principal and Wayne's guidance counselor so they could properly help him when the holiday break was over. Tom knew after the display in the store that he was definitely in over his head and it would be best for everyone if they approached Wayne's needs as a team.

While Tom was in the bathroom, Taylor picked up the phone and dialed the number for the police station. To his surprise, the chief himself answered.

"Chief Embry?" Taylor asked.

"Evening, Mayor," the chief answered. "What's got you up so late?"

"Pies," Taylor sighed.

"Yeah, I saw you guys were doing a killer business the last couple days. I think my wife even ordered a couple."

"Tell her to be sure to drop by tomorrow and I'll make sure her order is taken care of myself."

"I'll do that," the chief said. "So, I'm guessing this isn't an emergency."

Taylor laughed. "Not exactly. We had a bit of an incident tonight."

"McInerney?"

Taylor frowned. "How'd you know?"

"Picked him up for drunk driving about two hours ago. He was spoutin' off about how his son had shacked up with…well, I'm sure you know what he was sayin'."

"Yeah," Taylor agreed.

"You guys need to press charges?"

"No," Taylor said. "No, we don't want to do that. I was just going to ask you if your guys could keep an eye on him. I don't want him to cause a scene for Wayne. Things are hard enough for the kid, you know?"

"Yep, I know," the chief agreed. In the two years he'd been Mayor, Taylor had learned nothing but respect for the town police chief. He was as honest and decent a person as Taylor had ever known, focusing on the needs of each and every citizen with a natural, self-effacing grace that made him one of the most trusted people in the town. Taylor could never remember hearing him raise his voice—he just said what needed to be done and did it and expected everyone around him to do the same.

"He'll be spending the night down here," the chief said. "I think I'll have a talk with him in the morning and see if I can…change his priorities a bit. Don't you worry, though—I'll make sure someone keeps an eye on him for you."

"I appreciate it, Chief," Taylor said.

"Don't mention it, Mr. Mayor. Congratulations on winning the election, by the way. I voted for you."

Taylor smiled. "Thanks for the confidence, Chief, I appreciate it."

"You have a good night, Mayor."

"You too."

The line went dead and Taylor hung up the phone. As he did, Tom opened the bathroom door and he winced in the bright light. Tom had switched to a T-shirt and boxers, but Taylor still wore his open dress shirt and slacks. He laid the phone on the bed next to him as Tom sat on a corner at the end of the bed.

"Who was that?"

"Chief Embry."

"What did he want?"

"I called him," Taylor admitted.

Tom frowned. "You did? Why?"

Taylor looked at him directly. "We need to have them keep an eye on McInerney. I don't want him showing up here or at the school and making more threats. Next time, there might not be a bunch of guys there to protect Wayne."

"What did the chief say?"

Taylor chuckled. "They picked up Wayne's dad two hours ago for driving under the influence. He's going to spend the night in jail and the chief is going to have a talk with him in the morning."

Tom pondered the idea. "Do you think it will make any difference?"

Taylor shrugged. "I have no idea. The chief said they'll keep an eye on him anyway."

"Good. You ready to go to bed?"

"Just need to brush my teeth," Taylor said. He forced himself up, heading for the bathroom. Minutes later, he returned to find Tom already in bed with his side turned down and only the light on his nightstand providing illumination. He turned off the light and slid under the covers, pulling Tom into his arms.

"I already called the school and left a message. I'll get together with Steve in the morning and take care of things. We're off Wednesday anyway, so it'll just give Wayne an extra day off," Tom explained.

"Sounds good," Taylor said, exhaustion taking hold. He rested his head against Tom's, their arms intertwined. "It's all going to work out, right?"

"Yep," Tom said. He turned to kiss Taylor, who kissed him back, and then he nuzzled in and closed his eyes. Taylor took a deep breath and let it go, feeling himself relax after the tension of the day. Nothing felt better than getting to fall asleep with Tom in his arms, with the exception of waking up the same way. Their business duties covered for the morning, for once, Taylor had nothing to think about…and it felt wonderful.

Taylor awoke to the sound of the phone ringing somewhere in the room. Overnight, their positions had reversed, he stretched out flat on his stomach and Tom partially straddling him, his head right next to Taylor's on his pillow. Taylor remembered having set the phone on the bed the night before and realized it must be somewhere between them. Gently, he rolled over and felt the handset on top the covers.

"Hello?" he managed, voice still froggy. Tom shifted, his arm still over Taylor's chest, pulling Taylor in tighter.

"Hi, T. It's B. Did I wake you?" His younger brother Bryce's voice was awake and cheery—a double insult since he was actually an hour earlier than Taylor, living just outside Chicago.

"Yeah," Taylor admitted. "We were up really late at the bakery."

"How's that going?"

Taylor sighed. "Long story. What's up, Bryce?"

"Just checking to make sure you're still planning to pick up your favorite family at the airport."

Taylor paused, catching up with the day. "Oh, right," he said. "Yeah, it's Tuesday. Yeah, I'll be there."

"T, tell me you weren't going to leave us standing at the baggage claim."

"No, I wasn't. I just woke up. Honestly, B, I don't even know what day it is half the time. But, I know you guys are coming in today. Tom's parents are getting here tonight. Mom and Dad will be here tomorrow. It's all set."

Bryce laughed. "At least, that's your story. We're still staying with Gen, right?"

Taylor winced. He'd meant to call his mom for a week. "Actually, you're all staying with Gen. Part of the long story is we've got a kid—a guy—living with us right now. He works at the bakery and he's been going through a really rough time with his family. I think Tom and I have been about the only friends he can count on."

"So you put Mom and Dad over with us?"

"We figured it made sense. They know Gen and Tom's sister and her friend were still going to be on our sofas anyway. This way, his whole family will be here and our whole family will be there—no one is split up."

"Sounds good to me. Will Mom buy it?"

Taylor sighed. "B, do me a favor and don't say anything. I don't want to give her an excuse to back out."

"It's your call, T."

"She'll be okay when she sees everyone. Especially once she sees Dylan—she'll melt like buttah!"

"He's looking forward to seeing Grandma," Bryce agreed.

"Great," Taylor said. "See you in a few hours. Have a safe flight."

"Looking forward to it, T. Say Hi to Tom, okay?"

"Best to Ellie, too," Taylor said. They hung up and Taylor dropped the phone next to him. Closing his eyes, he pushed himself closer to Tom who tightened his hold reflexively. Taylor gently caressed his strong arm, the soft hairs playing against his fingertips.

Bryce was right—his mother would probably be grumpy that they would have to stay at Gen's, but he couldn't see any other solution. He was not going to put Wayne out of his room and it didn't seem fair to ask Tom's family to stay with someone who they'd never even met. Taylor sighed. His mother was just going to have to deal with change—just like he did.

As he started to slide back off to sleep, he heard a light tapping at the door. Since Wayne had started living with them, they tried to remember to close the door at night. Felix wasn't so thrilled with the plan, but it was better than being rude to their guest.

"Wayne?" Taylor asked.

"I didn't mean to wake you," Wayne whispered from outside the door.

"It's okay. Come on in."

Wayne opened the door gently, cautiously peeking inside. Taylor gave him a big smile and a wave, gesturing to Tom.

"I'm going to have to wake up sleeping beauty here soon anyway."

Wayne was in a gray T-shirt and plaid pajama bottoms. His medium-brown, medium-length hair was tussled and he generally looked like he just woke up.

"I thought I heard the phone ring," he said.

Taylor nodded. "You did. It was my brother, Bryce, who is coming to spend the holiday here. He'll be here later tonight."

"Oh. Cool. Are you going to need my room?"

Taylor shook his head. "Nope. Your room is yours. Don't even worry about it. Bryce and his family will be staying at Gen's."

"Okay." Wayne ran a hand through his hair, making it worse. "I guess I forgot to set my alarm last night. We're still supposed to have school today."

Taylor slid his legs over, freeing up the end of the bed. "Here, sit down," he said. Wayne looked uncomfortable just standing by the door. "Tom called in last night and told them neither of you would be in this morning. He's going to go talk to the school today."

Wayne sat at the end of the bed, bringing his knees up and wrapping his arms around his legs. "I don't mean to cause you guys so much trouble," he said.

Taylor smiled. "You're no trouble. Remember, you got me out of morning bakery duty—I owe you a lot for that alone!"

"I know the principal yelled at Tom yesterday, though. Then my Dad came in—that could have been a disaster. Maybe I should just go home."

Taylor freed himself from Tom and sat up, looking directly at Wayne. "Listen to me—you are not a problem. Tom and I are glad to be here to help you. And no matter what, you *are not* going back to that house."

Wayne smiled weakly, his uncertainty no doubt from never having had someone on his team before. "I'm scared my Dad is going to do something bad," he admitted.

Taylor nodded, drawing his own legs up to rest his elbows on his knees. "I was afraid of that, too. I talked to the police last night. Your Dad spent the night in jail." Wayne's eyes snapped up, fear on his face. Taylor shook his head. "It wasn't us," he promised. "They'd already picked him up for driving drunk. I told the chief what had happened and he said he'd have a talk with your father. They're going to keep an eye on him. You'll be okay."

"I shouldn't have said what I said," Wayne said. "It'll just make him madder. When Teddy finds out…I shouldn't stay here."

"Let the police do their job," Taylor said. "This is your home now. It will be your home until you're ready to be on your own. I know Tom said you can use the apartment, and you can, but we think it's better for you to have some people around right now. We're not worried about your father or your brother. We want you here."

"You don't know them," Wayne objected.

"You're right," Taylor agreed. "But being there for someone isn't just about when it's convenient or safe—it's a full time thing. This is your home now and we're here for you. We want you to be able to feel safe and comfortable."

Wayne smiled. "I do feel safe here, but I can't put you guys at risk."

"Let us worry about that," Taylor said. "I'm the mayor of this town. If I can't get the police to watch over me when I need it, then the rest of the town is in real trouble."

Wayne sat for a moment, lost in his own thoughts, staring at his fingers. Taylor watched him, letting him work through his inner struggles. He had never gone through what Wayne faced, nor anything like it. His parents, if sometimes a little distant, were good parents who cared for him and loved him. They had seen to his needs and ensured he would be able to continue to be successful. They had put him through his undergraduate degree and helped with his law degree. He was the oldest, with Bryce being about five years younger than him, but they had a close, caring relationship. His entire family had been very supportive of him his whole life, including when he revealed his sexuality. He couldn't even fathom how he would have dealt with what Wayne faced. His father loathed his differences, the fact that he wasn't like every other kid. He physically abused him out of his own displaced aggression and frustration. Taylor was no psychologist, but that much he could see on his own.

When Taylor looked at him, he saw someone entirely different. Here was a young man struggling to find a place in a world that had rejected him his entire life, but still he fought. Taylor knew Wayne thought himself weak, but he knew he was really among the strongest—someone who could survive in a family like his and still be able to function was worthy of the highest honors imaginable. Tom had confirmed that Wayne was a very bright kid, as long as he didn't think anyone was looking. It would be part of their challenge to get him to feel comfortable with letting people seem him for who he really is—and Taylor also was smart enough to know that would take a very long time.

Taylor remembered him standing there, bare-chested, bruised, tears streaming from his eyes, but not defeated. Even then, being confronted by someone he barely knew, his strength guided and protected him. It was only when he felt safe that he allowed himself to melt into Taylor's arms. Taylor knew it was that unconditional acceptance that Wayne clung to and it was the caring he felt for them in return that caused him to want to protect them from the man who had beaten him for so long.

Softly, Taylor asked, "So, are you staying?"

Wayne looked up, then smiled broadly, tears at the edge of his lids. "Okay," he said.

"Okay," Taylor repeated, returning the smile. He lowered his legs to sit Indian-style, the covers over them. "You may wish you'd said no, though."

"Why?"

"Well," Taylor began, "with everything else that has been keeping us busy, we kind of lost track of the week. As of tonight, Tom's parents, his sister, and a friend of hers will all be staying here. My brother and his wife and son are staying with Gen. Then, my parents are flying in tomorrow and they'll also be staying with Gen. Thursday, we're going to have the biggest Thanksgiving shin-dig you've ever seen, and I can tell you right now, you're going to get snagged into helping with something."

Wayne actually laughed. "I haven't had a Thanksgiving dinner in years."

"No getting around it when you're a part of this family," Taylor said. "Trust me, when you meet my Mom, you'll understand." Wayne looked at him, a question in his eyes. Taylor went on. "And yes, you *are* a part of this family now...if you want to be."

Wayne nodded. "I'd like that a lot."

"Then no more talk of leaving," Taylor said.

"I promise."

Taylor gave him a hug and realized he now had a new, even younger brother. That didn't bother him a bit. He turned and looked at Tom and was surprised to see him smiling back at him.

"How long have you been awake?"

"Long enough to hear you warning poor Wayne about your Mom. Really trying to scare him off, huh?"

"She can't be that bad," Wayne said, standing up for Mrs. Connolly.

"We'll see," Taylor said. He looked at the clock. "Okay, it's eight-thirty now. Let's get this day in gear. You guys have to take care of some stuff with the school. I'm going to check in with Pete and the chief and see how things are going, then I'll head over to the bakery and take my shift with the baking. Bryce called and they'll be here around six." He looked to Tom. "Your parents are getting in around eight, right?"

"Yeah, the last time I talked to Mom."

"Okay, in that case, why don't you stay here for their arrival?" He looked at Wayne. "You want to come with me to pick up Bryce?"

"What about the baking?" Wayne asked.

"The crew will be in tonight. They know we've got a bunch of people coming in. You, Tom and I can take the late shift once everyone is here and that way they can all get home early."

"Okay, sounds good," Wayne said.

Taylor nodded, a plan in place. "Good. Okay, let's get this party started!"

Wayne jumped up and headed down the hall to the bathroom he used, closing the door behind him. Taylor pulled the covers back, ready to get up himself.

"Tay?" Tom said. Taylor turned to him. "I heard you talking to him from the minute he came in."

"Sneak," Taylor said.

Tom grinned. "I thought it was good for you two to get to talk, too. You were really great."

"He's a good kid. He deserves to have things go his way for once."

"Yeah, but what you said to him was really great. It made me feel really proud to be with you."

"You're the one who took him in."

"And you're the one who supported me. We really are a good team, aren't we?"

Taylor rolled his eyes. "That's what I keep *saying*," he insisted.

Tom sat up and leaned over. "Thanks, Tay," he said, giving him a quick kiss. He hopped off the bed. "Shower dibs," he said, reaching for the bathroom door.

"Oh no you don't!" Taylor said, chasing after him. They crashed into the bathroom, like two kids at play, for once able to let the responsibilities of their life be forgotten, if only for a few minutes.

"I've never been to the airport," Wayne said. He sat next to Taylor in the Jeep, smelling of soap and cologne. They had all gathered at the house earlier in the afternoon to get ready to receive the respective family travelers. Wayne had asked what he should wear and Tom told him he could feel free to borrow stuff from Taylor and him. When he'd made his way back down the stairs, Taylor could immediately see he was waiting to test their reaction. He'd opted for a gray cable-knit turtleneck with black jeans and his well-worn black shoes, complete with a fresh coat of polish. He's gelled his hair into a more trendy style and borrowed some of Tom's cologne.

"Wow," Tom had said, grinning. "I wish I looked that good in those clothes."

"Yeah," Taylor agreed, "I wish he looked that good in those clothes."

Wayne blushed, but was clearly proud to have chosen well. When they went to leave, Taylor gave him a black leather P-coat, then grabbed his long black wool coat for himself.

As Wayne sat in the seat next to him, Taylor realized he was already recovering—and growing. Cracks had appeared in his shell and the real Wayne McInerney was starting to peek out…and see a world that was quite a bit different than the one he'd faced before. It was a world that was ready to accept him and care for him. Taylor was glad he and Tom were a part of it.

"You've never been to the airport?" Taylor asked, switching lanes to pass a slower car.

"Nope."

"Soooo…you've never been on a plane?"

"Uh-uh," Wayne said.

"Wow!" Taylor exclaimed. He immediately felt bad, not wanting to make Wayne feel like an outsider for never having flown, but he was truly surprised. He'd been flying since he was three and couldn't imagine any other means of travel. He spoke quickly, trying to cover his comment. "Okay, where do you want to go?"

"Go?" Wayne asked, looking at him.

"Yeah, where do you want to fly to?"

"What do you mean?"

"I mean," Taylor said, "If someone were to get you a plane ticket right now, where would you go?"

"I've never been anywhere," Wayne said. "Where should I go?"

Taylor smiled. "That's partly the point. If you've never been anywhere, there must be a place you would like to see. Where would you go?"

"In the U.S. or in the world?"

"Do you have a passport?"

"No," Wayne said, looking at him like the answer should have been obvious.

"Then let's stick to the U.S. for now."

"How about Washington?"

"D.C.?"

"Yeah. I mean, it's the capital. It would probably be a good place to see."

Taylor nodded. "You'll like Washington," he said.

"I will?"

"Yep. Everyone leaves Friday. That gives us two days, three if we take Monday off. We all need a vacation, so Washington it is."

Wayne stared at him wide-eyed. "Taylor, you can't!"

"Oh yes I can," Taylor said. "Just you watch me."

"No, it's too expensive. And what about the bakery?"

"The bakery is closed for the holiday."

"Since when?"

Taylor picked up his phone and hit Tom's speed dial. "Hi. Great. Yeah, almost there. Hey, swing by and put up a sign in the window—we're closed for the holiday. Yep. I'm taking you and Wayne to D.C. Yeah. It was all Wayne's idea."

"Hey!" Wayne objected. Taylor gave him a wink, then continued.

"Yeah, check on hotels, will you? Arlington or Alexandria would be good. Just use the platinum card. Cool. I'll get tickets while we're at the airport. Great! Thanks, hon. See you in a little while. Bye." He turned to Wayne. "See, no trouble at all."

"I don't know what to say," Wayne said. "You're nuts."

Taylor laughed. "I'm not nuts. We all work ourselves like crazy. If we don't enjoy the fruits of our labors now and then, it's a big waste of time. Tom didn't object—in fact, he thought it was a good idea."

"Well, if Tom thought it was a good idea…"

Taylor smiled. "You're learning."

About an hour and a half later, they pulled into the driveway and found the way to the garage blocked by a large, capped pickup truck.

"Tom's family's here," Taylor announced.

"We might as well take our stuff over to Gen's, don't you think?" Bryce asked. He had let Wayne take the front seat, opting to sit in back with his wife, Ellie, and son, Dylan.

"In a minute," Taylor said, turning off the car. "Let's go in and say hi first. I'd be willing to bet Gen will be over here anyway, if I know her."

Bryce stopped to help Dylan out while Wayne held the door for Ellie. They walked up the steps to the porch and Wayne led the way in.

The living room was alive with activity. Tom's mom and dad were seated on the couch, while his sister and her friend had the two chairs. Tom was sitting on the floor, leaning against the wall, and as Taylor had predicted, Gen had pulled a chair in from the dining room. As Taylor's troupe made their way in, Tom rose and made introductions.

Bryce was nothing but a more athletic version of Taylor. While Taylor was in good shape, Bryce clearly worked out, the football player to Taylor's runner. He had the same stunning blue eyes, rich tan (even in November) and blonde hair. Dylan, to all appearances, was going to take after his father and uncle.

Ellie was the picture of quiet serenity and dignified grace, with rich auburn hair in ringlets, pulled back with an antique clip. Her green eyes twinkled on her smiling face, her porcelain skin a bright contrast to the Connolly boys. She was nearly Taylor and Bryce's height, though she somehow seemed smaller and more delicate. It was only when she spoke that she stood out, her accent from Mississippi, faded but still present.

Tom's parents were the quintessential Midwestern couple, both clad in blue jeans. His dad wore a dark long-sleeved polo, while his mom had a cheery pink sweater over a white shirt. Both were more sturdy people, though Taylor would not have termed them fat. He could see where Tom took after both of them and neither of them at the same time. His mom had what would probably be considered dark blonde hair and blue eyes, while his dad had darker hair and brownish eyes. Taylor realized the combination probably gave Tom his peculiar hazel gray eyes that would go violet whenever he felt strong emotion.

Beside them sat Tom's sister, their daughter, Mandy. Mandy was a thin female version of her brother—shorter, but balanced, with lighter blonde hair that Taylor felt was probably more fashion than natural. She was thin, with bright blue eyes and a natural, friendly smile. He realized she was watching him closely and he flashed her a quick grin.

Last of the new arrivals was Mandy's friend, who Tom introduced as Eric Driskell. Eric was a freshman at the college Mandy was attending. His family was from California and he hadn't been able to afford to go home for both Thanksgiving and Christmas, so he opted for the longer break. Mandy had asked if it was okay if he joined the McEwan's for the holiday, so he got to come along for the trip. Taylor wondered if anyone had told him what the situation was between him and Tom before he got there, then thought, a little culture would be good for him.

Tom's mom got up to give Taylor a hug, which he readily returned, while his Dad gave him a good firm handshake. Taylor always thought families should hug, but he'd cross that bridge later. For all his parents' often distant behavior, they always hugged their boys and their boys'…significant others. Internally, Taylor grumbled at himself—he really did need to find a title for Tom's relationship to him. Later.

"When do your parents get here?" Tom's mom asked.

"Tomorrow afternoon," Taylor said. "We'll pick them up right after we close the bakery."

She smiled. "I can't wait to see this bakery. I can't believe you boys have been working and running this place all on your own."

Taylor gestured to Gen and Wayne. "I wouldn't say we're all on our own. In fact, now that everyone is here, we need to get you guys situated, then Tom, Wayne and I have to work. Gen's fiancé, Miguel, and a couple of our other friends have been holding down the fort while we collected everybody."

"Go, go," Don, Tom's dad, said. "We can find our way. Tom showed us to our room and Mandy and Eric will make do down here. You boys need to keep your business in business."

"I'll take care of showing Bryce's group around," Gen volunteered. "Will you ask Miguel to give me a call before he heads home?"

"Sure," Taylor said. He turned to Wayne. "After they get the Jeep emptied out, will you bring it down to the store?"

"Will do," he said, taking the key.

Taylor nodded. "Then we're off. We'll see everyone in the morning. Help yourselves to anything you want. Bryce," he said, turning to his brother, "Do not touch anything chocolate in Gen's house. She's still getting the blood out from the last person who did."

"Good night, Taylor," Gen said, holding open the door.

Tom followed him out and they started walking down the street. Once they were out of earshot, Taylor turned to Tom. "So, everything okay with your family?"

Tom smiled. "Yeah. Dad even seems more relaxed this time. I think this will be okay."

"I know it will," Taylor confirmed.

"So, what's this about D.C.?" Tom asked.

Taylor explained that Wayne had never been on a plane and he thought it was time for them all to get a break. Following the general train of thought, Tom agreed. "You like him, don't you?"

Taylor nodded. "For all he's been through, he's a great kid. We have so much and I feel so lucky for it, I feel like we need to share it with someone in need."

Tom took Taylor's arm in his, feeling not the least bit self-conscious in the darkness. "You're amazing," he said.

"Oh?"

"Three weeks ago, you were afraid to have this kid around for what people would think of us. Now, you're protecting him, going head to head with the school district and his father, not afraid of anything."

Taylor nodded. "I keep thinking of our discussion about having kids. Here's a kid who has known little love in his life and here we are wanting to be able to give that love to a kid in need. It's sort of like fate."

Tom hugged Taylor's arm tighter "Well, I know *I* feel lucky to have you."

"There's not a day that goes by that I don't find a reason to be thankful I found you, too," Taylor said. "Which brings to mind the other thing that has been bothering me lately."

"What's that?" Tom asked, looking at him as they walked.

"It just bugs me that we can't do anything to make our relationship 'official.'"

"Like what?"

"Like our parents."

"Married?" Tom asked. He glanced at Taylor, but Taylor just watched the sidewalk, talking as he walked.

"Yeah. Sort of. I don't know. That's the problem, there is no word, no status for people like us."

Tom shrugged. "So? That hasn't stopped us yet."

Taylor shook his head. "I don't even know what to call you. I mean, here you are, the man I plan to spend the rest of my life with, and I don't even have a word to describe you."

Tom laughed. "You mean like 'spouse' or something?"

Taylor stopped dead in his tracks. Tom jerked to a stop beside him, not expecting his action. Taylor looked at him wide-eyed, epiphany in his expression.

"That's it!"

"Huh?" Tom said, confused.

"Tommy, I have been trying to come up with a term to describe your relationship to me for weeks. I hate all the trendy terms like 'partner,' which is our business relationship, or 'lover,' which is nobody's business, or 'boyfriend,' which doesn't sound very permanent. You're not my husband because I'm not your wife, and vice versa. I couldn't think of anything that worked—but 'spouse' is perfect! It's gender neutral, non-denominational, non-confrontational, and non-offensive!"

Tom nodded, happy to have made Taylor happy. "But we're not married," he pointed out.

Taylor's eyes narrowed as he pondered the point. They weren't married, nor could they be, legally, thanks to the state's "Defense of Marriage Act." Taylor often wondered if the homophobes who created such legislation had any idea of how counter it was to their own goals. He set the thoughts aside. He had his word—his term—for his Tom. Now, he just had to take care of one other thing...

With a knowing grin, he slowly lowered himself to one knee and took Tom's hand in his. Tom's eyes widened as he realized what Taylor was going to do and he bit his lip.

"Tom McEwan, will you marry me?"

Tom slowly lowered himself down so he was on one knee as well and he stared deeply into Taylor's eyes.

"Taylor Connolly, will you marry me?"

Taylor realized immediately what Tom had done—theirs was to be a marriage of equals and Taylor wouldn't have it any other way. As he watched Tom, he smiled. Together, they spoke as one...

"Yes."

Chapter Seven

The Night Before the Day Before

Taylor slid a completed tray of unbaked pies into a waiting rack. He rolled the rack to stand next to the oven, ready to begin shifting the next batch in as the finished pies came out. He and Tom had arrived to find a very tired Pete and Anita doing the baking. Rob and Mel were boxing while Miguel handled the people coming in and sorted the finished pies to keep everything organized. Since Pete and Anita had volunteered to open in the morning, Tom had wanted to be sure they got some sleep. Taylor wasn't sure what they were going to do to thank their friends yet, but he knew it was going to be big.

He saw Tom glance at him and grin from across the room and he smiled back. They had decided to wait to say anything about their decision until everyone was there and the time was right. Tom worried over how his father would react, but assured Taylor it would work out for the best. Taylor just said they had to live their own lives and he'd be there no matter what.

The back door opened and he heard Wayne's voice call a hello. To his surprise, he heard additional voices as well and stuck his head out into the hall to see who was there. Behind Wayne, Tom's mom, sister, and sister's friend followed.

"They wouldn't let me leave them," Wayne explained, standing at the door to the baking room as the trio invaded.

"We didn't come all the way over here to sit at your house and watch TV," Donna explained. "Besides, your friends have all had to work their butts off. Here are three willing and able sets of hands, ready to help."

"What do you know about baking, Mom?" Tom asked.

"You think you learned how to bake all these pies from your father?" she asked, hands on hips.

"Mom, you were baking black-bottom cupcakes before they were fashionable," Tom objected.

"I'll bet Rob and Mel wouldn't mind having someone take over boxing duties," Taylor interjected.

"We'll help with that," Mandy said, guiding her mom out front.

"What can I do to help?" her friend asked.

"Eric, right?" Tom clarified.

"Yep," he said. He had a navy blue turtleneck sweater under his brown leather jacket, with dark blue jeans and brown shoes. His dark wavy hair came down to his collar, giving him a casual, model look while his dark brown eyes gazed penetratingly at Tom.

"Wayne and I can use a hand in here. You're probably going to be pretty warm in that sweater, though."

Eric smiled. "No problem," he said. He took off his coat and pulled off his sweater, revealing a white T-shirt under it. "Where can I put this stuff?" he asked.

"There's a coat rack in the bathroom, across the hall," Wayne said.

Satisfied that the baking was handled, Taylor said, "I guess I'll go spot Miguel so he can get home."

"Don't forget Gen wanted him to call before he leaves," Tom reminded.

"I'll let him know," Taylor assured, then walked down the hall.

In the store, Rob and Mel were handing over the boxing reigns to Mandy and Donna, showing them how to assemble and properly label the boxes. The flow of customers had stopped, leaving Miguel to help box and organize as well.

Taylor relieved all of them, thanking them again for the help. As they said their goodbyes, Taylor locked the door behind them and pulled the blinds—they were closed for the evening, finally.

"What a neat place, Taylor," Donna said, gesturing to the store. "The pictures Tommy sent just don't do it justice."

"It's usually a lot more sane than this," Taylor said, arranging the boxes on the tables out front, readying them for the day that would start in a few short hours. "I haven't even wanted to know how many pies we've assembled, baked and sold. I'm really looking forward to a vacation."

"A vacation?" Mandy asked. "Do you have plans?"

"Just today, as a matter of fact," Taylor confirmed. "On the way to pickup Bryce's family, Wayne mentioned he'd never been to the airport and had never flown on a plane. So, I decided it was high time for us to get away and we made arrangements to spend the rest of the weekend in Washington."

"Just like that?" Donna asked, watching Taylor.

"Working all the time has to have some benefits, or it's not worth it," he reiterated, using the same argument he'd given Wayne.

"So what's Wayne's story?" Mandy asked. Taylor moved to stand with them, knowing the exhaust fans from the baking room would mask their discussion. He had no intention of gossiping about Wayne, but he also didn't want him to feel self-conscious about Tom's family knowing what was going on.

Taylor gave them the brief run-down of what had been going on and Tom's mom just shook her head, horrified that anyone would treat his own son that way. Mandy was amazed he was doing so well, saying, "he seems so normal."

"He is normal," Taylor defended. "He's just had to get there through a really crappy life."

"I'm so proud of you boys," Donna said. "That's a really nice thing you're doing for him."

"I feel lucky for what I have, and so does Tom. We want to share our good fortune with someone who hasn't been so lucky."

Mandy smiled, moving a stack of completed boxes. "It'll be interesting to see how Wayne and Eric get along."

"How so?" Taylor asked.

"Eric's gay, too," she said, confirming Taylor's suspicion. "But he's barely out of the closet. They should have a lot in common."

"Because they're gay?" Donna asked.

"Because they're both nice, smart guys," Mandy said, giving her mother the patented "oh, mom," look. She turned to Taylor. "Eric hasn't had to go through anything like what Wayne has lived, but it was pretty hard for him to come out, too. His family is Catholic and not all of them dealt well with it. They weren't violent physically, but they've been a little cold. I think that's part of the reason he didn't care if he went home."

Donna smiled. "Well, he picked the right family to come to if he wants warmth," she said with a big grin. "There won't be any judging here."

"That's right," Taylor said. "How is Mr. McEwan handling things?" He couldn't bring himself to call Tom's dad by his first name, knowing he still hadn't fully warmed up to Taylor nor his lifestyle.

"He's doing okay," Donna said. "He'll come around. Remember, he really hasn't seen much of you guys together. From his perspective, it's still a lot more new."

Tom appeared, a complete tray of pies in his glove-covered hands. He slid them on the rack, looking at the conspiring trio. He could tell from the guilty expressions on all their faces that they'd been talking about the rest of them.

"What am I missing?" Tom asked.

"Nothing much," his mom said, looking away.

"Uh-huh," he said, unconvinced. Lowering his voice, he turned to Mandy. "Is Eric on our team?" he asked with a glance to Taylor.

"Yeah," she said.

Tom brightened. "Cool—he and Wayne have been talking up a storm in there. I feel like the fifth wheel."

"It's going well, huh?" Taylor asked.

"Real well," Tom confirmed. He turned to his sister again. "Did they tell you about Wayne?"

"Yeah," she confirmed. "Don't worry—Eric won't do anything to hurt him."

"He'd better not. Between Taylor and Mom, he'd never be able to meet anyone again."

Taylor and Donna looked at each other, then turned to Tom. He flashed them both a version of the Taylor Smile, then took off back to the baking room, proud of himself for zinging both of them at one time.

"Like this?" Eric asked. Several completed pies sat in front of him, awaiting inspection from the new "master" baker. Wayne had caught the smirk Tom had tried to hide as he bestowed the title on him, but let it go. If it was one thing he never doubted, it was that Tom and Taylor were his friends, so he didn't have to be sensitive to their teasing. Teasing from friends was, after all, just friendly teasing.

"They look perfect," Wayne said, inspecting the finished product. "Just the right amount of filling, perfect thickness on the crust. You'll be a baker in no time."

Eric smiled. "I don't know about that, but this is kind of fun. How long have you been doing it?"

Wayne stopped to consider the question. At the speed everything had been moving, he hadn't really given much thought to the actual amount of time that had passed. He was shocked when the reality of it struck him. "Almost four weeks," he said.

"Only four weeks? I'd have thought you'd been at it for months, maybe years."

Wayne laughed. "Sometimes it feels that way. It's been a fast four weeks."

Eric nodded. "You're still in high school right?"

"Senior year," Wayne confirmed, moving the pies to a tray. Eric pulled fresh pans from a rack and started preparing them.

"I can't imagine working like this while I was in school. Between classes and football, I was maxed out."

Wayne looked over. "You played football?"

Eric smiled broadly. "Quarterback, actually. My parents wanted me to try for an athletic scholarship, but I told them I wanted to be able to just focus on school while I was in college. They weren't thrilled, but they didn't force me. I think they just figured if I had a talent that could make me wealthy, I ought to go for it. Sometimes there's more to life than money, though."

Wayne nodded. "I've never had to worry about that—we've barely had enough money to live on most of my life. My parents divorced a few years ago and I wound up living with my dad. Things kind of went downhill from there." He paused, realizing he'd said more than he really meant to. Eric was very easy to talk to.

Reaching for the bucket of filling, Eric asked, "So you live with your dad now?"

Wayne froze. The thought of his father was something he had actively avoided over the last few days. His time with Tom and Taylor had been like an extended vacation in fantasyland—warmth, love and acceptance replacing hatred, loathing and abuse. Wayne thought again of Taylor's comments the day before—"you are a part of this family now." What was the point of hiding anymore? With Tom and Taylor, he could be who he was...and if someone didn't like it, he knew they'd be there to support him.

"No, I live with Tom and Taylor now," he said. "My father was...things weren't going well, and they offered to let me stay with them."

There was something in Eric's expression, but Wayne couldn't quite make it out. He didn't think it was bad, but it was at least...curious. "How's that working out?"

Wayne didn't even hesitate. "Best thing that's ever happened to me. They're the best friends I've ever had."

Eric smiled, but Wayne was even more sure there was something else behind it. "You're very lucky," he said. "Things with my family have been a little rocky the last couple of years. They had certain expectations of what I should do and when I had other ideas, my Dad wasn't too keen on my ideas."

"Like what?" Wayne asked, trying to draw him out.

"My oldest brother was a star baseball player, went on to get a scholarship, and is in the minors right now. My next oldest brother, just two years older than me, is studying to be a priest. My family is pretty strongly Catholic. So, when I turned my back on a sports scholarship and said I was going to go into design, they weren't thrilled. Then...well, let's just say I've done a few other things to cause trouble."

There it was. Wayne had been pretty sure, but he was almost certain. He kept the conversation moving. "Design, huh? Anything in particular?"

Eric's eyes flicked in his direction, but he kept his attention on his work. "I've been doing a little bit of interior and architectural, deciding where I want to specialize."

Wayne tried to keep the conversation light, not wanting to appear to be grilling him. "They're kind of different, aren't they?"

"Yeah," Eric agreed. "I just can't decide which direction I want to go. I'll have to make up my mind soon, though."

"You're only a freshman," Wayne objected.

Eric nodded, looking at him briefly. "My dad doesn't want to pay for wasted credits, though. He's already mad enough that he's having to pay at all."

"No worry of that from my dad," Wayne said. They were both quiet for a moment, busy making and filling pie crusts. His curiosity got the best of him, though. "So, what other things have you done to cause trouble?" he asked innocently.

Eric coughed, clearing his throat. "Oh, you know…being Catholic, pretty much anything gets you in trouble."

"Marijuana," Wayne said, as though everything was clear.

"No!" Eric objected, turning sharply. Wayne's knowing grin told him he'd been caught and he smiled back. "Nothing like that," he said, more subdued.

"Oh, come on, am I going to have to guess all night?" Wayne asked. Even as he said the words, he was amazed he was the person saying them. Just a week ago, he would have gone out of his way to avoid the subject altogether. Yet somehow, by being more or less out himself, he wanted the people around him to feel comfortable showing their true colors, too.

Eric turned, his face slightly flushed, facing Wayne. Wayne could see the uncertainty on his face—he'd felt it himself, plenty of times. In truth, he was sure he would feel it again, especially if he had to decide if someone would accept his revelation. Even if his situation was different, Eric would have his own demons.

He opened his mouth to speak just as Tom came back into the room. Immediately, his mouth clamped shut and he turned back to the pies. Wayne frowned, turning back to his own racks as Tom realized he must have walked in on something.

"How's everything going?" he asked.

"So far, so good," Wayne said. "Eric has picked up the business in no time. At this rate, I'll be out of a job."

Eric smiled, recovering from the previous track in their conversation. "No danger of that. After all, you're the master baker," he said, letting the words hang there in the air.

Wayne realized he'd been had and turned back to the pie shells. "We're just about done for tonight," he said, gesturing to the completed racks. "Once these are boxed, we can shut down."

"Wonderful!" Tom said. "With all this help, it'll be an early night."

"How late do you usually go?" Eric asked.

Tom chuckled. "I'm not sure we've been closing much at all lately," he said. "I think we're just rotating people in and out."

"Cool. Well, if we're done assembling, I should probably help box," Eric said.

"Go to town," Tom said, gesturing toward the store. He left and Tom gave Wayne a knowing look.

"What?" Wayne asked.

"Nothing," Tom said, face the picture of innocence. "Need any help?"

"No, I can take care of this stuff. The sooner these racks are done, the sooner we can go."

"Okay," Tom said. He took one of the rolling racks and pushed it out the door.

Alone, Wayne wrinkled his nose, wondering if he'd overdone it. Eric was right that they needed to get things done so they could go home, but it was also equally possible that he just wanted to get away from Wayne's questions. He knew he shouldn't expect miracles—he'd already had more than his fair share lately. Oh well, time would tell—it always did.

The tables were again covered in boxes. It was nearing midnight and the bakery would be open again in about six hours. Normally, Tom didn't like to have baked goods sit overnight, but there was simply no option with the volume of orders they were servicing. He knew he'd hear about it sooner or later from Taylor, but that was okay. Disagreements were part of the game—Taylor had asked him to marry him, and that was all that really mattered.

"Everything square back there?" Taylor asked.

"Yeah," Tom said. "He kicked me out. I guess it was bound to happen sooner or later."

"You'll be okay," Taylor said, a glimmer in his eyes.

"Isn't the point that you *want* him to be able to kick you out?" Tom's mom asked.

Tom shrugged. "Still, you're never quite ready for it to happen."

"Wait 'til you have kids," she said, closing a box. Her hands stopped and she realized what she'd said. Tom caught Taylor's glance, then he looked away, moving a pile of boxes. Tom's mom gave him a guilty look. "Well, you know what I mean," she said, trying to gloss it over.

"So how long have you guys been at this?" Mandy asked, swiftly jumping in to shift the conversation.

"About a week," Tom said, thankful she had realized the silence that had descended in the room. "People kept asking if they could order just one more and you know how bad I am at saying no."

"Which, in turn, meant the rest of us showed just how bad we are at saying no," Taylor filled in with a grin to Tom.

"I have to admit, everyone really sailed in to bail me out," Tom said.

"Your friends all seem very nice," Tom's mom said, rejoining the conversation after her earlier *faux pas*. "That Gen is really something."

"She's been amazing to Taylor and me," Tom agreed. To his amazement, his mom seemed pretty comfortable. He knew she was always kind toward Taylor, but she was acting like everything was perfectly normal—which, in fact, it was, except that she'd never really been around them together.

There was a knock at the door and Tom looked over to see Bryce waving at the window. Taylor made his way over and opened the door.

"What are you doing here this late?" Taylor asked.

Bryce smiled, looking so much like Taylor that it really surprised Tom. "I didn't want the McEwan's to have all the fun. Ellie and I got Dylan to go to sleep, then Gen told me where the bakery was. Ellie stayed at Gen's in case Dylan wakes up. Really, I think she's just tired," he confided.

"Okay," Taylor said. "I was going to bring everybody by in the morning, but since you're here," he said, gesturing broadly, "welcome to Downey McEwan's."

"Why Downey?" Bryce asked, looking at the sign behind the counter.

"The original owner's name was Downey. The bakery was just called Downey's until we took it over. Then, we thought it would be kind of cool to update the name to represent the new ownership and Downey McEwan's just sounds kind of cool."

"I think it sounds more like a pub," Mandy said from behind the counter.

"And yet we're okay with that," Tom said.

Bryce looked around, taking note of the pictures of little league teams on the walls. "You coach?" he asked, looking to Tom.

"Yep. I've been coaching for about the last five years," he said proudly.

"Looks like you've been winning for about the last five years, too," Bryce noted, seeing the trophies in the pictures.

"Tommy was quite a baseball player in high school," his mom revealed, smiling. Tom felt himself blush a bit, but let her have her moment.

"Taylor was more the brains of our family," Bryce said.

"I ran track," Taylor defended.

"That's true," Bryce said, letting the potential argument rest. "Nice antiques," he commented. "Is the décor original?"

"Mostly," Tom said.

"Feels homey," he said, standing next to Taylor. "So, any free samples?"

"Not on your life," Taylor said, swiping a pie away. "Every pie we eat is one more we still have to bake."

"You're not honestly going to make me stand here with all this great food and not even get a sample." Bryce and Taylor were the same height and Tom could see some sibling interaction going on behind their conversation.

"You'll have to work for food," Taylor said. "If we get everything boxed by twelve-thirty, we'll cut a pie and share it with everyone."

Bryce nodded. "I'm up for a challenge." He took his coat off and hung it over the back of one of the chairs, then reached for a pie. Taylor stopped him.

"Hands, mister," he said. "Sink is behind the counter."

For a moment, Tom thought Bryce would object, but then he turned and went to the sink. Seconds later, he stood next to his brother, packing boxes. Tom looked from the Connolly's to his mom and sister and realized he really was enjoying the scene. Beside him, Eric pulled the last pie from their rack and rolled the rack to the back, ready to get what Tom hoped was the last one for the evening.

Wayne was in the process of breaking down the mixer to clean it when Eric reappeared. He rolled the empty rack into the room and stopped to look at Wayne bent over one of the large sinks. Realizing he was waiting, Wayne stopped the water.

"Hi," he said.

"Hi there," Eric responded. He gave Wayne a friendly smile, which helped restore his confidence. "Taylor's brother just showed up, so they've got a fair number of hands out there. Do you need help here again?"

"I'm just cleaning up for the night," Wayne said, gesturing to the baking equipment waiting for its trip through the sink.

"Can I help?" Eric repeated.

"Sure," Wayne said. Truth be told, he was used to cleaning things up himself, but if Eric was willing…

"Okay, let me roll this other rack out there and I'll be right back. Is this the last of it?"

Wayne shook his head. "No, there will be a few more coming out in the next few minutes. I'll stay and wrap up, though—there is no need for everyone to be here."

Eric nodded. "Cool. I'll stay and help out if you'd like. After all, I don't have to get up in the morning and it sounds like I've had a whole lot more sleep than you guys have."

"Okay," Wayne said. He tried very hard not to appear too eager. Taylor had warned him not to rush himself. He felt such elation and freedom from being away from his father and brother, in a house with such warm, caring, accepting people. He felt like nothing could ever hurt him again, but Taylor warned that was exactly what he had to be wary of. Taylor said he would do well, but it wouldn't happen overnight. He had no choice but to believe him. Maybe he would take Taylor up on his offer to have him talk to Rick's friend Steve. More perspective couldn't hurt.

Eric reappeared, clapping his hands and rubbing them together, ready to work. Wayne showed him how to rinse out the equipment once he had scrubbed it down. He seemed perfectly at ease working among people he had just met and Wayne respected that. In new situations, he tended to be reserved and quiet, never quite sure what to expect. Eric seemed to have none of those inhibitions.

"So," he said, rinsing out one of the large mixing bowls, "Mandy gave me a little bit of the story, but I'm curious. Tom and Taylor are a couple, right?"

"Yep," Wayne said. He was surprised by the sudden shift in the subject, but decided to go with it and see where Eric wound up.

"And the town accepts them?"

Wayne nodded. "Most of the town. My dad's friends made a few rude comments here and there, but with Taylor as the mayor, they pretty much kept their thoughts to themselves. This town seems to have a good idea of what really matters in life. Of course, it's not perfect, but it's pretty good."

"So they just live together like a normal couple?"

Wayne wasn't sure how to answer that. His own experience with what constituted normal was pretty limited. But, if his dreams were anything to go on, what Tom and Taylor had seemed like it would fit the bill. "Fairly normal," he admitted. "Of course, having both of them working two jobs and Taylor being mayor on top of that doesn't exactly make them average."

"And now you're living in the middle of all of it, too," Eric observed.

"Best thing that ever happened to me," Wayne said.

"Doesn't it make you uncomfortable?"

Wayne stopped, looking at him. "Why should it?"

"What if people think you're gay, too?"

Wayne realized he'd inadvertently been caught in his own trap. Eric was investigating him, just as he had been investigating Eric a short time before. On the one hand, he was annoyed that it had been turned around on him, but on the other, maybe it would be a better way to draw out Eric's feelings on the matter.

"Why would I care what people think?" he asked.

Eric looked a little nervous, as though maybe he had gone farther than he meant to, but couldn't turn around now. "I, uh, I mean, would you want people to think you're gay if you're not?"

"People make wrong assumptions about me all the time," Wayne said. "I can't stop them."

Eric considered his words. Wayne watched him, knowing he was making him face his own inner turmoil. He had spent so long as the object of derision, it was nice to just not care anymore. Tom had told him that no one ever really said much to him—they just assumed he was shy and quiet and that he'd find a girl he liked sooner or later. When he finally came out, it had been almost ignored by most of the people he knew. They just figured instead of him being shy looking for a girl, he'd be shy looking for a guy. Then they found out he'd already found a guy and it just kind of went away.

Wayne expected his own coming out to be a little more problematical than that, but he would deal with it. So far, no one really knew what was going on at school and Wayne would prefer it stayed that way. He knew, though, that if it didn't, Tom would be there for him and that knowledge alone was worth more than he could imagine.

Eric finally looked at him, his eyes a little dark and Wayne knew it was time. Slowly, Eric worked up the courage and spoke. "Are you?"

No. Of course not. Absolutely not. The old answers welled up in his throat, denizens of a life that was already becoming a memory. He didn't have to lie anymore. He didn't have to hide anymore. He was free.

"Yep," he said, a grin appearing on his face. It was the first time anyone had asked him since he and Tom and Taylor had held each other in this very room, just over a week before. It was amazing to him how far he'd come in that short time—how much better he felt, like he could take on anyone or anything. Right then, though, he said nothing more, just watching Eric, letting him make up his own mind about how he wanted to proceed.

Finally, Eric turned his attention to the bowl in his hand and Wayne thought the discussion was over. He reached for the soapy rag he was using to wash with when Eric spoke.

"Me too."

*   *   *

Tom's mom closed the lid on the final box and Taylor turned to look at the clock. He smiled.

"Twelve thirty-one," he said, turning to Bryce. "Too bad, B."

Bryce held up a threatening fist and shook it at Taylor. Taylor nodded and smiled. "What flavor?"

"Apple," Bryce, Mandy, and Donna all said at once.

Taylor looked at Tom, who shared his surprise. His mom spoke up.

"Have you smelled those things as you put them away? Honestly, it was all I could do not to dig in to one right on the spot."

"Go for the French Apple," Tom said. "Let's just take it back to the house. Dad will already be asleep, so he won't notice when we all get there. Then Bryce can just go back over to Gen's from there."

"Sounds good," Donna said. They all hung up their aprons and Taylor went to the baking room to see how the final round was coming. He found Wayne and Eric, facing each other, expressions serious. Eric caught sight of him standing at the door and promptly gave a broad smile.

"How's everything going?" Taylor asked.

"Last batch will be out in about ten minutes," Wayne said. "We've gotten everything ready so Mrs. Johnson and Emmy can handle regular morning baking."

"Great!" Taylor said. "We're going to head home for a little apple pie. Want us to wait for you?"

Wayne shook his head. "That's okay. You can take the car and we'll walk back."

"You sure?" Taylor asked.

"Yep—just lock the door behind you and we'll go out the front."

"Okay," he said and followed after the rest of the crowd. He stopped to turn off the lights in the store, then collected his jacket and followed his brother and Tom's family out the door.

A short time later, everyone had eaten their token pie and gone their separate ways. Tom helped Mandy get the hideaway bed in the sofa ready so she and Eric would have a place to sleep. He smiled to himself as he thought of his sister sharing a bed with Eric. Normally, that would have left his dad incensed. The fact that he had said nothing told Tom that Mandy had already informed him about Eric. Poor dad, surrounded by boy boys.

Taylor showed Donna to the room they had designated for her and Mr. McEwan to share. She bid him goodnight with a kiss on the cheek, then closed the door quietly behind her. He glanced in Wayne's room on his way by and saw Felix sprawled out on Wayne's bed. He shook his head—he didn't know what it was about pets and him, but they always seemed to go in the other direction. Oh well.

In his own room, his bed was like a siren in the night, calling to him, promising to soothe his aching, tired body. For once, he didn't even care about tidiness, tossing his own clothes to the floor in readiness to let sleep overtake him.

In the darkness, Tom appeared, silently closing the door behind him. His clothes met Taylor's on the floor and he slid smoothly between the sheets as he melted into Taylor's arms.

"Hi, you," he said.

"Hi yourself," Taylor said. Their shared warmth was a welcome respite to the relative cold of the late night house.

"How were Wayne and Eric getting along?"

"Not sure," Taylor said. "I think I walked in on something."

"Really?"

"Yeah. They were kind of staring at each other, very serious. Eric kind of jumped when he saw me standing there."

"Hmm…" Tom intoned contentedly. "Maybe the game's afoot, eh?"

Taylor pulled Tom a little tighter. "Do you think he's ready?"

Tom shrugged under Taylor's arms. "It's not really for us to know," he said. "He'll know when he's ready. We'll just be there to pick up the pieces if it falls apart."

"Fun."

Tom laughed. "That's what having kids is all about, honey bunny."

"Honey bunny?"

"Sweetiekins?"

"Ugh."

"Shnooky?"

Taylor laughed in spite of himself. "Okay, just stop that now."

"Puddinpie?" Taylor pinched him. "Ow! Okay!"

"Eric seems nice, though," Taylor said.

"They'll be fine. And, just think, as of tomorrow, no more pies. Wayne has clearly mastered running the bakery, so that means…more Tom and Taylor time."

Taylor hugged him close. "I'll take all of that I can get."

"Careful what you wish for…love muffin."

Taylor laughed out loud, giving Tom a good push. Tom rolled right back into his arms, laughing himself. Relaxing in the one place he loved being more than any other, Taylor drifted off to sleep, the world finally going his way, for at least a short while.

Chapter Eight

The Day Before

A subtle tap at the door brought Taylor out of a very pleasant dream into an even more pleasant reality as he awoke to feel Tom's arms wrapped around him, his head gently resting against Taylor's. For a few brief seconds, he just enjoyed the feeling of awakening to find Tom there, rather than the usual empty bed. Then he heard the tap at the door again and Wayne's voice call his name.

Gently, he turned enough to make sure it was okay to invite someone in the room. Aside from their clothes strewn at the end of the bed, they were presentable. "Come on in, Wayne."

He softly opened the door, coming in with a phone in his hand.

"Sorry to wake you again. Your mom is on the phone and Tom's mom made breakfast. She was about to send me to wake you guys anyway."

"It's okay," Taylor said with a smile. He accepted the phone. "We'll be down in just a minute."

"Thanks," Wayne said, returning the smile. He pulled the door closed behind him as he left.

Taylor released the mute on the phone. "Good morning, Mom," he said, trying to disguise the fact that he'd just awakened.

"You just woke up, didn't you?" his mother said, no greeting intended.

"It was a long night, Mom," Taylor moaned. He felt Tom rustle next to him and reached up to gently rub his arm. Tom held on to him a little tighter and he smiled. "We didn't get to bed until about one."

"You're going to have to stop working like that, you know," his mother said.

"Yeah, we're on that plan."

"And who is Wayne? Where's Tom? Has something happened?"

Leave it to his mother. She could never just ask one question, but would instead ask the next three or four down whatever worst-case scenario train of thought she was on at any given time.

He decided a little shock value might be called for. "Tom is currently wrapped around me, still trying to sleep," he said. "Wayne is a friend who works with him at the bakery and needed a place to stay."

Undaunted, his mother didn't miss a beat. "What happened to the apartment above the bakery? Can't he stay there? Why does he need to stay in your house?"

Taylor groaned. Whose idea was it to have both sets of parents there at the same time? He couldn't really remember—whoever's idea it was, they should both be flogged for letting it happen.

"Mom, was there a point to this call? Otherwise, I'm really not in the mood to discuss the finer points of how Tom and I are managing our life right now."

There was a pause at the other end of the phone as his mother decided if she was going to make the situation into a case. Taylor really hoped she wouldn't. After all, he hadn't had to hang up on her in a while. Couldn't she have just talked to Bryce?

"I was calling to make sure you would be there on time to pick us up at the airport."

"And yet we're only just now getting to that topic. Yes, we will be there to pick you up. Your flight lands at six thirteen. None of us would forget."

"I hope you'll be in a better mood by then."

"So do I," Taylor agreed.

"Why don't you see if Dylan would like to come with you? I'm looking forward to seeing him."

"I'll mention it to B," Taylor said. *In fact,* he thought, *maybe I can get B to pick you up himself!*

"Good. I'll see you tonight."

"I'm looking forward to it," Taylor lied. He clicked the phone off and dropped it on the floor beside the bed. In two days, he would be off with Tom and Wayne in Washington and he would spend the next two days reminding himself of that fact.

"Good morning," Tom whispered in his ear.

"I love you," Taylor said. "More and more with every passing day."

"It's only two days," Tom said, echoing his thoughts.

"Thank God," Taylor said. He gave Tom a quick kiss. "Your mom made breakfast."

"Then we should probably get down there and eat, huh?" Tom said.

"'K," Taylor said. He tossed aside the covers and they both pulled on sweatpants. Standing in the bathroom, they brushed their teeth, then stared at each other in the mirror.

"Not very often we're both up at the same time, huh?" Tom commented.

"More now that Wayne is here," Taylor said. "Nice hair."

"Same to you," Tom retorted, laughing. They both looked like they had messy bird's nests on their heads. "I say it's a look."

"Let's go with it," Taylor said. He put an arm around Tom and they walked downstairs, hand in hand.

"It's about time," Tom's mom greeted as they appeared at the back stairs. The kitchen was alive with activity. Tom's dad sat at the table, newspaper in hand, steaming cup of coffee before him. Wayne and Eric sat on one side of the table, looking mighty chummy, while Mandy and Dylan sat on the other side. Taylor glanced in the dining room and saw his brother and sister-in-law having a conversation at the other table with Gen and Miguel.

"We were up as late as you and managed to get out of bed a lot earlier," she pointed out.

"You haven't been living this for the last week, Mom," Tom said. He noticed his dad's glance at the two of them standing together, but merely greeted it with a smile. His father grinned thinly, turning his eyes back to the paper.

"You're just in time," she said. "What'll it be? Pancakes? Bacon? Sausage? Eggs? Grits? Toast? Fruit? Juice?"

Taylor watched as she gestured to the various food choices. He hadn't even realized they had that much food in the house. Leave it to a mother to whip up a breakfast like that. Well, leave it to Tom's mother. He wasn't sure his mom would be able to do it.

"Is that biscuits and gravy?" Tom asked.

"Of course," his mother said. "It's your favorite, Tommy."

"I'll call the cardiologist," Taylor deadpanned. Tom elbowed him in the stomach.

"How often do I get homemade biscuits and gravy?" he asked. "Certainly not from *you*."

Taylor elbowed him back. "Just for that, I'll have some, too."

Tom leaned back against him and his mom smiled. "There's plenty to go around, Taylor. What else will you have?"

Taylor laughed. "Oh, what the heck, let's go for the full artery blocking package. Biscuits, gravy, bacon and eggs, and grits."

"We'll have you eating like a real boy in no time," Tom's mom said, serving up the plate. "To drink?"

"Diet Coke."

"Oh! So close," Mandy said. "No points for Taylor."

"Diet Coke with breakfast?" Donna asked.

"Breakfast of champions," Taylor defended. He reached down and picked up Dylan, setting him in his lap. "How 'bout you sit with your uncle?"

"Okay!" he said happily, reaching for a piece of bacon.

"Hey, B, is it okay if Dylan eats all this stuff?"

"Sure," Bryce called from the other room.

"Okay, then," Taylor said, sharing his plate with his nephew. Tom took the other open chair at the table as his mother served him. Her boys fed, she made her way around, serving Mandy, her husband, and Wayne and Eric. The other room had already been fed, taking the more healthy fruit and toast route.

Taylor nodded appreciatively at Tom's mom. "This is really great!" he said between bites. "What do you think, Dylan?" he asked.

"Yummy!" Dylan said, happily crunching down another piece of bacon. Taylor worked to get him to eat some of the other stuff while the rest of them watched and laughed at Dylan's antics.

Tom's dad laid his paper aside and ate his breakfast, quietly observing the people around the table. Taylor felt compassion for him—his generation had never had to deal with diversity in the way he faced it today. In his time, growing up in the Midwest, there had been few people of other races, men were dominant, and women still often stayed home. Here, his son was living with another man, and had another man like them living with them. His daughter had brought yet another gay man along for the ride. His son's best friend was a black woman, who was marrying a man of Hispanic and black descent. Bryce and Ellie, at least, fit the image of "normal" Mr. McEwan would have.

Taylor decided it was time to engage the man, rather than just have him sit there.

"Sleep okay, Mr. McEwan?"

He nodded. "Slept great," he said. "Nice house you guys have here."

"Thanks, Dad," Tom said. "We were glad to get it."

"Quiet area," his dad observed.

"It's a nice block," Taylor agreed.

"So your parents are coming in tonight?" he asked.

Taylor was pleased to see him joining in a bit. Maybe he just needed a little longer to warm up.

"Yes," Taylor confirmed. "We have to pick them up just after six. Tom and I were thinking it might be fun to take you guys into the city for a few hours this afternoon. We have to work at the bakery for a couple hours this morning. We thought we'd go into the city and look around, then we'll go get my parents and you guys can either spend more time in the city or come back here. Gen has volunteered to come along and provide extra shuttle service."

"That's good of her. Sounds like it should be interesting," he said. Taylor wasn't sure he was excited, but at least he was going along for everyone else's sake.

He saw Wayne look down at his plate. He knew Wayne had been planning to work—before he met Eric.

"Wayne, you've been working awfully hard. Why don't you ask Emmy if she can deal with the last of the baking today?" Tom asked.

Taylor glanced over at him and caught the tiny wink as they made eye contact ever so briefly. He reached under the table to give Tom's hand a little squeeze, then resumed seeing to Dylan's dining needs. Not missing a beat, Mandy reached over and picked up the phone, which she promptly handed across the table to Wayne. Taylor saw Eric's mood brighten at the idea of having Wayne along for the day and he smiled. It was going to be an interesting holiday, that much was sure.

"Dylan, come back here," Ellie called, turning to chase after the running four year old. Bryce turned to follow them, commenting to Taylor, "Science museum. Great idea."

"Whiner," Taylor shot back and Bryce ran after his wife and son.

Wayne and Eric had disappeared in search of one of the large dinosaur exhibits while Tom's parents went in search of the aquarium. There was a large temporary exhibit on bugs, one of Dylan's current fascinations. Gen and Mandy were taking in the gemstone exhibit, leaving Tom and Taylor a welcome moment of respite.

"I think they're having a good time," Tom said.

"At least they don't look like they're having a *bad* time," Taylor said.

Tom turned to face him, leaning against an exhibit rail. "That's a fairly pessimistic view coming from my usually optimistic fiancé."

"My mother is on her way here now," Taylor complained.

"You like your family."

"I like my family being an airline flight away."

Tom laughed. "You know we're leaving them all in their respective towns for Christmas."

Taylor nodded vigorously. "Oh, we are *so* leaving them on their own for Christmas."

"What do you want to do?"

"Worry about it later," Taylor said, standing shoulder to shoulder next to him, watching the people as they walked by. With so many people off work, the museum was actually fairly busy. "And speaking of worrying about things, what do you want to do about our pending nuptials? We have to tell them."

"You're not getting cold feet, are you?" Tom asked, his hand gently brushing up against Taylor's without being too obvious.

"Oh *hell* no," Taylor replied emphatically. "You couldn't get rid of me if you tried. I was just wondering what we want to tell them and when."

Tom rubbed his chin, thinking. "Let me get back to you on the when part," he said. "But we're definitely going to tell them over the holiday."

"What are we telling them?"

Tom looked at him like it was obvious. "We'll tell them the truth—that we're getting everyone together somewhere insanely romantic to have a ceremony joining us together forever, at least to each other, even if the laws haven't caught up with us yet."

Taylor nodded. "Okay, this plan is working for me. Where will qualify as 'insanely romantic?'"

"I would either think something like a sea shore, or overlooking the Grand Canyon, or maybe a cruise in Alaska. There's always the French Riviera, somewhere in Italy or one of those tropical paradise places in Thailand. Then there's the Caymans. I've always wanted to go there for as long as I can remember."

Taylor looked at him, the light on over his head. "The Caymans…that would certainly fit the bill. Find some nice secluded resort, maybe stay in those little huts."

"Can we afford it?"

"Sure. We can dip into the money Pete and I used to start the firm. Even with me hardly ever being there, we have a bunch of cases bringing in a good chunk of change."

"Who do we invite?" Tom asked.

The question sparked a thought in Taylor's mind. "Hey, did Gen ever talk to you about the wedding?"

"No," he said.

Taylor rolled his eyes. "I'm not supposed to say anything because she wanted to talk to you first, but she wants us to stand on her side in the wedding."

Tom frowned. "I'm not wearing a dress, gay or not."

Taylor laughed. "Me either. I already told her. She's got it all worked out. My point, though, is that we should probably have her in the wedding party."

"And Pete and Anita," Tom said.

"Probably John and Sandy," Taylor said.

"Do you think they'd be able to come? What about the kids?"

Taylor nodded. "Good point. But we should probably invite them anyway and let the decision be theirs."

"Wayne and my sister," Tom said.

"Rob and Mel," Taylor said. "And Bryce."

"This is getting out of control."

"What about guests?" Taylor asked.

"You know, I was kind of envisioning this being a small thing."

"Just family?" Taylor asked.

Tom nodded. "We could always have a reception when we get back."

Taylor gave him a knowing look. "Okay, so who qualifies as family?"

"My parents and Mandy. Your parents and Bryce. Ellie and Dylan. Gen and Wayne," Tom said, trying to shorten the list.

"Pete is my business partner in the firm," Taylor said.

"And we're god parents to Taylor Thomas. Maybe this isn't going to be so easy."

Taylor laughed. "Sounds like the definition of every wedding I've ever attended."

Tom gave him a devious look. "We could elope."

"That would kind of defeat the purpose, wouldn't it?" Taylor asked. "I mean, we could just go to Tiffany, buy a couple rings, and say that's that."

"But we have to go to the Caymans," Tom reminded him.

"We need to bring people along to clap and throw simulated rice at us."

"Good point. It's just not a wedding without rice." Tom looked across the room at Gen and Mandy. They were both standing in front of a large dish, staring back at them. "What are they doing?"

Taylor looked at them and the girls started walking toward them. "I dunno," he said. Both women wore broad smiles as they walked up, causing answering looks of bewilderment from the guys.

"So, how are you two?" Mandy asked.

"Fine," Tom said. "Just enjoying a moment of peace and quiet."

"Quiet?" Gen asked.

"Yeah," Taylor said, "What about it?"

"Something you want to tell us?" Mandy inquired.

"About what?" Tom asked.

"Going someplace?" Gen prompted.

"Going where?" Taylor asked.

"Maybe a little beach action, a swim," Mandy said.

Tom turned to look at Taylor, then stopped. Taylor followed his gaze, falling on the object behind the rail they had been using as a support. He looked across the room and saw a nearly identical object on the other side—a large, parabolic dish, nearly perfectly centered on their position. They'd been had.

"How much did you hear?" Taylor asked.

"Not much," Gen confirmed. "Just something about eloping and the Caymans."

"You two had better not be planning to sneak off without us," Mandy said.

Tom shook his head. "Nothing of the sort. Actually, we were trying to plan who to bring along."

"Then you are…getting married?" Gen clarified.

Taylor nodded. "That's the plan. But don't say anything. We're waiting until everyone is here to tell people."

"Our lips are sealed," Mandy said. Tom groaned and shook his head. "Don't give me that look, big brother. Gen and I can keep a secret."

"A secret about what?" Bryce asked, walking up from the other side.

"Nothing," Taylor snapped. "Okay, let's round everybody up. We're going to have to get something to eat, then split up to go get Mom and Dad."

"What secret?" Bryce asked.

"Later, B," Taylor said. Wayne and Eric appeared at the far end of the gallery, trailed by Tom's parents. Ellie and Dylan showed up from the other direction, bringing their little group together. Taylor sighed, realizing the odds of their secret surviving the night were low. As though sensing his concern, he felt Tom's hand slip into his, hidden between them as they stood at the head of the little group. Everyone headed for the parking structure, then paired off to their respective cars. *Two more days*, Taylor thought. *Two more days.*

Taylor and Bryce relaxed on a bench, awaiting their parents' flight. Dylan was curled up with his head on Bryce's leg, napping. Changes in airline regulations meant they could no longer meet their parents at the gate, so they waited in the baggage claim area. Their mother had promised that she would call as soon as they were off the plane to let them know they were on their way. Taylor knew better than to be late getting them, so they had gone directly from the museum while the rest of the family went on to one of the more tourist-oriented parts of the city. They agreed they'd all meet up for dinner once the Connolly's were in.

"I really like Tom," Bryce said. "He's really a great guy."

Taylor smiled. He and his brother had always been close, but had the sort of competitive relationship brothers often did. Taylor, being older, was usually in the lead or indifferent, a fact that had often caused friction between them. He came out while he was in college, and so hadn't spent a lot of time around Bryce since then. Bryce had met most of the people he'd dated, certainly all with whom he'd ever been serious, but it was the first time he openly endorsed Taylor's…friend. *Soon to be spouse*, he thought and smiled again.

"Thanks," Taylor said. "I'm pretty fond of him."

Bryce laughed, his face lighting up like Taylor's did when he smiled. "I can tell. I've never seen you so…happy…before. You two were made for each other."

"So it would seem."

"How long has it been now?" Bryce asked. His hand rested on Dylan's back, gently massaging it as his son slept.

"Just over two and a half years."

Bryce shook his head. "By the time Ellie and I had known each other that long, we were married and Dylan was on the way."

Taylor chuckled ruefully. "That's not quite an option for us."

Bryce looked up, realizing what he'd said. "T, I'm sorry. That's not what I meant."

Taylor nodded. "I know, it's okay. Don't worry about it."

Bryce frowned. "But you know, it's not fair. I have plenty of straight friends who haven't got half of what you guys have, get married, get divorced, and lead pointless lives. You guys have a great relationship, but you can't be together."

Taylor turned to his brother, surprised at the level of thought he had given the matter. He had no idea Bryce would even think of such a thing or care. "We're actually luckier," he said. "Look at your friends and their failed relationships. Marriage did nothing for them except complicate their eventual departure. Our commitment to each other is so genuine that it doesn't require government sanction to keep it alive."

He stopped himself, hearing his own words. For so long, he had been disappointed about the very fact that Bryce had raised, yet as they sat there he realized it really wasn't important. He and Tom *were* committed to each other. What difference would a ceremony or a document make? Their commitment to each other was revitalized with each passing day, as they looked out for each other, cared for each other, and loved each other. For many people, marriage was a constant reminder that their status had changed, that they were tied to another person. Tom and Taylor needed no such reminder because their bond was its own strength and its own reward.

"Still," Bryce went on, "It's not fair that you aren't able to share that commitment with the rest of the world. What if something happens to one of you? You have to go through a mountain of red tape to get anything done."

"That's true," Taylor agreed, "But it's getting less complicated as it becomes more common. We've already taken care of a lot of that, and we'll continue to take care of it as we go. The laws are constantly changing, more often to our benefit than our detriment."

Bryce shook his head. "Call me old fashioned, but I still think I should be able to stand with my brother and have him be able to take vows with the person he loves, like Ellie and I did. It's not fair. It's not fair to you, to me, to our families. It sucks."

Taylor stared at his brother, slack jawed and dumbfounded. In all their years, he'd never felt closer to Bryce than he did in that moment. Clearly, he had put *a lot* more thought into the situation than Taylor had given him credit for.

"Wow, B," he said.

Bryce looked at him, realizing the force behind what he'd said. "Well, that's how I feel," he said.

"You don't know how much it means to me that you care that much," Taylor said.

"Of course I care. You're my brother and I love you. You know that."

"Well, yeah, I mean, sure I do," Taylor stumbled. "I just had no idea you'd thought about Tom and me that much."

Bryce just watched him. "Of course I have. You may not have the dictionary definition of a traditional relationship, but it's not really my place to define what traditional is anyway, is it? How about if we define traditional as a loving, caring relationship between two people who care more about each other than they do themselves? By that definition, you and Tom are the picture of traditionalism. Of course, then more than half the population would be outcast and they wouldn't like that at all, would they? Our society could use more couples like you and Tom."

Taylor was speechless. No one, except maybe Gen, and certainly Tom, had ever endorsed him so strongly. He just watched Bryce, feeling the energy radiating from him.

"I'll tell you something else that might surprise you," Bryce said. "Ever since you came out, I have not voted for a single political candidate that didn't actively support same-sex issues. You may be my big brother, but I have to look out for you, too. I was lucky because the person I love fit the model, but that doesn't mean I don't have to look out for you. And if you really want to be surprised, I'll tell you that Mom has been the same way."

"Mom?" Taylor asked.

"Yep. We've talked about you a lot more than you might think, actually. She worries about you, T. She wants to be sure you're happy. When you were with that other guy, it about drove her nuts. She was nervous because you met Tom so soon after finally unloading him, but it all worked out in the end. And you don't need to worry, she really loves Tom. It's definitely like he's a part of the family." Bryce looked directly at Taylor. "No, it's not *like* he's a part of the family—he *is* a part of the family."

Taylor took a deep breath, considering his words carefully. He'd intended to wait, but it just seemed like the right time. He had to tell Bryce.

"Actually," Taylor started, "we were going to talk about this tomorrow, but I feel like I need to tell you now."

Bryce watched him, silently prompting Taylor to go on. "Tom and I decided that we're going to have a wedding…type…thing…down in the islands. Sometime next year."

Bryce's eyes widened and his face lit up. Taylor continued. "I mean, I know we can't do anything officially, but like you said, it's more about just doing it and sharing it with the people we care about."

"Taylor, that's awesome!" Bryce exclaimed, pulling him into a hug. "I wish it could be legal, but at this point, I'm not going to be picky."

Taylor laughed, surprised by his brother's reaction. "I'm so glad you think it's a good idea," he admitted.

"I think it's a great idea!" Bryce said. "It will just help both sides of the family to get more comfortable with the idea of the two of you together. Let's face it, our parents are still pretty tradition oriented. At least this will force them to quit sidestepping the issue."

Taylor frowned. "Do you think they do that?"

Bryce shrugged. "Not too much, but a little. I mean, half the time, no one is even sure how to refer to Tom—you know, what is he? Boyfriend, partner…"

Taylor laughed out loud. "You have no idea how much I have tried to figure out that exact thing. I can tell you, though, that as of tomorrow, you can refer to him as my fiancé."

His brother smiled. "Works for me."

Taylor felt his phone vibrate in its cradle on his waist. A quick check showed the words "Mom Cell" on the display. With a nod to Bryce, he stood, opening the phone. Bryce reached down to wake Dylan as Taylor heard his Mom's voice.

"We're here!" she said cheerily.

"So are we," Taylor said. "We'll be waiting for you just inside the baggage area."

"We're already there," his mom said. "We decided not to make you stand around. Where are you?"

Taylor turned, looking at the entrance. Sure enough, his mom's blonde head was visible next to his dad's salt and pepper. "Looking at you now, from the windows to your right."

She turned and he waved. She waved back. "We're on our way," she said and hung up. Bryce picked up Dylan and pointed to where Grandma and Grandpa were. His face brightened as he saw them and he leapt down to run in their direction.

Their mom scooped her only grandson into her arms as he ran to her. She carried him while their dad rolled two carry-on suitcases behind him. They joined their sons, waiting while the luggage carousel was loaded.

"Hello boys," their dad said, pulling them each into a hug. "How are my favorite sons doing?"

"We're great, Dad," Taylor said.

"Did you have to wait long?"

"Nope," Bryce said. "We've been here about a half hour. Gave us a chance to sit and talk a little bit."

"Still busy baking?" their mom asked.

"No," Taylor said, voice slightly defensive. "We got some people to cover the store so we could show everyone around today."

His mom patted his face. "You look thin. You need to be eating more of your product."

Taylor laughed. "Don't worry, Mom, I'm getting plenty of food. And, things will be a little calmer with the holidays over."

"As long as Tom doesn't take so many orders at Christmas," she corrected.

Their Dad located their luggage as it came around. Bryce pulled both bags from the conveyor, handing one to Taylor and taking one himself. He also reached for one of the carry-on bags, leaving his Dad with only one and leaving his Mom free to fawn over her grandson.

"Mom, make him walk," Bryce said. "He's too heavy for you."

"He's not too heavy," his mom complained.

"He's too heavy," Bryce said. "He can walk."

She put Dylan down, but he happily held his hand up to her so she could walk with him. Finally together, the Connollys headed for the car.

Taylor was again drawn to Bryce's words. He could only hope that his parents would be as welcoming to the idea of him being married to Tom, even if in practice only. He smiled as he thought about Bryce. He'd seen very little of his little brother in the last few years, but he realized he'd blossomed into quite a man. Gone was the competitiveness, replaced with genuine caring and concern for Taylor, and by association, Tom.

Taylor realized his only dilemma was going to be who to have as Best...Person. He'd thought to return the honor bestowed upon him by Gen. But, Gen was an only child. He had to consider Bryce's feelings and, in truth, he felt a renewed sense of loyalty to his brother. He hoped Gen would understand when the time came.

With everyone loaded into the car and Dylan happily seated between his grandparents, they headed back to the city and Taylor prepared himself for reality—the Connolly's were about to meet the McEwan's for the first time.

Chapter Nine

Thanksgiving Day

Taylor awoke to the dull light of day and realized it must be cloudy out. He smiled as he realized it would be a typical November day. With the recent cold spell, the weather forecasters said it was even possible they would get snow. Tom thought it would be a good idea to put up some of the Christmas decorations while the family would be there to enjoy them. Taylor couldn't remember the last time his family had been around to help dec the halls, so he had agreed it would be a nice way to spend an otherwise quiet evening.

As he became aware of his surroundings, he felt Tom's hair brush his chin and looked down to see his head resting in the crook of his neck. He was straddling Taylor like a body pillow and had pinned Taylor's left arm under him. Taylor realized he was in for a good case of pins and needles when the circulation was restored, but didn't rush to move his sleeping…fiancé.

The next thing he noticed was the smell…and the noise. Clearly, the family was already up and someone was cooking. He'd be willing to bet it was Tom's mom, if only because of her general mom-like behavior. As much as the last week had left him wishing for a few days of peace and quiet, he had to admit Tom's family was a welcome change from the norm.

Meeting the Connollys had gone fairly well. By the time they finished dinner and made it back to the house, both sets of parents seemed content to beg off to bed. Gen had taken his parents to her house while the "kids" stayed at his house. Tom and Taylor had finally headed off to bed around eleven, still beat from their hectic schedule. Taylor had heard Wayne make his way upstairs sometime around two…and wondered if he'd been by himself.

All of a sudden, the bedroom door burst open and a small form rushed into the room. Taylor jumped and in so doing, woke Tom.

"Uncle Taylor, wake up!" Dylan's young voice called as he bounded onto the bed. "Come on, Uncle Taylor, wake up. You too, Uncle Tom! It's time to get up. Grandma said."

Taylor pulled his arm from under the very groggy Tom and wrestled his nephew down, tickling him.

"Do you always listen to what Grandma says?" Taylor asked.

"Yes!" Dylan replied dutifully. Bryce appeared at the door, smiling as he saw the commotion his son had caused.

"Come on, D," he said. "Let your uncles get up."

"Grandma Donna said not to let Uncle Tom stay asleep either," Dylan objected.

"Uncle Tom is awake, Dylan," Tom managed, his voice gravelly.

"Come on, Dylan. Back downstairs," Bryce said. Dylan crawled off Taylor and hopped down, headed for the door. His dad gave him a pat on the butt as he flew by.

"Sorry, guys," Bryce said.

Taylor laughed. "It's okay. We need to get up anyway."

"You're darned right you do," his mother's voice called from the hallway. Bryce backed out of the way and she stuck her head in the door. "Do you think that turkey is going to cook itself? We do want to eat *today*, you know. Do you want me to get it started for you?"

"*No*, Mother, I do not want you doing anything. Tom and I will cook dinner," Taylor said. "Look, just let us get up and we'll be down in a couple minutes."

His mother pursed her lips. "Well, you'd better get moving. The day isn't getting any younger, you know."

"Got it," Taylor said. "Thanks for the help."

His mother pulled the door closed and Taylor dropped his head back on the pillow. Before he could even say anything, Tom kissed him and smiled.

"It's only one day," he said.

Taylor groaned. "It's going to be a *very* long day."

Tom threw the covers back. "Come on, let's go. You'll feel better after you take a shower."

"Are you sure?"

Tom held out his hand and smiled. "Yep."

A short time later, they appeared at the back stairs, dressed and coiffured, ready to impress. To their surprise, the kitchen was alive with activity. Eric and Wayne sat at the table, Tom's mom was turning out breakfast, as expected, but Taylor's mom was also wearing an apron, running back and forth serving the various guests. Both fathers, Bryce, Ellie, Mandy, Gen, and Miguel were seated at the dining room table and Dylan ran back and forth between rooms.

"What'll it be, boys?" Donna asked.

"The usual?" Tom said.

"Lucky for you, there's just enough left," his mother said, pulling two dishes from the warm oven and ladling thick sausage gravy over them. Both the late arrivals took seats at the kitchen table and dug eagerly into their breakfasts.

"You're spoiling us, Mom," Tom said between bites.

"Nonsense," his mother said, washing out the finished pots and pans. "You boys can cook yourselves a good breakfast anytime. You obviously have the stuff."

Tom shook his head. "Taylor won't let me. Too fattening."

Donna eyed Taylor as she scrubbed the dishes. "You boys could do with a little fattening up."

"I said the same thing," Taylor's mom interjected from the end of the table.

"There is not a man alive who is ever *healthy* enough for his mother," Taylor defended.

"My mom is always trying to fatten me up, too," Eric offered.

Taylor's mom gave him a once over and nodded. "Good for her. And the same goes for you, young man," she said with a glance in Wayne's direction. "I'm sure your mother says the same thing."

Taylor choked on the bite of food in his mouth and Tom put a hand on his back, looking at Taylor's mom like she'd just sworn. With effortless grace, Wayne said simply, "Actually, my mom lives in California. I haven't seen her in years."

Between Taylor's reaction and Wayne's soft-spoken statement, she got the hint and let the subject go. Donna stepped in, ready to further deflect attention away from Wayne.

"So, what's the cooking plan? You've got plenty of cooks, ready to work."

Tom nodded, turning to his mom. "Yeah, I'd say we may have a cook or two too many. Taylor and I will have kitchen duty. The rest of you suix chefs can work at the dining room table. There are vegetables to peel, dishes to prepare, etc."

"Surely you'll want more help in here than just to two of you," Taylor's mom said.

Taylor shook his head. "No, the two of us will be just fine," he said. He looked at Wayne. "How 'bout you and Eric run up to the bakery and pick up our baked goods?"

"Sure, Taylor," Wayne said. Taylor saw the distance in his eyes and made a note to talk to his mom later.

"You can take the Jag," Tom said, tossing him a key.

"Cool!" Eric said.

"Great," Tom said. "Moms, you and Gen can start prepping vegetables. I'll help you get setup while Taylor gets ready to cook the turkey." The women followed him into the dining room to clear things off while Eric went to get his and Wayne's coats.

Wayne helped Taylor clear the remaining dishes from the table and he turned to Wayne at the sink.

"Sorry about that."

Wayne offered a half-hearted smile. "It's okay. It just kind of reminds me, you know."

Taylor nodded. "When you're being reminded, just remember what we talked about yesterday morning, okay?"

"I remember," Wayne promised. He gave Taylor a quick hug, then Eric walked in with his jacket. "Ready to go?" Wayne asked.

"Can I drive?" Eric asked.

Wayne looked at Taylor, who nodded, knowing better than to disappoint them. Clearly, they were getting along very well indeed.

"Just be back within an hour," Taylor said.

"We're only running up to the bakery," Wayne said, confused. When he saw Taylor's expression, he realized what he'd said. "Oh. Got it," he said, smiling. They headed out the door just as Tom peeked in from the dining room.

"Need anything in here?" he asked.

"Nope," Taylor said. "I'm just going to get the turkey in the pan and start the oven."

"Okay," Tom said and pulled the door closed behind him. The sudden quiet was a welcome break. Taylor hadn't noticed how noisy the house had gotten. The guys had turned on the TV in the living room, watching one of the parades being carried from somewhere around the country. Taylor generally preferred the Macy's parade, but it just never seemed quite as magical as it had when he was a child. He missed the childlike innocence of youth and hoped he could find a way to recapture it one day.

Wrinkling his nose as he always did, he pushed up his sleeve and reached inside the carcass to retrieve the "innards." An unconscious "yuck" escaped his lips as he pulled the parts out and dropped them into a waiting pot. Boiled into stock, they would make a rich and tasty gravy, but Taylor hated reaching inside the cold body, seeing it for what it really was. His mother, the original health nut, always insisted she wanted stuffing inside the turkey. So, as he always did, Taylor put just enough in to make it look like he had stuffed the turkey. When he pulled it from the oven, he would stealthily dispose of the questionable stuffing and replace it with fresh stuffing made on top the stove. For the past three or four shared Thanksgivings, she'd never noticed.

He reflected on the past few days in the relative quiet. They had actually gone better than he expected. The families seemed to get along well, and the few people who had learned of his and Tom's plan to formalize their relationship had been very supportive. As Tom said, Taylor was usually optimistic about things, but he had to admit, he'd been dreading the holiday. With the day actually upon him, he found Tom's unswerving optimism was probably the better choice. Whatever the case, the next few hours would be interesting.

Three "discussions" about how to prepare various dishes and six hours later, the family was seated around the extended table, all waiting expectantly as Taylor brought the completed turkey in from the kitchen. He smiled proudly, the large golden brown bird surrounded by vegetables, exactly as the picture had shown in the cookbook he'd selected. If it was one thing he understood, it was presentation.

"Son, that is one good looking bird," his dad said from the other end of the table.

"Thanks, Dad, I thought the turkey looked pretty good, too," Taylor quipped, straight faced. At first, no one caught the double entendre, but the thin approving smile on Mr. Connolly's lips confirmed he had.

"Before we begin," Tom said, standing beside Taylor and catching his hand as he reached for the carving knife, "The McEwans have a tradition."

"Oh, come on, Tom," Mandy objected.

"Amanda, let your brother be," his dad said, speaking up for the first time. He gave his son a smile and a nod and Tom continued.

"Every Thanksgiving, before we dig in, we go around the table and each person has to say one thing for which he or she is thankful. Taylor and I will go last. Gen, you start," he said, looking to Gen, who was sitting to Taylor's left.

"I'm thankful that Miguel and I have gotten to spend this wonderful day with my second family," Gen said.

Miguel nodded and added, "I'm thankful to have met all of you, through Gen, and to have been welcomed into your holiday."

"I'm thankful to get to spend this holiday away," Mandy said, "Even if it does mean having to bring this silly tradition with us."

Donna gave her daughter's hand a light slap as she spoke. "I'm thankful that I got to meet all of Tom's wonderful friends and family and share this day with them."

They looked at Tom's father expectantly. He had remained fairly quiet throughout the day, occasionally joining casual conversations as they happened, but generally just observing.

"I'm thankful," he said, matching Tom's gaze, "to see that my son has found such a great person to spend his life with."

Tom beamed as his father finally endorsed Taylor, who offered a gracious nod.

"I'm thankful Tom can put up with Taylor so he doesn't have to spend his life alone," Taylor's dad said, a verbal poke in the ribs.

"Thanks, Dad," Taylor said, glaring.

"I'm thankful to get to spend the holiday with my family and my new extended family," Taylor's mom said, nodding to the McEwan's.

"I'm thankful everyone is healthy and happy," Bryce said.

"I want pie," Dylan said, causing everyone to laugh. His mom gave him a hug and offered her words. "I'm thankful I finally got to meet all of you and had the chance to get to know you," she said.

Eric spoke next. "I'm thankful Mandy invited me to spend the holiday with all of you and gave me the chance to meet all of you." At the last, his glance fell on Wayne, who gave a shy smile.

"I'm thankful for the warmth and love I have received from all of you, but especially Tom and Taylor," Wayne said. "This is the first time I've truly felt like a part of a family. I really do feel like that now."

Tom put a hand on his shoulder and gave it a pat. With a broad knowing smile he turned to Taylor.

"I'm thankful Taylor asked me to marry him," he said.

Taylor nodded, smiling back as he faced their combined family. "And I'm thankful he said yes."

Taylor realized their timing was perfect. Hungry people had their minds more on the great bronze turkey at the end of the table than the two turkeys standing behind it. The mêlée lasted only a couple of minutes, thanks to the fact that only the parents were really in the dark about the situation. Handing over the fork and knife to Tom, Taylor announced that he would be doing the honors and sat as Tom carved the turkey.

For their part, the fathers were both fairly quiet, letting their wives barrage the hosts with questions about how they would handle the event. Their sons survived, Taylor saying he would only commit to whatever Tom wanted and Tom only willing to commit that they would announce the plans after Christmas.

Dinner went smoothly as the hungry family summarily dispatched the mountain of food. Conveniently, they had positioned the parents at the opposite end of the table, making it difficult for them to corner the boys about their announcement. For their part, the siblings kept everything light and festive and Taylor found himself smiling as he sat back and observed the interactions.

Bryce and Ellie spent a large part of the dinner keeping Dylan entertained until his grandmother finally couldn't stand it anymore and put him on her lap. There he sat happily, picking at her food and earning his father's ire. Beside them,

Wayne and Eric managed to stay largely off in their own little world, occasionally sharing their conversation with Mandy, who had been relegated to sit between her parents and Miguel on the other side of the table. Miguel was, as always, quiet and contemplative, choosing to observe rather than interact.

The parents managed to entertain themselves for the most part, though Taylor wasn't convinced either set was truly comfortable with the other. His parents were far more urban, given to appreciate culture and convey themselves as people who appreciated culture. Tom's parents were more earthy, the kind of people who went to a movie once in a while, but otherwise enjoyed their quiet time at home. Taylor knew that he and Tom were both somewhere in between. Thankfully, neither of them seemed particularly interested in upsetting that balance.

The "kids" cleared away the dinner dishes and the real treat of the evening was dessert. Since they had worked so hard for the last few weeks, Tom and Taylor decided it was only fair that they get to bring a sampling of the desserts from the bakery. In short order, the table was covered in pies, cookies, and pastries. They had kept the true magnitude of the spread hidden so that everyone would be surprised.

"T, how can you expect us to eat all this?" Bryce asked.

Taylor shook his head. "Don't worry, there's no hurry. We figured we'd put everything out and let people come back to it as they please all evening."

"We are going to be so fat," Mandy complained.

Her brother turned to her. "You don't have to eat any. It's okay."

"Right!" she said, reaching for one of the cherry pies.

As Taylor reached for a slice of apple, the doorbell rang. He shot a questioning glance to Tom, who shrugged and shook his head. Curious, Taylor excused himself and made his way into the living room to see who was at the door.

"I was wondering if we could buy a pie," John said, standing at the door holding out a twenty.

Taylor broke into a broad grin. "Nope, not today. But you're welcome to come in and have a piece or three."

"You're sure? We don't want to interrupt," John said. His oldest son, Chad, stood next to him.

"Of course not!" Taylor said. "It's no interruption. Where's my godson?"

"In the car," John said, "with his mother."

Taylor pulled Chad inside. "Well, get them in here. It's cold out there. The more the merrier."

Tom appeared behind him and saw who was at the door.

"John! Hi! Where's the family?" he asked.

"He's just going to bring them in," Taylor interjected.

John turned to go back to the car while Taylor helped Chad out of his coat and boots. While Tom waited at the door, he took Chad to meet the family.

"We have some extra guests," Taylor said. "This is Chad Atkins. His mom and dad are old friends of ours. They just had a new baby who was named after Tom and me and we're his godparents."

"The baby is here?" Taylor's mom asked. In an instant, she had disappeared into the living room.

Bryce picked up Dylan and turned to Taylor. "Well, I'm stuffed for now anyway. Let John and Sandy have some pie and we'll get a piece later. Dylan and I will see what's on TV."

"Me, too," Ellie said, following along behind him.

"Eric and I can work on dishes," Wayne volunteered. They disappeared into the kitchen and Mandy followed them.

John and Sandy made their way into the room, John carrying their two year old daughter, Wendy, and Tom carrying his godson, Taylor Thomas. Tom made introductions as Gen and Miguel came around to greet their old friends.

"This sure is a welcome surprise," Gen said, sitting with Sandy.

She nodded. "Taylor had said something about everyone getting together, but we didn't know how little Tay would be doing, so we couldn't commit. He's been in a really good mood today, though, and John thought we ought to just drop by."

"You're sure we're not an imposition?" John asked again.

"Will you stop asking that?" Tom complained. Little Taylor had wrapped his fist around Tom's right forefinger as he watched the activity going on around him. Taylor's mom was mesmerized by him and kept talking to him to see if she could get him to smile.

"What is it about women and babies?" Tom's dad asked.

Donna patted his arm lovingly. "Like you were any better when the kids were little," she commented.

Taylor picked up his piece of pie and sat across from his friends, next to Tom's mom. "So, he's been doing good?"

Sandy smiled proudly. "He's been doing *great*," she said. "He's way ahead, both physically and in his perceptive abilities. He can already make out faces and knows his family. He can push himself up a little and he rolls over on his side."

"So you're saying he takes after his mother?" Taylor asked.

Gen laughed. "Well, he obviously doesn't take after his father," she said.

"Wait a minute!" John objected.

Taylor's dad made a wave of his hand. "Don't bother, John," he said. "With these women, you can't possibly win."

"Evan's right, you know," Gen agreed.

Dejected, John said, "Yeah, I know."

Sandy laughed. "It's okay, dear. Here, have more pie."

Taylor's dad nodded. "Just like a woman to offer—"

"Dad!" Taylor interrupted.

"What?" he asked, face the picture of innocence.

"Why don't you go watch TV with Bryce?"

Grumbling, he walked into the living room. Sandy watched him go and turned to Taylor. "Your dad's cute."

"He's something," Taylor agreed, taking a healthy bite of pie himself.

John pushed his plate back. "So, now that this whole holiday is done, do you think we might actually see you guys once in a while again?"

"I hope so," Tom said. He sat next to Sandy, watching little Taylor as he cooed and shook his fists up and down. Every now and then, he would catch Tom's gaze and break into a big smile. "I can't believe how much he's grown."

"He's coming up on two months old," Sandy said, smiling proudly at her son.

Taylor turned to John. "So, what's new around the firm?"

"There's a new partner."

"Really? Who?" John smiled broadly. "You? John, that's fantastic!" He reached across the table to shake his friend's hand. "When?"

"Last week," John said. "I was going to call, but then we decided to just come by."

"Congratulations," Taylor said. "It's about time."

"I'll say," John agreed.

The doorbell rang again and Taylor glanced toward the door. Bryce rose to answer it and Taylor watched his body language. Whoever it was must be unexpected. To his surprise, he saw Miguel walk to the door and heard their voices slightly raised.

"Excuse me," Taylor said. Nearing the door, he realized what the commotion was about. "What are you doing here?" Taylor asked.

Wayne's father stood on the porch, face serious. Taylor could see his beat up pickup truck on the street, Wayne's brother at the wheel. At his feet was a brown paper grocery bag and a cardboard box.

"Mayor Connolly," he said. They were the most polite words Taylor could ever remember hearing the man speak.

"What can I do for you?" Taylor asked. Bryce and Miguel stood immediately behind him while several other people crowded in to see what the fuss was about.

"I'm…sorry…about the other night," he said. "The chief and me…we had a talk." Embarrassment showed on the man's face, bright as day, and it surprised Taylor. He watched the senior McInerney silently, neither offering support nor aggravating the situation. The man coughed a couple times, then continued.

"Anyway, the reason I came here tonight is to, uh, well, give Wayne his stuff. His brother, Teddy, and me, we're leavin' town. This ain't the kinda place we belong no more and we don't wanna cause no more trouble."

Taylor frowned, uncertain how to take the news. "Where are you going?"

McInerney shook his head. "Wherever the good Lord takes us, I guess. We pretty much packed everything we got in the truck. I ain't had a job in about a year, neither has the boy, so we'll just have to see what we can do. Maybe construction—they're still building down south, where it's warm."

Taylor nodded. In a way, it was a relief to know they'd be gone, but in a way he knew it would only reopen many of Wayne's wounds. It was also going to mean an even greater responsibility for Tom and him.

McInerney looked up and Taylor realized his eyes were red. The onslaught of emotion from such a belligerent man took him aback. It was easy to think of Mr. McInerney as nothing more than an abusive, hate-filled man, but Taylor knew enough about people to know they didn't usually become that way without some influence to drive them. He found himself wondering what had happened to Mr. McInerney in his life to turn him into the man who had so beaten and abused his own son.

"You'll look after my boy, won't you Mayor? Make sure he don't get into drugs or do anything dangerous. I mean, I don't know much about guys like you, but the Chief tells me you're a good person and Wayne is lucky to have you and your..." his face took on a look of confusion as he struggled to find the words. "...And Mr. McEwan as friends. I mean, I can see you like him and all. Just try to be better to him than I know how to be, okay?"

Taylor let out the breath he'd been holding. "Of course, Mr. McInerney," he said. "Wayne *is* our friend and we do care about him. You know, he wants to go to college next year and we're going to help him do that."

McInerney smiled, nodding to himself. "That's great, Mr. Connolly," he said. "I'm much obliged." He gestured to the things in front of him. "This is all Wayne's stuff," he said. "Will you please give it to him?"

"Of course," Taylor promised.

He felt hands on his shoulders and turned to see Wayne behind him, with Eric having joined the throng of people by the door. Gen stood with Eric and he realized she must have told them what was going on.

"Dad?" Wayne said. Taylor realized more than offering a physical barrier, he was actually helping to support Wayne as he faced his own nemesis—his father.

"Hi, Wayne," Mr. McInerney said. "I was just talking to your friend Mr. Connolly here."

Wayne saw the truck in the street beyond, soft white flakes of snow illuminated in the headlamps, a cloud of exhaust streaming from the back end. The truck was painted a dark orange color, but darker patches of actual rust showed through the paint and it was questionable whether it had ever seen a carwash.

"Where are you going?" Wayne asked.

"I don't know yet, son," McInerney said. "Teddy and I's gonna head south I think, to see if we can get ourselves jobs and try to turn things around."

"What about me?" Wayne asked. He moved to stand next to Taylor in front of the door, still leaning on him.

McInerney looked confused. "Well, you're stayin' here, with these guys. They're your friends, right? I thought that's what you'd want."

"Yeah, you're right, but…" Wayne was overwhelmed. "Why are you leaving?"

"There's nothin' more for us here, boy," his father said. "It's time for us to go. You can live your own life and be the person you are. You ain't gonna want us here lookin' over your shoulder. I know I been tough on you, boy, but you turned out good, even if you're a…well, you know. Anyway, we gotta get to the interstate. You be good and mind your manners and do what the Mayor here says, you hear? We'll try and write now and then and let you know what's goin' on."

Wayne leaned into Taylor, who put a reassuring arm around him. McInerney took a step back, toward the steps back down to the sidewalk.

"Goodbye, son," he said. He turned and made his way down the steps, shuffling toward the truck, head low, gait uncertain. Taylor felt for both of them as he held Wayne, knowing that it was both the best and worst possible solution for them.

Wayne stood up and ran out the door in only his socks, nearly falling as he ran down the walk. "Dad!" he called. McInerney turned and Wayne hugged him. To Taylor's surprise and happiness, the man hugged him back. They said a couple more words to each other, then Wayne let go and walked back to the house. Tom handed Taylor a blanket and he put it over Wayne's shoulders as he came inside. Eric and Miguel went out and retrieved the things Mr. McInerney had brought as the truck squealed away into the darkness.

Taylor guided Wayne upstairs while the assembled guests tried to understand what had happened. He heard Tom and Gen quietly explaining what they knew of the situation as he closed the door.

He reached into a drawer and withdrew a fresh set of socks so Wayne could change out the ones he'd soaked from running in the freshly fallen snow. As he did that, Taylor sat next to him on the bed, saying nothing.

"I can't believe he's gone," Wayne managed as he sat back up. "I mean, I should be happy, right? We won't have to worry about him showing up anymore, causing problems, hitting me. Why don't I feel that way?"

Taylor nodded. He was out of his league, but the best he could do was offer reasonable guesses as would any friend.

"You're a good person," he said. "Maybe you're not happy because you hoped things would be different."

"I knew they wouldn't be, though," Wayne admitted.

"Maybe the time apart will help," Taylor offered. "What your father did to you was inexcusable, but maybe being away from each other will give him the chance to gain perspective and understand you for the great person you are."

Tears rolled down Wayne's cheeks. "My life has been turned upside down. I feel alone," he admitted. He turned to Taylor. "I'm so glad you guys are here," he said, anticipating how Taylor would respond. "It's just the sense of finality, you know? Watching him walk away. It's like he was walking away from me."

"What if instead of walking away from you, he was trying to walk away from himself?" Taylor asked.

Wayne shook his head. "I don't know. What do I do now? I don't even know where to start."

Taylor smiled. "You start by being you. Live the life you want to live with the people you want in it. You're not alone, not even by a country mile. Tom and I aren't going anywhere—that's part of the reason Steve thought it was a good idea for you to live here. I think it will be good for you to talk to him and for the two of you to work through this together. You're going to be fine, Wayne. On that, I promise you."

Wayne fell into his arms and Taylor held him. Wayne was somewhere between a little brother and a son to him and he would accept the challenge of helping him. He had an innate sense of whether or not a person was good and there was no question in his mind about Wayne McInerney.

There was a soft knock at the door and Wayne pushed himself up, wiping his face. He saw a couple dark marks on Taylor's shirt where his tears had stained and he said, "sorry."

Taylor laughed and answered the door. Eric stood there, concern on his young face and Taylor knew what he thought he had seen over the last two days was true.

"Is he okay?" Eric whispered.

Wayne appeared behind Taylor and nodded. "I'm cool," he said. "I just had to change my socks."

Eric laughed. "We finished the dishes. I thought maybe you'd like to show me which pie I should try."

"They're all good..." Wayne said, leading him down the back stairs. Tom stood in the hall outside their room, a different sort of smile on his face.

"You did a good thing, Tay," he said. "Is he okay?"

"He will be," Taylor confirmed. "It'll take time and a few hours with Steve, but he's strong and somehow, he's gotten a solid foundation. He'll build himself up from there."

"He's lucky to have you as a friend," Tom said.

Taylor smiled. "He's lucky to have *us* as friends."

Tom took Taylor's hands in his, pulling them around his waist. "He identifies with you. He trusts you. That's important. We work together, but it's you who he confides in. I'm glad you're there for him."

"Not what we expected when we put out an ad for a baker, is it?"

Tom laughed. "It never is."

Together, they walked toward the stairs. "Well, I think we've survived," Taylor observed. "Meal came off okay, everyone got along, everyone is still speaking to each other. We did it."

"Do it again next year?" Tom asked.

"Not a chance," Taylor committed. They made their way down the stairs, holding each other, to the sound of happy people enjoying the festivities below. The moms had found the Christmas decorations and the dads had the tree partially assembled as they stood at the landing. The boys and Mandy sat in the dining room with Gen and Miguel as the two families enjoyed their first holiday evening together and Taylor knew he was truly thankful for the wonderful people with whom he'd been graced that day.

Chapter Ten

The Aftermath

Taylor heard the back door close and felt a cool draft over his bare feet. Reflexively, he pulled them back under the blanket covering his legs as he turned to the next page in the paper. In the weeks since their return from Washington, the weather had taken a decided turn for winter and it looked as though it was going to be a very cold year.

The kitchen door closed and Taylor looked over the top of his newspaper to see Tom's eyes smiling back at him.

"You're home early," Tom observed.

"Business has been slow with the holidays," Taylor said. "Pete was out of the office, so I decided to take the rest of the day off."

"I'm glad you did," Tom said. He curled up next to Taylor and pulled the blanket to cover him as well. "Are you going to take time off while I'm on break?"

"Of course," Taylor confirmed.

"What do you want to do?"

Taylor shrugged. "I'm open to suggestions."

The slamming of the back door interrupted Tom's response as Wayne came through the kitchen, his cheeks and nose red.

"Sorry!" he said, dropping his books on the floor next to him as he sat in one of the chairs. "It's starting to get really windy and *cold* out there."

"It's bound to snow sooner or later," Taylor observed.

"They're calling for it tonight," Tom confirmed.

Wayne pulled off his shoes and rose to put his coat in the closet. "I hope it doesn't screw up the roads," he said.

"Going somewhere?" Taylor asked. Wayne looked at him like it was the dumbest question he'd ever heard.

"Eric's coming into town tonight," Tom reminded, patting his leg.

"Eric who?" Taylor asked. Unfortunately, he could contain the smirk no longer and Wayne nodded, realizing his friend was just teasing. "Oh, *that* Eric."

"Yes, *that* Eric," Wayne said. "He's driving in from school. Have you checked the weather?"

"Not yet," Tom said, reaching for the remote. He turned on the news, which was preempted by the ever-present commercials. "When was he expecting to get here?"

"Sometime around four, he thought," Wayne said. "He wasn't sure when his final would end."

"Come on, I'll help you make up the guest room," Tom said. "Taylor can watch for the weather."

Taylor glanced up from the paper, having fallen out of the conversation. "Huh?"

"Weather. Watch. Get report," Tom said, handing him the remote.

"Okay," Taylor said. With a sigh, he set his paper aside, realizing his chances of actually getting to read it weren't that good. The slower season had also meant a reduction in the number of high profile cases, for which he was grateful. He was thankful for the business and the prosperity it afford Tom and him, but a break was good now and then, and he didn't mind missing his name on the printed page.

He smiled to himself as he considered Eric's pending visit. Wayne had come flying down the stairs, shortly after their return from DC, and announced that Eric wanted to come back for a visit. His request for permission for him to stay with them had been nearly frantic and Taylor and Tom quickly agreed to let the young man come back. A couple days later, a long weekend turned into a week that turned into the whole of their Christmas vacation. Tom and Taylor had already been considering closing the bakery for the holidays and that cemented it.

In the weeks Wayne had been living with them, his personality had undergone radical improvement. Taylor watched as he became more confident, both academically and socially. He had started participating in social events with Emmy and her friends, all of whom appeared to have accepted him readily and warmly. Tom said he'd more or less been "out" at school, but recent events had made it a certainty. To their mutual surprise, Wayne seemed very much at ease with the whole situation, a point Steve attributed to their support and his burgeoning relationship with Eric.

Taylor was glad for Eric. He could only imagine what his life might have been like if he'd met someone at such a young age. Eric was only nine months older than Wayne and they seemed to have a great deal in common. Since Thanksgiving, Tom had quietly had a second phone line installed for Wayne to use and they bought him a small laptop computer to keep in his room to access the internet. Eric had provided a grounding, centering force in Wayne's life and they felt it was good for them to stay in touch. Steve warned them that young relationships often failed, too, so they had to be prepared. For once, though, the "long distance" nature of the relationship probably helped—they *couldn't* spend all their time together, so Wayne was forced to seek out other friendships as well.

Emmy had been amazing. She took in all the chaos of their various situations and came out a staunch ally. To Taylor's eye, she was a Gen-in-training for Wayne. He truly hoped they would stay friends once they had both gone off to their respective schools. Emmy had a very good life and Taylor thought learning how other people lived probably helped her gain a little more perspective on the world, so it was a win-win situation.

Outside, he heard the wind whistle and glanced through the shutters. In mid-December, as the shortest day of the year fast approached, it was already getting dark. The warm comfort of summer had given way to the chilling cold of winter and, as always, Taylor wasn't ready. The cold of the wood floors under his bare feet reminded him once again that it might be time to finally cave in and wear socks around the house. Maybe.

The bushes rustled in the force of the wind, smacking the fencing around the porch with house-shaking force. Taylor shook his head and walked to the kitchen. Nothing like the cold of winter to inspire a warm beverage; if Eric was indeed driving through this weather, he would no doubt appreciate some warm cider, too. Taylor just hoped there was some left from the weekend.

As his hand touched the kitchen door, he heard the doorbell ring. Reversing, he headed back through the living room.

"I'll get it!" Wayne called from upstairs. The sound of his footfalls rolled like thunder as he bounded down the stairs and landed in front of the door. Taylor stood in awe, watching the display. With unabashed zeal, Wayne flung open the door, his eyes bright with excitement. "Hi!" he said.

"Hi," Emmy answered, her expression confused, no doubt thanks to the sound of Wayne's arrival.

His face fell as he saw who stood outside the storm door and he stood frozen in place. Taylor came up behind him and moved him out of the way to open the door.

"Hi, Em," he greeted. "Come in out of the wind. Don't mind Wayne."

"I know, he's waiting on Eric," she said. "He's been babbling about him all week."

"Sorry, Emmy," Wayne said. "I just thought, you know…"

"I know," she said. "Don't worry, I just came over to talk to Taylor for a minute. You can go back to pining."

"Okay," Wayne said, oblivious. He made his way back up the stairs, albeit more slowly than he had come down, and disappeared around the corner.

Taylor turned to Emmy. "So, Em, what's up? Can I take your coat?"

She shook her head. "Sorry, I've got a big test tomorrow. I just stopped by on my way home."

"Okay," Taylor said. "What can I do for you?"

She smiled. "Actually, there's something I can do for you."

"Oh?"

"My parents have a cabin in the mountains, about three hours from here. We usually go there for Christmas, but this year my Dad decided to take us all on a cruise since I'm a senior. Mom told me to come over and see if you guys would like to use it while Tom's on vacation."

Taylor's smile broadened at the offer. Emmy's parents had turned out to be among the more supportive people in the town and had gone out of their way to be kind to Tom and him. Emmy had worked with Tom for almost four years, so they were like extended family.

"What a great gift," Taylor exclaimed. "Are they sure it's okay?"

"Definitely," Emmy said with an affirming nod. "Mom thinks you guys need to get to spend some time without the distractions of town."

Taylor smiled. "That *would* be nice."

"The cabin has three bedrooms and two snowmobiles. It's on a private lake. There isn't anyone else around for miles. You'll be completely alone and completely secluded."

"It sounds wonderful."

She held out a set of keys. Taylor took them and pulled her into a hug. "We'll come by and thank your parents later."

"It's okay," Emmy said. "Merry Christmas."

"Merry Christmas," Taylor said. He showed her to the door and was surprised by the force of the wind as she made her way back out. Making sure the door would stay closed, he went upstairs and found Tom and Wayne getting the guest room situated.

"What was Emmy up to?" Tom asked.

Taylor held up the keys. "Her parents just loaned us their cabin for Christmas," he explained. "I guess we know where we're going."

Tom's eyes bulged as he saw the keys. "I've been there once before," he said. "That place is awesome!"

"It's ours for the duration," Taylor affirmed.

The doorbell rang again and Wayne again disappeared in a thunder of running feet. Tom moved to follow, but Taylor caught him.

"Emmy said it has three bedrooms."

"Yeah?" Tom said. Taylor glanced in the direction of Wayne's departure. "Oh," Tom said. "Yeah, that would be nice for them, too, wouldn't it?"

"It's that or leave them here," Taylor said.

Tom shrugged. "I don't really think it matters leaving them here."

"Me, either," Taylor confirmed, "but I do think it would be nice for Wayne."

"What would be nice for me?" Wayne asked, once again returning from the front door without Eric. This time, Gen trailed behind him, still shaking her head from getting a greeting similar to Emmy.

"Think you and Eric might want to join us at Emmy's cabin?"

"Really!?" Wayne exclaimed, face lit with excitement. "That would be *awesome!* Emmy talks about that place all the time. Eric loves to do things outside—it'll be perfect!" He actually jumped up and down, throwing his arms around Taylor in his zeal.

"Then I guess that's that," Tom deadpanned, watching his young friend's antics.

"Cabin?" Gen asked.

"Emmy's family just loaned us their cabin for the holidays," Taylor explained.

"Oh. That will be nice, won't it?"

"Yeah," Tom agreed. "What are you doing ringing the doorbell, anyway?"

Gen smiled. "I didn't want to just *barge in*, you know. Who knows what could be going on around this place?"

"Not much right now," Wayne grumbled as he fell into a chair, his cheer for his vacation plans quickly replaced by once again waiting for Eric's arrival.

"Eric is late," Tom explained, leading the way out the door and down the back stairs to the kitchen.

"He's coming here for the whole time?" Gen asked. She sat down at the table, watching as Taylor resumed his plan for hot cider.

"I guess his parents were a little hesitant," Tom explained, taking the seat next to her, "but he told them he wanted to spend the holidays with Wayne. They were talking about maybe going to his parents' place for a few days."

"In California?" Gen asked.

Tom nodded. "It's up to them. We told Wayne we'd send him out as part of his Christmas gift, if that's what he wanted."

Gen chuckled. "If they have a choice between spending a week together in a secluded cabin or staying with his parents…"

"Right," Taylor confirmed. He started pulling out mugs for the cider. "You staying?" he asked.

Gen shook her head. "No. Miguel should be home any time. We're going out for dinner tonight."

"You've been doing that a lot lately," Taylor observed, putting one of the mugs back.

"I haven't felt like cooking as much," Gen admitted. "It's easier to let someone else clean up the mess."

Tom nodded from beside her, giving Taylor a pointed look. "Yeah, that would be nice."

Taylor returned his stare, one eyebrow raised and Tom broke under his gaze, laughing. Taylor turned back to scrounging around for ingredients. In short order, it turned into a cacophony of banging pots and pans.

"What are you looking for?" Tom asked.

"Cinnamon. You'd think it would be easy to find—we just made this stuff a few days ago."

Tom reached into the pantry and pulled out the jar of spicy sticks. "Here you go."

"Why was it there?" Taylor asked.

"I'm guessing mainly to confuse you," Tom said.

"What else is new?" Taylor said. He put a pan on the stove and poured the rest of the cider into it along with a couple cinnamon sticks, then turned it on low heat.

Yet again, the doorbell rang, but this time, the earth shattering sound of Wayne's travel was missing. Taylor and Tom glanced at each other, then made their way into the living room. Still no Wayne to be found, they saw Eric's waiting form at the door. Tom opened the door to let him in.

"Hi, Tom," he greeted warmly. "Taylor, Gen," he said, acknowledging the two other people. He wore a heavy black wool coat with a red scarf around his neck. Taylor remembered it being the scarf Wayne had sent him a couple weeks before, as the weather had really started to turn cold. "Where's Wayne?"

"Great question," Tom said. He turned and called up the stairs, "Wayne?" At the second lack of response, they all made their way up, turning to the guest bedroom. Tom stopped short, backing up to let Eric by him.

On the bed, stretched out on the diagonal, Wayne was fast asleep. With a knowing smile, Eric sat down next to him, gently rubbing his back. Slowly, Wayne's eyes opened, then snapped wide as they betook Eric's warm features.

"You're here!" Wayne exclaimed, jumping up to pull Eric into a hug. "Sorry I fell asleep," he said, his face buried in Eric's shoulder.

"It's okay," he said, laughing.

"How was the trip?" Wayne asked.

"Long," Eric said. "The weather west of here is not good."

Wayne took an end of the scarf in his hand. "You wore the scarf," he observed, happiness radiating from him like bright sunlight.

"Heck yeah. It's cold out," Eric reminded, unwrapping the scarf and unbuttoning his coat.

Taylor cleared his throat. "Why don't you get situated, then come on down. I've got some warm cider on the stove and we'll figure out what to do for dinner."

"Sounds good," Eric said.

"Thanks, Taylor," Wayne said, barely able to steal his eyes away from Eric.

Tom, Taylor, and Gen turned and made their way back downstairs, leaving the two some time to get reacquainted. Gen paused at the front door.

"I should be going, too," she said. "Miguel will be home anytime. Come on by whenever you like."

"We will," Taylor said. "My guess is they'll want to stay in tonight, but soon."

"When is school out?" Gen asked.

"End of the week," Tom said.

She nodded. "I'll be around. Tell Eric if he's bored to come on over. We can go into the city or something."

"Things are light at my place, too," Taylor said. "How 'bout tomorrow we go shop downtown? We can make a day of it."

"Sounds great to me," Gen said. Shopping was a fulltime sport for her, and Taylor held his own well.

"You guys just go have your fun while we're working," Tom sighed from behind them.

"Dinner at Mike's on the River?" Taylor said, putting his arm around Tom.

"Okay," he conceded.

"You're buying," Gen said, remembering the price.

"What I do for a little love," Taylor complained.

"More than a little," Tom corrected.

Gen shook her head. "I'm outta here. See you boys tomorrow."

"Bye, Gen," Taylor said, closing the door behind her.

Outside, the wind had died down a bit, but thick white flakes fell from the sky. He and Tom stood together before the large window, watching the picturesque image before them. The street lights and Christmas lights helped to light the snow into a Capra-esque image of the world.

Tom turned to look at Taylor. "I feel like going for a walk," he said.

"We'll freeze," Taylor said.

Tom smiled. "That's half the fun—getting to warm up afterward."

"Where do you want to go?"

"Let's walk to Alberto's, have dinner in town, then come back and watch old black and white movies in front of a roaring fire."

Taylor held him close, wrapping his arms around him as he hugged him tight. "You're a romantic."

"So that's a yes?"

"Of course."

Tom relaxed back into Taylor's embrace, reaching up to put his hands over Taylor's. They turned to the sound of two sets of feet coming down the stairs. Wayne and Eric came into the room, both wearing big smiles. Tom filled them in on the evening plan and their smiles grew even wider. Taylor covered the cider and left it for later and they were off, boots leaving heavy prints in the already deepening snow.

"What a night," Alberto breathed, shaking his head. He absently tossed his ever-present towel over his shoulder, skulking back from the door.

To Taylor's surprise, they had turned out to be the *only* residents of the town to brave the weather. In the town's defense, he wasn't sure he would have wanted to drive in the near blizzard conditions, but walking wasn't too bad. Fortunately, Eric and Tom had insisted the two less weather savvy people, namely he and Wayne, wear warmer clothes. Taylor had been about to object but one look at Tom's face told him it would be pointless. He'd loaned one of his other warm coats to Wayne, who apparently didn't have a warm coat to his name.

By the time they got situated and left, it was already coming down heavier thanwhen he had first noticed the snow. Tom checked the weather and found that a good storm was indeed heading in their direction. However, since the house was only four blocks away and they wouldn't have to drive, he felt pretty safe.

An hour and a half later, thick ruts marked the paths of the few cars that had passed through the downtown area. Even for the middle of the week, traffic was unusually light.

"I hope people are being safe out there," Alberto said, eyes still on the windows.

"Alberto, how far away do you live?" Tom asked.

He shrugged. "About ten miles. Not too far."

"Why don't you bring the check? There's no point in you keeping the place open on a count of us," Tom pointed out.

"No no, Tommy. You're my best customers. It's no trouble at all."

"We'd rather know you made it home safe and sound before it gets any worse," Taylor chimed in. He reached into his pocket and pulled out two crisp hundred dollar bills. "Will this cover it?"

Alberto shook his head. "That's too much. It's on the house."

Taylor smiled. "Not a chance. Use it to buy your wife something special for Christmas, okay?"

The other three men took the cue to rise and put on their coats. Alberto continued to object.

"It's the least we can do," Taylor said, pushing the bills back. "Consider it our contribution to a slow night, okay?"

Reluctantly, Alberto relented. "You're a good friend, Taylor," he said.

"So are you," Taylor agreed. "Now, lock those doors and get home before it gets worse."

"Want me to give you a ride home?" Alberto offered.

Tom shook his head. "No thanks. We're kind of enjoying getting to go for a walk."

"Have a good night, then," Alberto said, walking them to the door. As they started down the sidewalk, he waved again, then bolted the door. Taylor glanced back a few moments later to see the lights go out.

"Hey, Tay," Tom said, taking Taylor's arm in his against the blowing cold wind. "Do you think the skating rink is open yet?"

"Maggie mentioned the Chief had declared it safe," Taylor said, referring to the town's administrative secretary, who did most of the actual running of the town while "Mayor" Connolly was off running his business. She didn't mind and Taylor saw to it that she was well taken care of. He'd even mentioned getting the town council to give her a better title and she had flatly rejected the idea, saying it would just bring more responsibility. He continued, "And, it *is* the first major snowfall."

"Let's go down there," Tom said, looking at him expectantly.

"One, it's really cold and that's a fair walk. Two, we don't have skates."

"Don't be a party pooper," Tom said. "We're all dressed for it, no thanks to you, and I can tell from the roads that we're not going to have school tomorrow."

Taylor glanced back to the other two members of their party. Wayne's hair was white with snow, as he had opted to only wear earmuffs. Both he and Eric were hunched over, pressed up against each other to share warmth—not that they seemed particularly bothered by it.

"Wayne doesn't even have a hat," he objected. Eric reached into a pocket and withdrew another hat that he handed to Wayne.

"Planned ahead," Eric explained.

Taylor laughed. "I'll take that to mean you want to go?"

"Yeeessssss, but leetttt's gggoooo," Wayne said between chattering teeth. "It's cold."

"Maybe I should run back and get the Jeep," Taylor offered.

"It's just down the street, Tay," Tom said.

"Are you sure?" Taylor asked Wayne. "You look like an icicle."

"I'll warm up when we're moving," Wayne said.

Eric put his arms around him. "I'll keep him warm."

"See?" Wayne said.

"Okay," Taylor said. Tom nodded and led the way, arm in arm with Taylor, gloved hands in his pockets.

Even after two winters in the town, Taylor forgot how much the townspeople enjoyed the first major snow. Fortunately, the weather had been cold enough long enough to freeze over the pond area in the park, leaving it ready to be converted into a skating rink. In the few hours the snow had been coming down, people had already come out, cleared the ice, and were skating around like kids on holiday.

The foursome made their way down to the pavilion at the edge of the pond and found the facility was open for business.

"They don't waste any time," Eric observed.

"The town waits all year for this," Tom explained. "Last year, we only got a few dustings of snow before Christmas and it was a big let-down. This year, with this kind of snow, the turnout will be pretty big."

"Looks like more than just the schools will be closed in the morning," Taylor observed.

Wayne glanced over at Tom, an expectant question on his face. Tom continued to survey the people swirling about on the ice and nodded to himself. He leaned back against Taylor, who took his cue and encircled his arms around him.

"The roads don't look like people will be driving much in the morning," he said.

Taylor caught the message. "People aren't going to want to get up early anyway, after being out late tonight."

"We should probably just shut down for tomorrow, huh?" Tom asked, still watching the melee on the ice.

"Makes sense to me," Taylor agreed.

Tom smiled. "And we won't have to get up early, either."

"Fancy that," Taylor said.

"Cool!" Wayne cheered, then he looked sharply at Tom. "I mean, too bad." He grabbed Eric's arm. "Come on, let's go get skates!"

The duo ran off, leaving Tom and Taylor alone on the edge of the pond in a rare quiet moment together. As always, Taylor appreciated the lack of attention their relationship drew from those around them. Watching the skaters, he realized few, if any, had even taken notice of their arrival. All were enjoying their own activities and were focused on the experience.

"Hey, guys," a voice called from the ice, breaking the moment. Standing at the edge of the ice, Mel waved them over, a big smile on her face.

"Hi, Mel," Tom greeted.

"We weren't sure if you'd make it down or not," Mel said. "We went by the house a little while ago, but the lights were out."

"We had dinner at Alberto's," Tom explained. "Eric is back in town visiting Wayne, so we decided to go for a walk in the snow."

She smiled. "Always a good night to be out, the first snow," she said.

"Where's Rob?" Taylor asked.

Mel gestured out at the center of the pond. "Still trying to teach Amanda to skate. She's in one of those awkward times where her coordination just isn't very good."

"Some of us never outgrow that," Tom said, with a pointed glance in Taylor's direction.

"Yeah…well…so what?" Taylor stumbled.

"Come on, Taylor," Mel encouraged, "Tom and I will take you out and you and Amanda can work together to learn."

"Poor Amanda," Tom said.

"Hey! You're supposed to be on my side," Taylor complained.

"I'm always on your side," Tom said.

"Uh-huh. Now I'm going to have to go skate circles around you," Taylor said.

Without another word, he turned and marched in the direction Wayne and Eric had gone. They waved at him as they made their way onto the ice, both stumbling around, but able to stay on their feet. Tom followed along behind, knowing better than to let Taylor do anything athletic without backup.

Two hours and five snowdrifts later, the foursome made its way back from the pond. Even in the cold weather, they had managed to get pretty wet. Taylor was by far the wettest, having lived up to Tom's prediction, finding turning to be a bit of a challenge. Feeling bad about having teased him, Tom had been quick to help guide him and keep him on his feet, offering nothing but words of genuine encouragement.

In the end, Taylor finally threw in the towel and acknowledged sometimes the effort had to be its own reward. Seeing Tom and Taylor turning in their skates, Wayne and Eric had decided to call it a night as well and they walked back to the house together.

School would definitely be closed, as would many of the town's businesses. The snow had continued to come down heavily the entire time they were out and the ground was covered with at least six inches. The county snow handling equipment would be focused on keeping the interstates clear, meaning the town's streets would likely go unplowed until sometime in the late morning or early afternoon, if they were lucky.

Reaching the house, they all made their way upstairs and changed into warm clothes. Even after the exertion of skating, the fact of the day off the following day left no one eager to go to bed, so they continued with the original plan of an old movie. Wayne retrieved firewood from the back porch and they were bathed in a relaxing warm glow minutes later.

Taylor finished the cider and brought four mugs out to share. He went to sit on the couch in his usual spot when he saw Tom glance at the chair beside him. Taylor gave him a questioning look and he in turn glanced at Wayne, who was stoking the fire, then at Eric, who was sitting at the far end of the couch. Taylor did the math—let the youngsters have the couch—and did as Tom suggested. Usually it was they who shared the couch, but there would be plenty of time for them later.

As he sat, Wayne turned and saw the remaining seat was on the couch with Eric. For all his bravado, Taylor saw hesitation in his eyes, and he saw a certain amount of it on Eric's face as well. He was reminded again that they were both quite a few years younger and considerably less experienced. In some ways, he envied them the experiences they were about to share, but in the end, he was much happier for the stability and fulfillment of his life with Tom.

"So, what's playing?" Eric asked, easing the tension as Wayne sat at the other end of the couch.

"The Bishop's Wife," Tom said, wielding the remote. "Cary Grant and Loretta Young. It's one of our favorites."

"Didn't they remake that one?" Eric asked.

"Sort of," Taylor said, face unimpressed.

The movie played, Cary Grant carrying on as he often did, providing charming comic relief to David Niven's stern single-minded bishop. As Tom's antique grandfather clock chimed twelve, he stood with a yawn and stretched, and looked pointedly at Taylor.

"I don't think I'm going to make it any longer," he said.

Taylor nodded. "Yeah, I'm pretty spent myself," he agreed. Eric and Wayne remained at opposite ends of the sofa, neither apparently comfortable enough to be closer, even after their evening together on the ice. They exchanged "good nights" and Tom and Taylor headed upstairs.

As Taylor closed the door behind him, Tom abandoned his clothes to the floor, as he usually did. For once, Taylor followed suit—he could put things away in the morning. Under the cold sheets, they lay in the darkness with only the distant sound of the television breaking the silence.

"So, where do you think Eric will wind up sleeping?" Taylor asked.

Tom propped himself up on an elbow, facing Taylor. "Taylor Connolly, I'm surprised at you. We raised our Wayne to do the right thing."

Taylor nodded. "So, if we find the guest room occupied in the morning..."

"Then you'll simply have to take Wayne aside and remind him that he's an adult and we're not a bunch of old prudes."

Taylor turned to look at Tom in the darkness. "And so the reason for making up the guest room?"

"We do have a responsibility to offer our guest the option," Tom said. "Emil Post, Rule 2374."

"Emil Post?" Taylor asked.

"Gay Etiquette."

"It took you over four months to admit to me you were gay and now *you're* the expert on gay etiquette?" Taylor inquired.

Tom leaned in close to Taylor. "I learn fast," he said.

In the darkness, Taylor heard the TV go silent and the sound of footsteps up the stairs. He paid little attention to the noises, as he and Tom were making a few noises themselves, but his last recollection was of hearing only one door close in the hall.

Chapter Eleven

A Better Choice

Tom's boots crunched the morning snow as he made his way from the house to the garage. With Wayne's help, the Jeep was nearly loaded. It would be a tight fit for the four of them to make the three-hour drive to the cabin, but they knew it would be worth it.

He heaved the heavily laden cooler into the back, sliding it into the small space that had just enough room to accommodate it. Behind him, Wayne appeared with two more duffel bags. Emmy had told them the cabin had the basics—linens, dishes, heat and running water. Everything else was for them to bring. There was a small store about ten miles away, but she didn't know whether it would be open or not. The nearest town was a little over a half-hour away. Since their goal was to not use the car for a week, they had packed heavy.

"Eric's stuff and my stuff," Wayne explained, handing the bags to Tom.

"That should be about it," Tom said, placing the bags on top the cooler.

"We just need Eric and Taylor," Wayne agreed.

"Where are they?"

"Shower," Wayne said, leading the way back to the house.

"Together?" Tom asked.

"Better not be," Wayne said, opening the door.

Taylor turned from the microwave, a steaming cup in hand. "Better not be what?" he asked.

"Nothing," Tom said, standing on the rug at the back door. "Are you finally ready?"

"Hey, looking this good requires work," Taylor defended.

"Too bad," Tom countered, "I look this good after just five minutes."

Taylor walked over and gave him a kiss. "It's all for you, baby."

Wayne choked. "Please!" he complained. "Where's Eric?"

"Right here," Eric said, bounding down the back stairs. "Did you put my bag in the car?" he asked Wayne.

"Along with everything else."

"Rowrrr," Taylor said.

"Some of us got up when we were supposed to," Tom said.

"It's not a race," Taylor countered.

Tom gave him a look. "Just for that, you two get to ride in the back."

Eric looked up. "What did I say?"

"You were late, too," Wayne said, standing firm with Tom.

"But the bed was so warm and comfortable," Eric defended.

"And somehow I managed to get out of it," Wayne said. He couldn't help himself and started laughing. Eric hugged him and Wayne managed, "You're still sitting with Taylor."

"Since when is that a bad thing?" Taylor asked, washing out his emptied mug.

"Anytime the meal is too spicy?" Tom asked.

"Okay, time to go," Taylor said. Tom handed him his coat from the hook by the door.

"Where's Felix?" Tom asked.

"On the bed. Gen said she'll check in on him every day while we're gone."

"Great," Tom said. "All set?"

"Yep," Eric said, finishing tying his boots.

With Tom at the wheel and Wayne in the passenger seat, they made great time. Most of the holiday traffic was still a couple more days off and the weather had held out so the freeways were all plowed and cleared. The recent snowfall had made using the Jeep a certainty, though. The Jag handled well in the cold weather, but with the cabin as secluded as it was, Tom and Taylor agreed a sport utility would have a much better chance of getting them there safely.

Taylor watched the countryside pass them by as Tom explained various bits of scenery. He'd been to the cabin before and had a general idea of the area. The "town" consisted of two stores, a gas station, a greasy-spoon restaurant, and a couple small engine repair businesses, both of which appeared to be closed for the holidays. Tom noted that, at least that day, the convenience store was open if they found they'd forgotten something.

After the town, the road just stretched on, completely empty, winding through the steep hills. The deciduous trees were all bare, but the woods were still thick with various types of pine and spruce trees.

"Emmy said there is an old Christmas tree farm near the edge of the property," Wayne said, turning to face Taylor and Eric. "She said we can cut one down if we want to have a tree."

"She mentioned it to me, too," Tom said.

"We don't have a base," Eric commented.

"Em said there's one at the house," Wayne said.

"Decorations?" Eric asked.

"She said there are some. Her mom keeps all the heirloom stuff at their house, but she said there are some lights and bulbs and stuff," Wayne confirmed.

"I've never cut down a Christmas tree," Taylor said.

"Really?" Tom asked.

"Nope. We usually had an artificial tree. Mom didn't think it made sense to cut down a tree to put in the house for a couple weeks and then throw it away."

"That's why you have the one we put up at Thanksgiving?" Wayne asked. Taylor nodded.

"I can't imagine Christmas without a tree," Eric said. "I mean, I was okay with it for this year, but it's definitely more like Christmas with the tree."

Taylor watched as Wayne's face took on a more rigid appearance. "We only had a Christmas tree if I put it up," he said. "After my Mom left, my dad and my brother never really cared. They used to give me a hard time about putting one up. But, I did it anyway because I wanted one."

He sat back, facing forward again. Eric reached out and put a hand on his shoulder, a small gesture of caring. Taylor smiled; he was glad Wayne finally had someone who cared about him. There was no doubt that he and Tom cared about Wayne, but he needed someone in his life who was more than just a friend or parent figure.

Tom slowed, turning onto a snow-covered dirt road. Overhead, a canopy of trees was draped in heavy white snow, creating a tunnel of tree limbs. There were a couple other tire ruts in the road, but it was clearly not heavily traveled. In the early afternoon light, it was easy to believe they were on another world, without another soul for miles around.

"How many other people live on the lake?" Eric asked.

"According to Emmy, there are a few other houses, but they're all pretty far apart so it's like you're alone. It's a pretty big lake and she said there is almost never anyone at the other houses over the holidays," Tom explained.

"Sounds good to me."

"Hear, hear," Taylor seconded.

Tom slowed again and turned onto a small two-track driveway that led into a thick grove of trees. He stopped and reached for the keys he'd dropped in the cup holder. "Be right back," he said and hopped out. He ran forward to unlock the gate that obstructed their path.

Taylor felt the cold air as the door opened and realized the temperature was a few degrees colder than when they'd left. He reached for his jacket, which he'd tossed behind him a couple hours before. Eric did the same and he reached forward to hand Wayne his.

Tom hopped back in the Jeep, pulling the door closed behind him. "Wow, it's a heck of a lot colder out there," he breathed, rubbing his hands together.

"Your coat, sir?" Taylor said, handing it forward.

"Thanks, Tay," Tom said. "I'll put it on when we get to the house."

Taylor took the coat back and held it while Tom drove forward across the virgin snow. It was almost impossible to see where the "road" was, so he just aimed for the gap in the trees and hoped for the best. As they twisted around a couple large trees, it became obvious why the house wasn't visible from the road. It was painted a deep forest green, no doubt to help it blend into the surroundings. With the thick pine trees all around, it was the perfect camouflage color.

Tom turned them around in the driveway and backed up to the sidewalk leading to the door. He slid the shift into park and they were there.

"This is it, huh?" Taylor said.

"Not a bad place to spend Christmas, huh?" Tom said. They got out and Taylor held out his coat for him. "Thanks," Tom said, then reached out to hug Taylor. Taylor took the freebie, then turned to gesture at the house.

"Maybe we should get one of these."

"You'll get no objection from me," Tom said.

"Me, either," Wayne said.

"You think you'd get to use it?" Taylor asked.

"I'm family, remember?"

Tom laughed. "The boy's smart, no doubt about that."

Wayne grinned proudly. He opened the hatch, taking an armload of their stuff. "Let's get this stuff unloaded before we freeze."

"I'll get the door," Tom said. Taking a couple of the bags himself, he headed for the cabin while the rest of them unloaded the Jeep.

Inside, the "cabin" was anything but. Hardwood floors met warm earth-tone walls in a great room that faced the open white valley of the lake, through floor to ceiling windows that rose at least sixteen feet in the air. Beside the room was a kitchen fit for a king, complete with a professional grade gas stove and built-in refrigerator. The opposite end consisted of the two smaller bedrooms, one facing the lake, one at the back of the house, separated by a bathroom.

"Holy crap," Eric said, frozen in the middle of the great room.

"Wait 'til you see the master bedroom," Tom said. He took Taylor's hand and led him upstairs. The master bedroom was the entire top floor of the house. It consisted of a balcony sitting area looking out over the great room windows, with the actual sleeping quarters over the two lower bedrooms. The bathroom was palatial, with a two person shower stall, Jacuzzi bathtub, private commode and two sinks.

"What does Emmy's dad do again?" Taylor asked.

"Obstetrician," Tom said.

"He must get a lot of babies."

Together, it took the four of them one more trip to get the Jeep emptied. Wayne and Eric took the lower room facing the lake while Taylor and Tom were upstairs. Taylor knew they wanted the upstairs room, too, but sometimes rank had its privileges and they needed something to look forward to in their young lives…or at least that would be his excuse while he and Tom took the room.

Settled in, they sat in the living room, looking out over the lake. A light wind had set in and the snow stirred in great billows, speeding from one end to the other.

"Didn't you say something about snowmobiles?" Eric asked.

"Emmy said they're in the garage. They should all have gas and be ready to use," Tom confirmed. He sat on the couch, while Taylor lay with his head in his lap.

Wayne and Eric sat on the couch opposite them, not quite as relaxed. Tom was glad they'd at least chosen to share a room. He didn't want them to do anything they weren't ready to do, but he also didn't want them to feel like they had to live up to some false standard on his and Taylor's account.

"I'd like to try taking them out. It's been years since I was on a snowmobile."

"I've never been on one," Taylor said, staring up at the ceiling.

"You're kidding," Wayne said.

Tom laughed and waved a hand. "Wayne, you'll get used to it after a while."

"Hey, it's not my fault my parents never did anything like that," Taylor complained. "I knew most of the major pieces of classical music by the time I was fourteen and I can easily name at least a dozen artists' work in the museums."

"And to think, people were surprised when you came out," Tom chided.

"Right," Eric agreed. "Sounds to me like it's high time you had another new experience, then."

"How about a late lunch first?" Tom asked.

"I could eat," Wayne agreed.

"A quick lunch, then we'll go," Taylor said.

Tom slid his leg out from under Taylor's head and looked down as Taylor continued to lay on the couch. "Want me to make you something?"

He sighed. "Sure. Whatever you're having."

"Turkey sandwich?"

"Sounds good."

"I'll help," Eric said, following him into the kitchen.

As the two of them bustled about, Taylor got up and walked to the window. Wayne joined him there, looking out over the frozen water.

"What do you think?" Wayne asked.

"It's beautiful. A far sight better than just sitting around the house. What do you think?"

Wayne shook his head. "It's always hard for me to believe I'm in places like this. I mean, even when my Mom was around, we never had anything that was even a tenth as nice as this. It's like living a dream."

Taylor glanced in the direction of the kitchen and smiled. "Not a bad dream, huh?"

Wayne blushed and looked at the floor. "I can't complain."

"You guys seem pretty happy."

"We are. I know I am," Wayne said. "I couldn't even have imagined this, just a couple months ago. I keep waiting for the bubble to burst."

Taylor nodded. "I know what you mean. You'll get over it after a while. You deserve to have things go your way for a while."

Wayne shook his head again. "I don't know that I deserve it, but I sure do feel lucky to have things going my way for once."

Taylor smiled. "We'll try to keep them going your way as long as we can," he confirmed. "You *are* family, after all."

Wayne rewarded him with a big smile as Tom came back into the room, two plates in hand. Eric followed along behind, handing one to Wayne. They made their way into the dining room they had discovered at the front of the house, off the kitchen, on the way to the garage.

Taylor watched the three other people as they talked, and smiled to himself. Wayne had only been enjoying the peace he felt for a couple months. Taylor was lucky enough to have it for the almost three years. Tom was the most dynamic, caring person he had ever met and never a day went by that he wasn't thankful to have him in his life. Even when they teased each other, there was never a doubt that Tom wanted the best for him—he couldn't remember any other time in his life that he could be so trusting of another person, at least outside of his family.

Tom caught his gaze and smiled back, the same quirky little "Taylor Smile" he'd given Taylor since the day they met. It said everything, in one simple gesture—I love you, I want you, I want to be with you. Taylor winked and they went back to their lunches, Tom talking to Wayne and Eric about where to take the snowmobiles. Eric wanted to run flat-out across the lake, but Wayne was concerned about how thick the ice would be. Tom convinced them to stay near shore, at least for a while.

Taylor watched the interaction. There was no doubt that he and Tom were like older siblings, but they were friends, too, and he liked that. He'd often wondered if Tom's sister, Mandy, had engineered bringing Eric to meet Wayne. He couldn't remember if she knew about Wayne being in their lives or not, but he thanked whatever twist of fate had done it. Wayne would overcome the unfortunate things that had happened to him, growing stronger in the process, and Eric would be able to help him do it. As Taylor sat back, he knew things would be okay, and that was the greatest Christmas gift anyone could have given him.

"Okay, that should do it," Tom said, giving the end of the rope one final tug.

"Are you sure this is the best way to move the tree?" Wayne asked, gazing uncertainly at the six-foot spruce they had felled a few minutes before. Tom had used a rope they found in the garage to tie the stump end and first few rows of branches to the back of the large snowmobile Wayne and Eric were using. His plan was that they would drag it the half-mile or so back to the cabin.

"The rope will help hold it up and the snow won't provide much in the way of friction," Tom explained. "It's only a half mile on the flat surface of the lake. It should be okay."

"It'll be full of snow," Eric pointed out. All three of the other men faced Tom, uncertainty clearly evident on their faces. For his part, Taylor had chosen to stay quiet, letting the two younger men voice the questions that were on the tip of his tongue.

"We'll just shake it out when we get back," Tom said. For his part, he was in good spirits, taking their doubts in stride, rather than personally. "Don't worry, what's the worst that can happen? We'll come get another tree."

"You could always ride back with it between you," Taylor offered. Remembering he was trying to stay out of it, he looked down and tugged on the knot himself, as though he would be able to tell if it was right or not.

"Okay, let's go," Wayne said. Eric had driven for the ride out, so he took the front position for the ride back. Eric hopped on behind him, holding him tight in the cold of twilight.

"We'll be right behind you," Tom said. Wayne gunned the engine and they were gone, the tree dragging along behind them, just as Tom had promised.

"That *was* fun," Taylor said as the duo rounded a peninsula in the lake and disappeared on the other side.

"I knew you'd enjoy it," Tom said. In the silence, as darkness approached, he leaned back against the snowmobile and pulled Taylor to him. "It's nice to have a moment to ourselves."

Taylor relaxed in his embrace, resting his head on Tom's shoulder. "Yes, it is."

Tom pulled his arms around him tighter, sharing their heat to fight back the cold. Above, it was a cloudless night and the stars were starting to appear. In the distance, the moon just started to rise above the horizon, casting a blue glow over the fresh powder. The mountains appeared in jagged relief, completing the picture.

"I miss you," Tom said.

Taylor turned his head, his forehead still resting against Tom's chin. "What do you mean? I'm right here."

Tom laughed, hugging him tighter again. "No, I mean I miss being able to spend time with you. Just you."

"Because of Wayne?"

"Not just Wayne," Tom said. "Everything. We're still young, Taylor—too young to be this busy. We need to do this more—get away, just you and me."

Taylor chuckled in spite of himself. "You won't hear me complain."

Tom was silent again, just staring off in the distance, holding Taylor. For his part, Taylor seemed perfectly comfortable staying right where he was and made no effort to move.

"There are times I feel like we are so busy managing our lives that we're forgetting to live our lives. I mean, I love you and I know you love me, but I feel like I never get to be with you for more than five or ten minutes a day a few times a week. That's not how it's supposed to work, is it?"

Taylor sighed. Darkness was setting in and he could feel himself get sleepy as he rested in Tom's arms. "I don't know how it's supposed to work," he admitted. "I know I'd like to spend more time with you, too, and that I love you, too, and have no doubt you love me back. Let's face it, we got ourselves into this position, so only we can get ourselves out of it. It's getting better isn't it?"

Tom nodded, his late day stubble scratching lightly against Taylor's brow. "Yeah, it's better than it was. I guess I still just feel like we need more 'us' time."

It was Taylor's turn to tighten his hold on Tom. "I can never get too much 'us' time," he admitted.

"And I don't want to be greedy," Tom said. "Wayne needs us and we should be there for him."

Taylor shook his head. "Being there for him doesn't mean being there every minute of every day. He's doing okay and can afford to be on his own. He'll let us know if he needs us, either through words or through actions."

"Tuesdays and Thursdays," Tom said.

"What about them?"

"Dinner. Just you and me. We don't have to make a big deal out of it. We'll just go," Tom said. He leaned back to look at Taylor. "Do you think that will be okay?"

Taylor smiled and nodded. "I think it will be a great start."

Tears welled at the bottoms of Tom's eyes. "Just don't let us grow apart, okay? Promise."

Taylor felt his own eyes sting. "Is that what you think is happening? We're growing apart?"

"Maybe a little," Tom admitted and his lower lip quivered. "Not because of us—everything just keeps getting in the way."

Taylor blinked trying to clear his own eyes. "I have never wanted to be with anyone like I want to be with you. I will stop everything if that's what it takes to keep you. No more mayor, no more bakery, no more anything as long as you're still there. *That* is my promise."

Tom laughed and cried at the same time. "And I'm supposed to be the poet," he said. He kissed Taylor and Taylor kissed him back.

In the distance, they heard the sound of a machine approaching and saw the light of the snowmobile as it once again rounded the peninsula separating the cabin side of the lake from the old tree farm. Wayne and Eric appeared, Wayne still driving, and they pulled up beside Tom and Taylor.

"What happened to you guys?" he asked. "Everything okay?"

The two remained encircled in each others' arms, holding each other tight in the cold. Taylor spoke. "We were just talking, watching the moon come up," he said, indicating the glowing orb that had appeared and was now well above the horizon.

"Okay, well we got the tree back and shook it off and it worked just like you said," Wayne said. "We were going to actually set it up, but then we were afraid something had happened to you."

"We're fine," Tom confirmed. "But you're right, we should get back. We don't know this area that well and it's getting cold." He turned to Taylor. "You wanna drive?"

Taylor shook his head. "I'm fine with holding on for dear life."

Tom returned the grin and hopped on the machine. Taylor joined him and felt it roar to life beneath them. Tom revved the engine, then gunned it and they were off. They had surveyed the lake earlier and confirmed what Tom remembered—it was fed by the runoff from the mountains all around and had no river connections. He recalled that Emmy said it froze very deep over the winter, as it had no natural springs or other heat sources. She had told him it even froze all the way down a couple years ago, killing some of the plants and animals within it.

With a silent grin to himself, he steered off across the lake and opened the throttle all the way up. A glance in the rearview mirrors showed Wayne and Eric struggling to keep up with the older machine and he felt Taylor's laugh against this back as he continued to hold him tight.

A good hour later, they pulled the snowmobiles into the garage, parked them in their positions next to the Grand Cherokee, and closed the door. Wayne and Eric maneuvered the tree inside while Tom and Taylor made spiced cider and started a fire. Tom and Wayne went through the ornaments while Taylor and Eric had lights duty. They decided there was little point in going overboard since the holiday was only another day away and they'd wind up having to put it all back in the boxes a few days after that. So, for the first time since they'd been together, Tom and Taylor had a real Christmas tree, cut with their own hands, shared with their close friends.

"What should we do tomorrow?" Tom asked. He and Taylor had taken positions on one side of the fireplace while Wayne and Eric sat on the other. He was reclined casually against Taylor, while Wayne leaned against the opposite couch and Eric used his thigh as a pillow, facing the fire. They had all switched to comfortable sweaters and jeans, letting the fire and the cider warm them after the afternoon outdoors.

"I vote we try the other snowmobile," Eric piped up from the floor.

"I wouldn't mind seeing what really fast feels like," Wayne agreed.

"Sharing is only fair," Tom agreed. "You guys can have the fast one tomorrow."

"Is there any good hiking here?" Taylor asked.

Tom nodded. "Some, as long as the snow isn't too thick."

"Or we could just lay here in front of the fire and do nothing," Eric offered. His eyes were closed and he'd set his glass on the floor next to him.

Behind them, the room was dark, save the firelight and the lights of the tree. Taylor watched as Wayne's eyes got heavy, and he felt Tom's hand in his slowly relax. He leaned forward and quietly whispered into Tom's ear, "How about a little 'us' time?"

Tom's hand turned and gently took Taylor's. He leaned forward and Wayne's attention came back to the present.

"Looks like we're all pretty well beat," Tom said. "Just get up when you feel like it. I'll cook breakfast around nine or so, okay?"

Eric cleared his throat, his dark eyes barely able to keep themselves open. "If I don't beat you to it," he said. Though obviously tired, neither he nor Wayne made a move to get up. That was fine with Tom—he and Taylor had plenty of room to themselves upstairs.

"Good night," Taylor said, following Tom up the stairs.

Taylor closed the door and turned to find Tom pulling back the covers on the bed. Beyond it, the windows overlooking the lake were uncovered, revealing the pristine white beauty of the snow, illuminated by the blue moonlight, with only a few tracks from the snowmobiles to mar its beauty.

Tom lit the gas fireplace, then turned off the lights. He came up behind Taylor, who stood before the wall of windows, gazing at the darkness. Wrapping his arms around Taylor's middle, he lay his head between Taylor's shoulders.

"We really are the only ones here," Taylor observed. "There aren't any other lights on out there."

"There's one other house lit, at the other end of the lake," Tom said. "You can't see it from here."

Taylor turned in Tom's arms. "Then they can't see us, either."

Tom smiled, running his hands across Taylor's smooth skin under his sweater. "It's cold up here," he observed. "Think you can keep me warm?"

Taylor returned the smile, helping Tom out of his sweater…and everything else. "I'm willing to give it a try," he said.

They made their way to the bed, shivering in spite of themselves as bare skin hit cold sheets. Tom gasped a little and Taylor pulled the heavy covers over them, then turned up the temperature, just as he'd promised.

Chapter Twelve

Disaster

Taylor awoke with a start. What had he been dreaming about? The images had already faded into the clouds of his subconscious, but he felt a frown lingering on his lips and brow. Something seemed out of sorts, but he couldn't put his hand on it.

As daylight intruded on his thoughts, he felt Tom entwined in his arms. They often slept wrapped around each other. Early in their relationship, Tom had admitted it made him feel so safe and secure to know Taylor was there with him, each night. It was one of the ways Taylor knew they were not growing apart. Old couples slept on opposite sides of the bed; he and Tom slept together, always.

It had been just over a week since their discussion in the twilight of their first night at the lake house. Taylor felt the frown lessen as he thought of the week they'd had. He hadn't felt so relaxed in a very long time. Since they'd been away, there had been only three phone calls—Pete, Gen, and Eric's family. Even Tom's family and his own family had understood how much they needed not to be disturbed. He and Tom finally broke down and called them the evening of Christmas day, not wanting them to feel left out.

Wayne had taken it in stride, but Taylor knew it had bothered him to have all of them have people to talk to and be ignored by his own parents. Mandy had insisted on talking to him, making a point of asking all kinds of questions about how things were going with Eric. Taylor had watched how his face brightened as he recounted their exploits on and around the frozen lake. He'd even noticed how Wayne's face darkened at something she asked, and he quietly answered, "Yessss."

He and Tom had even managed a fair amount of 'us' time. It was a simple phrase, but Taylor knew it had stuck, from the moment Tom said it. He smiled thinly—it felt odd to admit it, but the fact that Tom missed him made him happy. It told him that even as he lamented their constant labors, Tom wasn't just sailing blindly through, oblivious. They were a team—that's what Taylor had always told him. Even the best teams have their up times and their down times. It was a testament to the strength of their relationship that their down times were something they were still able to share, without questioning the feelings they had for each other. They knew their love for each other was strong—they just had to be vigilant to never allow anything to get in the way.

Taylor looked at the blanket at the end of the bed and smiled. The night before had been New Year's Eve. Since moving from the city, New Year's Eve had taken on a completely different meaning for him. Gone were the parties and clubs he used to attend, replaced with good friends and good company. The first year had been at their place, the second at Pete's, and last year at Gen's. This year was a novelty in that they only shared the evening with one other couple, and that suited Taylor just fine.

What was better, though, was the time after the ball dropped in New York. Wayne and Eric were, as usual, barely able to stay awake, so Tom announced they were going to bed and took Taylor upstairs. To his surprise, Tom had laid out a blanket on the floor and surrounded it with candles.

"It may not be the islands," Tom had said, "But at least we can ring in the new year bathed in moonlight."

His slate eyes full of amorous intent, he'd pulled Taylor to the blanket and helped him into, or rather out of, his island attire. They managed to last an hour, in the wee hours of the new year, and as they both lay exhausted, Taylor had finally snuffed the candles and put Tom in bed.

He held Tom tight, his arms fully around him, feeling the soft puff of his breath on his cheek. The sun was coming up, slowly filling the room with light unobstructed by any coverings on the windows.

Beside him, he felt Tom stir and saw one gray eye peek at him from where he lay.

"Good morning," he said, lips barely moving.

"Happy New Year," Taylor answered, his own eyes still heavy.

"Sleep well?" Tom asked.

"After a fashion."

"Me, too." He nuzzled in closer to Taylor. "What time is it?"

A quick glance to the side provided the answer. "Eight thirty."

"What time did we go to bed?"

"About one thirty."

Tom lifted his head. "We're in bed," he observed.

"Yeah?"

He dropped his head back to the pillow. "I don't remember going to bed."

"You were already out."

"So you carried me?"

"Yep. Didn't want you to get a stiff back from sleeping on the floor."

Tom smiled. "You love me, don't you?"

Taylor shrugged. "I guess." Tom's hand found a vulnerable spot and pinched Taylor. "Okay! Yes, I love you!"

"You'd better."

Taylor kissed him. "Feels like we got some 'us' time."

Tom kissed him back. "Want some more?" His hand slid slowly down Taylor's side, heading for another vulnerable spot, just as a knock sounded on the door. Tom sighed, his head falling back to the pillow beside Taylor, but his hand didn't move.

"Tom? Taylor?" It was Wayne.

"Mornin', Wayne," Taylor greeted, reaching to remove Tom's lingering hand.

"Hey, I didn't want to wake you, but we're thinking we'll make some breakfast. Would you like something?" He stood at the door, his head just peeking inside.

"Why don't you give us about twenty minutes, okay? We just woke up." Taylor tried to keep Tom's hand at bay, but it kept moving.

"Okay, see you in a few," Wayne said. He pulled the door closed and Taylor let go the laugh he had been holding back.

"You are so *bad*," he said, poking Tom in the ribs. He recoiled, ever ticklish, and tried to push Taylor away. "Oh, it's not so funny when it's you, huh?" Taylor said, pinning him to the bed. "What are you gonna do now, tough guy?"

"Just this," Tom said and reached up to pull Taylor down to him. The sun rose above the horizon to touch their skin and it was indeed a new day in a new year.

At breakfast, everyone was relatively quiet. It had been a late night, and for reasons that defied the imagination, they'd all chosen to get up early. As promised, Wayne and Eric had breakfast waiting when Tom and Taylor made their way downstairs, twenty minutes, give or take, later. They'd both stopped to catch a quick shower, but hadn't taken any steps to perfect their appearance after. Tom wore a gray crewneck sweater, khaki's, and slippers, while Taylor had gone for a navy blue turtleneck and blue jeans. As usual, his feet were bare.

Wayne and Eric sat at opposite ends of the table and seemed a little reserved. Tom and Taylor chatted about nothing, as they usually did, but Taylor watched the two younger men. He realized Tom had picked up on it, too, though neither of them let on to the other two.

As the conversation hit a breakpoint, Tom turned to Wayne. "So, how late were you guys up?" he asked casually, as though nothing was the matter.

Wayne's attention refocused from whatever place his mind had been and he looked up. "Uh...I don't know, one o'clock or so?" he answered. It came out a question, but he didn't look at Eric.

"Big plans for the day?" Taylor asked.

Eric spoke up. "I was thinking I might go hike along that creek on the other side of the lake for a while and see if there's anything interesting," he said. He looked directly at Taylor, without even a glance at Wayne.

"I brought a couple books along," Wayne said. "I kind of feeling like reading."

"I've got a couple books to read myself," Tom said, eyes on Taylor.

Taylor nodded, as much to himself as Tom. "I was thinking about going around the lake some more," he said. He saw the very corners of Tom's eyes wrinkle. They were on the same wavelength, as usual.

"You're welcome to come along on the hike," Eric offered. Wayne glanced quickly in his direction, but his head never moved.

"Sounds like fun," Taylor agreed.

They finished the rest of the meal in silence. Tom said he and Taylor would take care of the dishes since the others had cooked. Eric went to the garage to ready the snowmobiles, while Wayne went to take a shower. As the doors closed, Tom started the water and scrubbed the pans.

"Trouble in paradise?" he asked.

Taylor shook his head. "They were fine yesterday, I thought."

"Yeah, me too," Tom agreed.

"Compare notes after lunch?"

"Sounds good," Tom said. "You can go ahead and take off. I'll finish this up."

Taylor stopped to look at him. "Did you really have books to read?"

Tom smiled. "I always take one or two with me, but I'd rather go off hiking with you," he admitted.

"Want me to come back in a couple hours?"

Tom's smile broadened. "How could I say no to you?"

Taylor kissed him. "That's what I like to hear," he said.

High clouds had begun to obscure the sun and the wind was picking up. Tom had checked the weather yesterday and told Taylor it might snow today. As he trailed along behind Eric, Taylor felt sure it would. Even through the heavy coat, snow pants, mask, gloves, scarf, and hood, the occasional waft of flakes managed to get in and sting his skin. As fun as it was to go fast on the snowmobiles, he wouldn't mind when they got to their destination.

Eric had taken the faster machine, offering it half-heartedly to Taylor when he came into the garage. Taylor was content to go a little slower—at most, he'd get there a minute or two behind Eric. As they headed off across the lake, Eric said nothing, just gunning the motor and disappearing in a haze of snow.

Taylor kept up, if a little slowly, and angled his approach to minimize the amount of snow that would be in his face. As they reached the shore, well out of view of the house, Eric slowed and pulled up on a shallow beach, turning to face Taylor.

"Sorry to leave you back there," he said, silencing the motor of the snowmobile.

"That's okay," Taylor answered, determined to remain magnanimous.

"I just needed to go fast," Eric continued, explaining himself absently as though Taylor was upset with him.

"I used to drive a Jaguar, remember?" Taylor said.

Eric looked up sharply, joining the conversation. "Yeah, how did that happen? A Jag to a Jeep?"

Taylor shrugged. "It was more important to Tom than it was to me, so I let him take it. When it's important to me, I'll just get something else…and he'll probably steal that, too. It's the nature of love, my friend." Taylor smiled, resting his arms casually in front of him. Eric looked down, expression anything but happy. He pressed on, hoping to draw Eric out. "So, you were pretty quiet at breakfast this morning."

"I was tired," Eric evaded. His shoulders slumped and he pushed the mask out of his face. "Taylor, can I talk to you?"

"That's why we're here, isn't it?" Taylor said.

Eric responded with a sheepish smile, realizing he wasn't as subtle as he thought. He hopped down from the snowmobile and rested against it with his arms crossed over his chest.

"I really like Wayne," he began. "I mean, I know he's your friend and all, but I want you to know that."

Taylor nodded, turning to face Eric in a like manner, slipping his hands in his jacket pockets. "I know."

Eric sighed, face heavy, as he looked at the ground. "He's just asking a lot from me, you know?"

Taylor frowned. "Actually, no," he said. "I'm not really following you."

Eric looked up. "He's been pressuring me to move out here with him. He wants me to transfer from OSU to go to college with him."

"He hadn't said anything about that," Taylor admitted.

Eric nodded. "He said he was going to talk to Tom about it, to see if we could take the apartment over the bakery."

Taylor looked away. He couldn't say he was surprised. It was no secret Wayne was head over heals for Eric, but he hadn't been expecting him to put pressure on Eric. To the contrary, he'd expected Eric to try to talk Wayne into moving to Ohio with him.

"I asked him why he didn't want to just move to Columbus with me," Eric said, interrupting Taylor's train of thought. At least he'd managed to see that one coming.

"What did he say?" Taylor asked.

"He wasn't ready to move away from you and Tom. You're the first real family he feels like he's ever had."

Taylor knew it wouldn't make Eric feel any better, but it warmed his heart to know Wayne had said that about Tom and him. He wasn't ready to be rid of their young friend yet, either, but knew that shouldn't be a factor in the situation.

"When did all this come up?" Taylor asked.

"We've talked about it off and on all week, but last night he started in on me when we went to bed. He kept saying our New Year's resolution should be doing what we have to so we can stay together. But, what he really meant was he wanted me to say I would move to live with him."

Taylor nodded. "And you don't want to do that?"

Eric looked up, eyes filled with pain, and threw his hands up in the air in frustration. "I don't *know*, Taylor. I don't know if I'm ready to be in that serious a relationship. I don't know if I want to leave Ohio State. I like it there; I have friends there and I'm doing well in my classes. I'll lose credits if I transfer here—there—you know what I mean."

His lip quivered and Taylor knew it was from more than the cold. He waited while Eric sorted through his thoughts, still holding himself tight with uncertainty. Eric looked up, his warm eyes practically demanding answers from Taylor.

"I think I love him, but I'm only nineteen. He wants me to make a commitment to him like you and Tom have made to each other and I'm not saying I won't want to do that, but I just don't know if I'm ready now. I mean, I've only even known him since Thanksgiving, for cryin' out loud. I love sending email and talking on the phone and coming to visit, but why does it have to be so fast?"

"It doesn't have to be that fast," Taylor confirmed. "It's okay to want to take it slow."

Eric rolled his eyes and looked back toward the forest. "That's easy for you to say. He's not staring you down, waiting for you to say you'll move your whole life to live with him."

"It's a big decision," Taylor agreed. "And I don't think it's something you should rush into if you're not sure."

"How do I tell him I want to think about it without him thinking I'm telling him I don't like him?"

"Honesty is usually my first choice," Taylor admitted, smiling.

"When I try to be honest, he just gets upset and thinks I'm going to abandon him like his family did."

Taylor's brow furrowed. "What has he told you about that?"

Eric shrugged. "His Mom divorced his dad, who was an abusive alcoholic, then got remarried and moved away. He had to live with his dad and older brother and they both used to beat him up when they got drunk." He looked at Taylor. "Man, it sounded really bad. I don't know how he survived."

Taylor smiled thinly. "He's a strong kid," he said. "The problem now is that all of us—you, me, Tom—we're the first people who have cared about him and made him feel like he has any self worth. I can't speak for his mother, but I know a thing or two about his father and brother, and they weren't particularly good people. Now, he's frantic to try to keep us in his life—Tom and I are like his parents, or at least older siblings. You're the first person who has ever expressed a love interest in him. He's scared if you leave that you won't come back, just like the other people in his life who he has loved and who were supposed to love him."

"Can't I be in his life without having to live right here, right now?"

Taylor smiled. "Of course you can. But, you're his first love. He wants you here all the time. Do you remember your first love? Didn't you want him around all the time?"

Eric nodded. "My first love was a kid I grew up with," he said. "He was straight. It just about killed me when we grew apart."

"Now put yourself in Wayne's shoes. Not many friends, no family, told you're worthless for most of your life. Now in walks a guy who you fall in love with, who seems to love you back, but has to go away."

Eric seemed on the verge of tears. "It's not like it's easy for me, either," he said. "I really do like him. I just don't know if I'm ready to uproot and move here and live together. That's a lot, Taylor."

"I agree, and that's probably the best reason not to do it."

Eric eyed him. "I shouldn't do it?"

Taylor shook his head. "You have to do what's best for you, Eric. Only you can determine that. If you do something just to make Wayne happy, the decision will haunt you later. When Tom and I chose to commit to each other, it was because it was what we both wanted and it was a mutual decision. If you were to move here just because you don't want to hurt Wayne, you'll eventually resent him for making you choose."

"It's not that I never want to do it, though. I just don't want to rush."

"Then that's what you say."

"But what do I do when he gets upset?"

"Wayne will have his own decisions to make. He will have to decide if he's willing to accept the terms you're offering. If he is, then you can go on slowly and get to know each other. If he's not, then he'll have to decide what he wants to do next."

"I don't want to lose him," Eric said.

Taylor looked at him directly. "You can't have it both ways, Eric. If you want to tell him you're not ready to move and you want to go slowly, you have to be prepared that he may not accept that. But, as I said, you have to do what's right for you. It's going to take Wayne some time, probably years, to work through the issues he has from his life. If you two do stay together, things like this will come up and you're going to have to be prepared to stand up for yourself, too. Wayne isn't a naturally violent person, but I expect some passive aggressive behavior is going to be likely as he mimics patterns he's seen in his own family. If you're not okay with what he wants, you have to be prepared to tell him, to stand firm, and deal with the fallout."

Eric paced in front of his snowmobile, rubbing his eyes with his gloved hands. "Why does it have to be like this?"

"No relationship is easy and they all have their challenges."

"It looks pretty easy for you and Tom," Eric shot back.

Taylor laughed in spite of himself. "It took Tom and me almost four months to even admit to each other we were interested in each other! That was nearly a disaster in itself. We moved in together pretty fast, but we're also older than you and Wayne. We've had our share of problems and we're not always thrilled with each other, but the feelings we have for each other always overcome. If what you and Wayne share is true, it will be the same for you."

"Can you talk to him?"

Taylor shook his head. "This is your relationship, Eric. If he comes to me, I'll listen to him, just like I'm listening to you, but it's up to the two of you to work this out between yourselves."

"So what do I do?"

"Be honest," Taylor said.

"I'm not ready to leave Ohio State."

"Okay."

"But I don't want to lose Wayne."

Taylor smiled. "Sounds good."

Eric looked hopeful. "And we can still come to see each other on holidays."

"Good plan."

Eric stood in front of Taylor, a question on his face. "Do you think he'll be okay with it?"

Taylor shook his head. "I honestly don't know. Nobody said anything about this to me before now, remember?"

"I really care about him, Taylor. I just want to take it slow. Is that so much to ask? I'm not telling him I don't love him or don't want to be with him, just that I don't want to rush. That's okay, isn't it?"

Taylor nodded. "Sounds okay to me."

Eric pulled him into a hug. "Thanks for listening."

"Anytime," Taylor said, returning the hug.

Eric let go and turned to look at the forest. "You know, I think I feel like going back. I need to talk to him."

Taylor nodded. "I thought that might be the case. Lead the way."

"You want the fast one this time?"

Taylor shook his head. "Nah. I can take the old grandpa one. You young pups should get the fast stuff."

"Okay," Eric said, offering no resistance. "See you there!"

Taylor watched as he disappeared in a cloud of snow, a rapidly diminishing spot against the uniform white field of the frozen lake. Taylor climbed back onto his own machine and started the engine. It roared to life and he was off, again following Eric into the cold.

They arrived back at the house a short time later, Eric having slowed to allow Taylor to catch him, and then riding in tandem. Taylor had no doubt that Eric didn't want to get back before him, anticipating as he was his conversation with Wayne.

Roaring up the hill from the lake, they rounded the curve and drove in toward the garage. As the opening appeared, Taylor saw the Jeep backed up to the door and Tom waiting, arms crossed in the cold. They pulled up and he could see on Tom's face a mask of concern. He parked the snowmobile and walked quickly to meet him by the car.

"What's wrong?"

"There's been an accident," Tom said.

"Wayne?" Eric asked urgently.

"No, I'm okay," Wayne said, appearing at the door from the house, arms full of their stuff. Eric moved to take part of the load from him.

"Who?" Taylor demanded.

"John and Sandy," Tom said.

"What? What happened?"

"Gen called just after you left. Pete was at the hospital. John and Sandy were out last night and were hit head on by a drunk driver."

"No," Taylor said. "How bad?"

It was then that he saw the water at the bottoms of Tom's eyes. "Sandy died on impact," he choked. He took a breath. "They don't expect John to make it."

"My God," Taylor breathed.

"Gen has the kids. Pete wants us to meet him at the hospital if we can get back in time."

Taylor turned to Eric and Wayne. "Close the garage. We're leaving now. We'll come back for the rest." Wayne went back in to close the house.

"It's all packed," Tom said. "We figured we'd get it done while we waited for you to get back."

"Let's go," Taylor said, heading for the Jeep. He realized the Jeep was already running. He got in to the driver's seat. Tom took the passenger's seat, leaving Wayne and Eric to sit together in the back.

As Wayne got in, Taylor shot out of the driveway and fishtailed onto the snow-covered road. The four-wheel drive caught them and he headed for the freeway.

"When did you tell them we'd get there?" Taylor asked, making the turn to carry them onto the freeway.

"I told Gen I'd call when we were on our way. I wasn't sure how long you'd be gone."

"We should be able to be there in about two and a half hours," Taylor said. "Which hospital?"

"General, on the north end of the city."

"Got it."

They drove in silence. How much things could change in so little time. Gone was the jovial atmosphere of the day before, replaced with sorrow and pain. Tom and Taylor mourned for Sandy and worried for John. Behind, Eric and Wayne struggled with their own feelings, though Taylor saw Eric reach over and take Wayne's hand as Wayne fought back tears. He hadn't known John or Sandy well, but they were friends of his "family" and loss was the last thing he needed. Taylor felt for Eric, knowing how he would struggle with his decision in light of the news.

Taylor was generally a cautious driver, but he made excellent time as they headed back from the mountains to town. They passed their regular exit, bound for the city. He secretly thanked the ethereal powers that be that the police seemed to have better things to do than patrol the interstate that day.

He thought back to when he had first met John. They were both green attorneys starting with one of the more prestigious firms in the city. John was a conservative business lawyer and Taylor was a liberal civil rights lawyer. Taylor liked to think they had both rubbed off on each other a little, John calming him down and he opening John's mind to the possibilities of new ideas beyond the needs of business.

John's wife, Sandy, had been instrumental in creating the situation that finally drove Tom and Taylor together. When Taylor broke up with his last boyfriend, Sandy had been adamant that he should date a friend of hers. As things warmed with Tom, Taylor had gone on a couple dates with Sandy's friend. Ultimately, when a woman from town confronted Taylor about his sexual identity, he ran off to New York with Sandy's friend. Tom finally came to terms with his own feelings and, together with Gen, pursued Taylor to New York.

Taylor shook his head. Pete and Gen were the only friends he had who he'd known longer than John and Sandy. He was absolutely numb to think that Sandy was gone and that he may lose John.

As they neared the hospital, Tom left a message for Pete, letting him know they were almost there. As good as his word, Taylor had made the trip in record time. He pulled up to the main entrance and turned to Wayne.

"You guys don't have to wait. Go ahead home. We'll have Pete drop us off when things settle down."

"Are you sure?" Wayne asked. "We don't mind waiting."

"Yeah, it's no problem," Eric agreed.

"They probably won't let you go up anyway," Taylor said. "We'll give you a call in a little while, okay?"

"Okay," Wayne agreed. As they got out, he turned to Taylor. "Promise you'll call, okay?"

"I promise," Taylor said. He gave Wayne a reassuring pat on the back, then ran around the back of the Jeep and followed Tom into the hospital.

"John Atkins," Tom said as they approach the security desk.

"Your names?"

"Tom McEwan and Taylor Connolly."

"I have Mr. Connolly's name here," the guard said.

"He's with me," Taylor said. "What floor?"

"He's not on the list," the guard said.

Tom faced him, eyes defiant. "Look, our friend is *dying*. What floor?"

"Third. Room 309," the guard said.

"Thank you," Tom said and led Taylor to the elevators. He punched the three button and they were carried up two floors. The doors parted and Pete was there waiting for them.

"How is he?" Taylor asked.

Pete shook his head. "He's not going to last much longer."

"Is he conscious?" Tom asked.

"A little," Pete said. "Come on. Anita is with him now."

He led them down the hall to a private room. Taylor had tried to prepare himself, but it was worse. Tubes and wires ran everywhere and a single shock of John's blond hair made him recognizable in the mess. Anita sat at his side, holding his hand.

Pete put a hand on Taylor's arm. "I need to talk to you before we go in."

"Yeah?" Taylor asked.

"John and Sandy executed a new will about a month ago." Taylor nodded and he continued. "John was planning to talk to you about it when the holidays were done."

"Okay?"

"In the Will, they named you as executor of their estate."

Taylor took a breath. "Okay, I can do that." He started toward the door.

Pete again reached out to hold him back. "There's more."

"Spill it, Pete," Taylor said. He didn't mean to be short, but the clock was ticking.

"They listed you and Tom as the guardians for their kids."

Taylor looked from Pete to Tom and back. "What? Us? How?"

Pete shook his head. "Obviously, they never anticipated this, that this would happen before they talked to you. But when little Tay was born, John was insistent that it be done immediately. I talked to them about it at length and they felt you and Tom would most be able to raise the kids as they would want. John is an only child and Sandy's brother already has three kids. Their parents are too old."

"I don't know what to say," Taylor said. Tom put an arm around him and Taylor pulled him close.

"John asked me to talk to you as soon as you got here. He's not going to make it, Taylor," Pete admitted.

"I don't know what to say," Taylor repeated.

"There's not much to say," Tom said. "We need to go talk to John."

"And tell him what?" Taylor demanded.

Tom met his gaze with assuredness. "And tell him we'll take care of his kids."

"Tom..." Taylor said.

"We have to," Tom said. "Come on, there's not much time."

He took Taylor's hand and led him through the door.

Chapter Thirteen

The Meaning of Family

Taylor slumped in his chair. It seemed like it was the first chance he'd had to sit all day. In the kitchen, Tom and Pete spoke quietly as Anita made a dinner for them. As he unbuttoned the top few buttons of his shirt, he reviewed the events of the week.

To their horror, Pete had been absolutely right about John's condition. Everyone agreed he had only managed to keep himself going long enough to see Taylor and Tom one more time. Taylor would never forget the pleading expression on his face or the intensity of his gaze as tears rolled from his eyes and he actually took precious time to apologize for not having talked to them sooner.

"John, don't worry about that now," Taylor had said quietly, his hand gently resting on John's right.

"Presumptuous," John coughed. "We should have asked first."

"The answer would have been the same," Tom assured him, resting against Taylor with his head just on Taylor's shoulder, facing John. Across the bed from them, Pete and Anita maintained silent vigil over their friend.

"Sandy loved you so much," John said, still holding Taylor's gaze. Then he looked to Tom. "Both of you. She was so happy when Taylor met you, you know, after the whole New York thing." They all managed a pained chuckle, causing John to wrack with coughs. He turned back to Taylor. "We left messages for our parents and Sandy's brother. Make sure they get them. They'll understand. Dennis couldn't take on three more kids. Our parents are just too old." He glanced to the left. "Pete and Anita will make their own babies," he said with a smile. They tried to return his smile through their tears.

"I promise," Taylor said, his most solemn vow.

"They're good kids, Taylor," John said. "They know you and Tom and they like you. Make them be good people."

"They already had the best example," Taylor reminded him.

John coughed again and his breath was raspy and short. Slowly, he blinked his eyes, and his face took on a distant calm. He sighed. "I think it's about time to go," he whispered. "Take care of my kids and tell them how much their parents loved them."

"You have my word, old friend," Taylor promised.

"And mine," Tom added from behind, reaching forward to take John's hand with Taylor.

The slightest hint of a smile fixed itself at the corners of John's lips and his eyes slowly drifted closed as though a comforting sleep had taken him. His chest rose and fell once, twice, then rose no more. Beside him, a machine sounded its dull tone, the twenty-first century harbinger of the afterlife. A nurse rushed into the room, followed by a doctor. The four friends backed out of the way as the professionals did their jobs. The doctor marked the time of death and they turned off the machines, leaving the room silent.

"Someone will be up for him in a little while," the Doctor told Pete, who had been acting as John's advocate. "You can stay as long as you like." Pete acknowledged him with a silent nod of thanks and the medical team left.

They held each other at the end of the bed, silent at their friend's passing. Pete swallowed and cleared his throat, not moving as he spoke.

"I'm going to miss him."

"Me, too," Taylor said.

Without another word, they turned and moved into the hall, walking slowly back toward the elevators. There was a waiting room off to the side and when Taylor realized it was empty, he guided everyone in.

"What do we need to do now, Pete?" he asked.

Pete sighed, rubbing his forehead. "Come down to the office tomorrow and we'll go through the Will. We'll have to contact someone to handle the services. The hospital will hold him until we send someone over."

"Where are the kids?"

"At home," Pete said. "When they didn't get back by a reasonable time, the babysitter called Gen, who they had listed as an emergency contact since you guys were gone. Gen went out at about two-thirty this morning. Once she and Miguel got the babysitter settled, she started calling police stations and that's when we got the news. She called me about four and I've been at the hospital since."

"Do you have any idea what she told them?" Tom asked, concerned for the kids' emotional state.

"No," Pete said. "I think she's been focused on just keeping them calm until everything played out."

"Until John was gone, too," Taylor said, staring numbly at the floor.

"No point in giving false hope and they're too young to see their dad like that," Pete said.

Taylor nodded. They all sat in silence for a few moments, processing everything that had happened. Truth be told, they were all in shock, but there was no time for that just then. Taylor had given his word and the meter had started in that instant. He stood.

"You and Anita need to get some rest," he said to Pete. The others stood with him and he continued. "We sent the boys home in the Jeep, so if you'll give us a ride back to town, we'll collect some things and then go to John's and take over for Gen."

"You might want Gen there when you tell them," Anita offered. "No disrespect to you guys, but a mother figure is probably going be more comforting to kids their ages."

"I thought she might be willing to help," Taylor agreed.

"Do you want us to come out too?" Pete asked.

Taylor shook his head. "No, I think too many people would just frighten them. Tom and Gen and I will talk to them. We're only going to tell them the minimum for right now, then we'll get together with Steve and see how best to talk them through this."

Pete had driven them home, then, and Tom made the call to Gen from the car. She agreed she would help talk to the children and they spent the first of what would no doubt be many nights with the kids crying and missing their parents. Little Taylor was their first concern, but he also seemed the most resilient. Gen had helped keep him on his feeding and sleep schedule and he was very content with his new family.

Taylor and Pete had made the calls to John and Sandy's family the next day, updating them on what had happened. It had been so fast that none of them had been able to fly to meet them in time. John's parents were the first to arrive, followed by Sandy's mom and then her brother. Her brother had left his wife and children at home, knowing logistics would be difficult.

Taylor knew John's family. They had only moved to Florida a little over a year before. They warmed to his position quickly, appreciating the steps he was taking on their son's behalf. Sandy's family had been more distant, but they also knew of her friends and accepted their involvement. The topic of the children had been an issue of discussion, but as John had promised, the letter left by Sandy and him had allayed their fears and concerns. As long as Tom and Taylor were willing to accept the responsibility, they were grateful for their aid.

And so it came to the day of the funeral. John's parents had stayed in the house, helping Taylor and Tom with the kids, while Sandy's family had chosen to stay at a nearby hotel. Sandy's mom said it was too hard to stay in the house and her brother stayed with their mom to support her.

The service was picture perfect and even Taylor was impressed by the number of people who came, both friends of John and Sandy's, coworkers, and people from the community. To Taylor's surprise, even Neil, the friend who had swept him off to New York City, came, along with his new, apparently very down to earth, boyfriend. Neil had spent a polite couple of minutes touching base with Taylor, but otherwise excused himself after paying his respects.

Pete had helped by organizing a tasteful gathering at a restaurant in the town where John and Sandy lived. Following the event, Sandy's mom and brother came up to them, to make their goodbyes.

"You're leaving?" Taylor asked.

Sandy's mom nodded. "It's time for us to go. You and Tom have a long journey ahead of you. Dennis and I will be available if there is anything we can do to help, but for now, it's time for you to have time to be alone with your new family."

Sandy's brother, Dennis, shook his hand. "John and my sister made a good choice in the two of you," he said. "I know we've only just met, but already you feel like family. I feel good knowing you'll be there to look after my niece and nephews."

"You'll be welcome anytime," Tom said, standing to Taylor's right.

"Thank you," the grandmother said. She gave them both a kiss on the cheek and they again shook hands with Dennis, and just like that, they were gone.

The throng thinned until it was just Pete and Anita and John's parents. Gen and Miguel had offered to stay at home with the kids, knowing the gathering was no place for them. Tom had insisted that they attend the funeral service, knowing it would be important to them later to know they had been there to say goodbye to their parents, though they didn't understand it then.

John's dad came up to them, loosening his own tie. "You did a good thing here today," he said. His wife joined him, taking his hand. "You sent our kids off well."

"Thank you, sir," Taylor said.

"We're ready to go, too, but I was thinking you might want a little help to get things settled," John's mom, Margaret, offered. "We don't want to get in the way, but we do have a little experience with raising children."

"I assume you're going to move them in to your house," his father, Ed, said.

"That was our plan," Taylor agreed.

Ed nodded. "Why don't you and Tom take a night off? Let the old grandparents look after them for a night. Tomorrow, I'd be happy to give you a hand getting things situated."

Pete and Anita had joined them, the room now empty. "We'll help, too," Pete said.

"You don't have to do that," Tom said.

Margaret smiled. "Honey, take the help while you can get it. You're about to have three kids pulling you every which way. It's been a long week for all of us. We don't get to see our grandchildren that often and you boys need some sleep."

"One good night would be nice," Taylor admitted.

"It's settled, then," Ed said, leading them toward the door. "We'll go take over and let Gen get home. Tomorrow, give us a call when you're up. I'll come out and we can start getting the rooms ready."

"Are you going to bring their furniture?" Margaret asked.

"We were planning on it," Tom said. "We thought it would help them feel more comfortable."

"Then maybe Anita and I can entertain the kids while you guys do the heavy lifting."

"I'll be happy to," Anita agreed.

"I'm sure Miguel and Gen will help out, too," Margaret concluded.

They reached the parking lot. Pete and Anita had ridden with Tom and Taylor in Tom's blue Jaguar. Ed and Margaret's Buick rental was parked a couple spaces over from them.

"Tomorrow, ten o'clock. No sooner. Later is fine," Ed said, helping his wife into the car.

"Yes, sir," Taylor said. He slid into the front passenger seat while Pete sat behind him and Anita sat behind Tom. The ride back was very quiet, punctuated only by Tom asking if Pete and Anita would like to come in for a few minutes and get a snack.

Taylor shook his head. Yes, what a week. Tomorrow, they would have another three children in their house, bringing it to a grand total of four children, two adults and a cat. It seemed like every time he and Tom tried to make their life easier, it got more difficult by an order of magnitude. He made a note to not try to make their life easier anymore.

As he thought about the children, Wayne's face popped into his head and he realized they hadn't heard from him since getting home. Eric had stayed around for the rest of the week, trying to help run interference as Taylor and Tom worked to settle John and Sandy's affairs. It would be an ongoing process as Taylor worked to sell their assets and move everything into a trust for the kids, but the first few days would be the hardest.

Wayne had been slightly more reserved, but clearly he and Eric had worked through enough of their differences to try to put on a bright face for the rest of the group.

Rising from the chair, Taylor walked back through the dining room to the kitchen and poked his head in the door.

"Have you guys seen Wayne?"

They each looked at each other, shaking heads, and Tom said, "No, we haven't. Is he upstairs?"

"I'll check," Taylor said, heading for the back stairs.

"You know, Eric's car wasn't here, either," Tom said as he walked upstairs.

Taylor made his way past the guest room that was soon to house the two older children. Their office would be converted to a nursery, leaving Wayne's room for him to keep. Quarters would be a little tighter for a while, but they'd make do.

He found Wayne's door ajar and gently knocked as he pushed it open. To his surprise, the room was empty. Perplexed, he walked back to the office, but it too was unoccupied. On a whim, he checked his own room, then the bathroom, but found no one. Taking the back stairs, he went back to the kitchen.

"They must have gone out," he said.

Pete looked up from where he sat at the table. "Do you guys usually leave lights on at the bakery? I thought I saw one when we came through."

Tom looked at Taylor. "There shouldn't be any lights on. We closed for the last couple of days because of the funeral."

"I'll go check it out," Taylor said, reaching for his coat.

"Want me to come with you?" Tom asked.

He shook his head. "No, I'll be fine." He looked out the back window. "I'm going to take your car since it's warm."

"Okay," Tom said.

Taylor made his way out to the garage and hopped into Tom's blue Jaguar. As it roared to life, he smiled, remembering Eric's question about why Tom got the Jag. "It's the nature of love," Taylor had said. And so it was.

By car, the trip to the bakery took only seconds in the dark hours of the night. Taylor made the turn at the end of the street, then swung wide to pull into one of the vacant spots out front. As Pete had said, there was indeed a light on at the back.

Taylor pulled up and turned off the car. He went in the front door, stopping to lock it behind him. Inside, the store was still, the cabinets empty. They had decided to stay closed for a couple days in observance of their loss and because most of the staff was tied up helping with the funeral. Emmy's family, back from their trip, had even offered to help, but they thought it easier to just not have to worry about it.

As Taylor rounded the counter, he saw the light was coming from the baking room. Slowly, he went down the hall, listening for any sign that he shouldn't be there. Except for a couple scraping sounds, he heard nothing. Rounding the corner, he stopped. There, in the middle of the room, Wayne sat alone on top of a stool, head down, hands crossed in his lap, silent.

"Wayne?" Taylor said gently.

He jumped, apparently so lost in his own thoughts that he hadn't heard Taylor come in.

"Uh, hi, Taylor," he greeted, clearing his throat. Taylor saw tearstains down his cheeks and realized he was trying not to be obvious as he sniffed and wiped at his face.

"What are you doing?" he asked, a question not a condemnation.

Wayne shuffled his feet, drawing a couple lines in the thin dusting of flour that perpetually clung to the floor. "I...you know...I just needed a little time to think...to get away. I didn't want to bother anybody."

"How could you bother us?" Taylor asked, slowly walking toward him, trying very hard not to appear in any way intimidating.

"You know...you've been busy...I didn't want to be in the way."

Taylor faced him, lowering himself down to Wayne's level. "Did we do something to make you think you're in the way?"

Wayne looked away. "Well, you've got three little kids you have to look out for. You don't need me taking up space."

Taylor chuckled in spite of himself. "Haven't we covered this?"

Wayne met his gaze, his eyes still full of tears. "But that was before."

"Before what?"

"Before you had a family."

He took Wayne's hands in his. "You mean before we met you? Because you're a part of this family, too." Wayne watched him, another tear escaping down his cheek. "And let me tell you another thing," Taylor continued, "We need you. We're about to have three little kids who are going to need a whole lot of love and attention and support and it would really mean a lot to Tom and me to have you there to help us."

"Really?" Wayne asked.

Taylor smiled. "Really. We want you to live your life, but we really want you to be a part of ours, too. You're as much a part of this family as those three kids, but that means you have to believe it, and you have to help them believe it. There may not be a Norman Rockwell painting to cover us, but I think we make a darned good family."

"I thought you'd want me to go," Wayne choked, leaning forward into Taylor's arms.

"Will you ever believe me when I tell you that's not going to happen?"

Wayne clung to him. "I believe you now," he said, his face buried in Taylor's shoulder.

"Good." They stood for a moment longer and Wayne made no move to let go, and suddenly Taylor realized how empty the room was and knew what was wrong.

"He left me," Wayne said finally, still holding on to Taylor.

"Eric?" Taylor confirmed.

"Yeah."

Taylor gently pushed Wayne back enough so he could see his face. "What did he say?"

"He said he doesn't want to leave Ohio."

"You asked him to leave Ohio?" Taylor asked, chancing that Eric wouldn't have told him about their conversation.

Wayne looked away, a little guilty. "I asked him to go to school here, with me, so we could be together."

"Are you sure you're ready for that?" Taylor asked, hoping he might have put a little more thought into it than just the emotion of having his boyfriend nearby.

"Yes! No. I don't know," Wayne looked miserable. "I know I love him. He's all I can think about a lot."

Taylor smiled. "There's nothing wrong with that. You care about him. Also, he's your first love, so you're bound to fall harder for him." Wayne didn't look convinced. "Did he tell you he didn't want to see you anymore?"

"No," Wayne admitted.

"Did he say he cares about you?"

Wayne nodded, sniffing back tears. "He said he loves me, too," he said and his face contorted with grief. "But then he left…"

"He left to go back to *school*, Wayne," Taylor said. Wayne's green eyes were dark and bloodshot from crying as they watched Taylor. "What did he say?"

"He said we'll still send email and talk on the phone and that he'll come and visit on Spring Break and I can come there on my break if I want. He said he still wants to be my boyfriend if I'll let him."

"What did you say?"

Wayne sobbed. "I told him I'd think about it."

"And now that you've thought about it?"

"I don't want to lose him."

Taylor smiled. "Maybe you should tell him that."

A look of panic started to set in on Wayne's face and Taylor's hand suddenly produced a mobile phone. Wayne let go a deep sigh as he accepted the phone from Taylor.

"Thanks, Taylor," he said. He gave Taylor a quick peck on the cheek, then turned to make his call.

"Make that quick, then I'll drive you home and you can call him from there," Taylor said, walking back out of the baking room.

He headed up front and took the store phone to call Tom. The phone rang and Tom answered on the first ring.

"What's going on?" he asked. "Is everything okay?"

"Yeah, everything is fine," Taylor said, a smile in his voice. "Wayne's here. Eric went home and he was a little upset about it. I was just helping talk him through it."

"Is he going to be all right?"

"He is now. I'll fill you in later," Taylor said, glancing to make sure he wasn't being overheard.

"Okay, sounds good. Anita made a light dinner. Are you going to be back in time?"

"Yeah, in just a minute. Wayne is on the phone with Eric now. He just needed to get the main words out now."

Wayne appeared in the doorway as Tom answered, "Okay, see you in five."

"We're on our way," Taylor said and hung up. Wayne met his questioning gaze with a sheepish smile.

"He said he feels a lot better to know we're still together," Wayne said. "He's going to come back out for a weekend once the semester gets going."

"Good deal," Taylor said, heading for the door.

"Thanks again, Taylor, for everything," Wayne said. "You know, I really love you guys."

Taylor smiled, holding the door open. "We really love you, too. And we're *really* going to love you when it's time to change little Tay's diapers."

"Great," Wayne said with a total lack of enthusiasm.

After dinner, Wayne went to call Eric and Tom and Taylor assumed their usual positions on the couch—Taylor with his feet stretched out on the ottoman, Tom using Taylor's leg as a pillow as Taylor surfed channels. Taylor held the remote in his right hand, where it rested lightly on Tom's lower chest.

"So, tomorrow," Tom said, leaving the statement incomplete.

"Tomorrow," Taylor followed, knowing what was on his mind.

"Are you ready for this?"

"Do I have a choice?" Taylor asked, a chuckle escaping as his thumb held down the channel button.

"Not really," Tom agreed. He gently ran his hand along Taylor's lower arm.

"I'll bet you wish I'd stayed in bed," Taylor said.

"Huh?"

"That first Sunday, after I moved here. Think about how much easier your life would be if I'd just stayed in bed."

"Easier?" Tom said. "Heck no, my life's been easier since I met you. More interesting, granted, but definitely not any more difficult."

"So you'll still marry me?"

Tom laughed. "We can't have our kids the children of unwed parents, can we? I mean, poor Wayne has had to go all this time with us living in sin, but the little ones…"

Taylor laughed with him, giving him a poke in the ribs with the remote. Tom grabbed his hand and held it down against his chest and for a brief instant they just enjoyed the laughter.

"So Chad is five and Wendy is two, right?" Tom said.

"Yeah," Taylor answered. "Chad's in kindergarten now."

Tom nodded. "That's good. The kindergarten teacher at my school is Mrs. Knight. She's very nice and will take extra good care of him."

"It'll probably help for him to know you're right there, too," Taylor agreed.

"What are we going to do about Wendy and Mini-Tay?" They had started calling Taylor Thomas "Mini-Tay" during dinner, to keep from confusing him with Taylor. Since he had both his new parents' names, there weren't a lot of options. It seemed like the new name was going to stick for a while.

"I haven't quite figured that out yet," Taylor said. "You have any ideas?"

"Wendy's the problem," Tom said. "Taylor will just sleep a lot of the time, but Wendy's going to want to play. I guess we'll have to see about hiring a sitter."

"That was the best answer I've come up with, too. With four more mouths to feed, we need to keep working."

Tom sighed. "At least the bakery is pretty well covered right now. Wayne has running it down cold. You think he's going to be okay?"

Taylor nodded. "He's going to be fine. I think he was feeling like an outsider with the little ones coming. I told him nothing could be farther from the truth and that we're really going to need whatever help he wants to offer."

"I was thinking," Tom said. "What do you want to do about Wayne's tuition?"

"His tuition?" Taylor asked.

"Yeah. He's been saving every cent we pay him to cover tuition at school."

"Are we paying him enough?"

Tom nodded. "He can cover tuition, but it's not going to leave him a lot of spending money. He needs to be able to get out."

"How much is it?" Taylor asked. Tom told him what it had cost for his last semester and figured rates would have gone up five to ten percent since then. Taylor thought for a minute, then shrugged. "You want to just pay it?"

"What do you think?"

"He's going to have to work less when he gets started. I want him to experience college, not just work and attend class and do homework. He helps out here all the time and never says a peep to complain. For a figure like that, I think it's the least we can do."

Tom smiled. "With an attitude like that, you're going to wreck your profession's reputation."

Taylor laughed. "I'm sure I already have."

"His birthday's coming up, too. Any idea what you want to give him?"

"Actually, yes," Taylor began, but was interrupted by the sound of Wayne bounding down the stairs. Gone was his melancholy expression, replaced with the cheerful radiance that was rapidly becoming his trademark.

"Hi!" Wayne said. He walked over and sat down next to the ottoman, his right arm resting on its edge, facing Tom and Taylor.

"How's Eric?" Tom asked, propping himself up with a pillow under his elbow so he could see Wayne.

Wayne smiled broadly. "He's good. He just got back to campus while we were on the phone. Said the trip went pretty smoothly, not much traffic."

"You two are okay now?" Taylor asked.

Wayne nodded emphatically. "Oh yeah, we're great. He said he'll try to come back out for a long weekend in a couple weeks. He doesn't have classes on Friday and his last class Thursday is at two. He could be here by seven."

"You, on the other hand, have class Friday, young man," Tom mock chastened.

"Yes, Dad," Wayne said, still unable to wipe the smirk from his face. "Hey, listen, while I was on the phone, Emmy called and wanted to know if I wanted to go see a movie with her and a couple other people."

"What movie?" Taylor asked. Wayne told him, but he hadn't heard of it. "What's it rated?"

"PG-13. It's a comedy," Wayne said.

"How late will you be out?"

"I don't know, midnight?"

"Twelve o'clock, on the button," Tom said. "Not one minute later."

"Who else is going?" Taylor asked.

"It's just Emmy, Katie, and Dan."

"Who's driving?" Tom asked.

Wayne glanced down for a minute, then looked up expectantly. "Me?"

"I suppose you think I should let you take my car, too?"

"Okay!"

"No drinking, no drugs, no sex," Taylor said.

Wayne made a face. "Duh. And besides, Dan's straight."

"And no smoking," Tom continued.

"Guys, I get it!" Wayne laughed. "You were a lot more fun before you were parents, you know?"

"Yes, we do," Taylor agreed. "But now you're stuck with us. You had your chance, but it's too late."

"I got the better deal," Wayne said, hitting Taylor in the leg as he got up. "Thanks guys."

"Drive carefully," Tom said.

"I promise. We'll be model citizens."

"You'd better be!"

Wayne took off out the back door, slowing just long enough to grab the spare key from the hutch in the dining room. They heard the door slam shut and saw the headlights as the car backed out a few seconds later. In less than a minute, all was once again quiet.

"Did we pass our first test as parents?" Taylor asked.

"I think we went too easy on him," Tom said.

"Me, too. Let's ground him tomorrow."

"Okay!"

"Make him do the dishes," Taylor said.

"Yeah yeah!"

"And mow the lawn!"

"Taylor, the lawn is covered with snow."

Taylor sighed. "You're right. Too bad."

Tom lay back down, resuming his original position. "How can a kid that good come from a family that screwed up?"

Taylor lay his head back against the padded cushion of the sofa. "I don't know, but I'm sure glad he's here."

"Me, too," Tom agreed.

They sat for several long moments, the television muted, no conversation between them, each lost in his own thoughts. Taylor reached over and gently took Tom's hand in his.

"You hear that?"

"Hear what?" Tom asked.

Taylor sighed. "The sound of silence."

"Yeah."

"We're not going to hear that much anymore."

"I know," Tom agreed.

"Let's go to bed."

Tom sat up and Taylor stood and held out his hand. Tom took it and rose up to put his arm around Taylor and have Taylor put his arm around him. Together, they went upstairs, their last night alone in their house for a very long time.

Chapter Fourteen

Easter

Taylor sat on the sofa, newspaper at his side, feet on the ottoman. Four months felt like four years. Upstairs, he heard the sound of Chad and Wendy at play. Little Taylor was down for his mid-afternoon, pre-evening nap. Who knew children could be so much work?

For better or worse, depending on his perspective, business was picking up at the firm. Pete had recommended they consider hiring another attorney. It had helped for a time, but word was out and the firm was continuing to grow. Though Pete never complained, Taylor knew his presence was missed and he needed to be there more than he was. The problem was, as it had been several times previously, that three young children were a full time job and they had trouble finding babysitters. Chad was in morning kindergarten, but Wendy and baby Taylor needed fulltime attention.

Their friends had, as always, stepped up to the plate, helping the two new parents adjust to their roles. Rob and Mel, as the only other friends with experience raising children, had been nearly a fixture for the first month and a half. Gen was once again stopping by more frequently, and Anita often had dinner waiting when Taylor and Pete had to work late. Wayne virtually ran the bakery by himself, with only the occasional help of Tom.

The week before, Tom had come home with an announcement, surprising Taylor.

"The college called me today."

"For what?" Taylor had asked. It had been a rare break when Wayne and Gen took the kids out for a couple hours to give their parents a rest. He had started setting the table while Tom finished making dinner.

"One of the English professors is retiring and they were wondering if I'd be interested in coming back there to teach."

"What about your job at the high school?" Taylor asked. He took two wine glasses and poured them each a glass.

"I'd have to give that up, obviously. This would be full time." Tom prepared the dishes, a light pasta with chicken and bleu cheese, and a Caesar salad.

"What do you want to do?" Taylor asked. The table set and the food presented, they both took their seats.

Tom shook his head. "I don't know. I worked hard to get this job, but I wouldn't mind continuing on at the college. I was honored that they offered it to me."

"You earned it," Taylor said, taking a bit of salad.

Tom ate, too, talking between bites. "It would free up my schedule a lot. They said I would only teach two classes the first semester and I'd have teaching assistants."

"Sounds good," Taylor agreed, sipping his wine. He smiled as he gestured with his glass. "You know I'll support whatever you want to do."

Tom nodded. "I know. The President said we could treat Wayne as our son, so he would be able to go to school for free."

"A bonus."

Tom smiled, digging in to the main course. "So would I. They have a Ph.D. program I would be interested in doing."

"You know I love it when you're smarter than me," Taylor said, his blue eyes sparkling with mischief as he watched Tom.

"You already have a doctorate," Tom pointed out.

"Yes, but you'd actually be called, Dr. McEwan."

"It would be a five thousand dollar a year pay cut."

Taylor just looked at him, waiting for more. When nothing was forthcoming, he shrugged. "Between you and Wayne, we'll make that back in tuition."

Tom nodded. "That's kind of what I was thinking."

"So you *are* interested?"

Tom nodded. "I think it would be a good thing for the family and I'd sure like to be able to get my Ph.D."

"So you're telling me I'm going to be living with a first grader, a freshman, and a grad student-slash-college professor?"

Tom smiled broadly this time, the gray of his eyes glinting in the subdued light. "What do you think?"

Taylor nodded. "I wonder if Gen still has that spare bedroom?"

Tom broke into a broad smile then and he nodded, knowing he'd been had. They enjoyed the rest of their dinner together like old times, before kids and jobs and all the stresses that had plagued them for so long. For a few minutes at least, it was just Taylor and Tom, sharing a meal and enjoying each others' company.

Taylor sighed and rubbed his neck as the memory faded. Old times indeed. If he felt any older, he'd be a grandparent.

"Want some help with that?"

Taylor jumped, looking toward the kitchen, where Tom stood smiling by the door. "I didn't hear you come in."

Tom laid his jacket on a nearby chair. "I was trying to be quiet in case the kids were asleep." He sat down next to Taylor and gently massaged his shoulders.

"They're upstairs. Chad and Wendy are playing, Junior is asleep. Wayne's not home yet."

Tom pulled Taylor to him as they relaxed into the couch. "And you're exhausted."

"I'm okay," Taylor said.

"I took the job," Tom said, resting his head next to Taylor's.

"Really?"

"Yep. I start in the fall. They've got me teaching introductory writing and honors English lit."

Taylor turned to face him. "That's great news. You'll love that."

"Now if we can just find a babysitter who'll last more than a couple weeks, we'll be all set."

The back door closed and Wayne came though the dining room. Seeing his two housemates on the couch, he stopped, dropping his book bag next to the chair as he sat down.

"What's up?" he asked. His expression was eager and light, a regular event for him in recent months. Wayne had readily taken to the three new additions to their family, going out of his way to help look after them. Steve had explained that being with the kids would only help Wayne as he continued to deal with his own, less than perfect childhood. He would protect them naturally, in the ways he felt he hadn't been protected himself. Sometimes, though, it meant Tom and Taylor had to virtually kick him out of the house in order to make sure he had a life of his own.

"I just accepted the teaching position at the college," Tom said.

"Really? That's great!" Wayne said. "Are you going to finish the year at my school?"

Tom nodded. "Of course. I start in the fall."

"Cool," he said, then took a breath. "I actually wanted to talk to you about something anyway."

"What's up?"

Wayne reached into his backpack and pulled out a sheet. "They're selling the remaining tickets for prom and they were passing around this flier at school."

Tom took the flier, printed on bright goldenrod paper, and read it. It gave the details of the event, including times and locations, and named the chaperones from the teaching staff and several parents.

"Are you planning to go?" Taylor asked, glad to see Wayne interested in doing something outside the house other than baking.

"I wanted to know what you think," Wayne said.

"Who do you want to take?" Tom asked.

Wayne gave him a look. "Uh, Eric?"

Taylor and Tom exchanged glances. "Ah," Taylor said, realizing what he was really asking. "You want to know if we think it's okay for you to take a guy to your prom."

"Well, yes, partly that, but I also wondered if you two would consider chaperoning. They're still looking for a few more people."

Tom nodded. "And then you and Eric wouldn't be the only gay couple at the dance."

"Well, yeah, pretty much," Wayne said. His face was expectant as his eyes moved from one friend to the other.

"I didn't go to my prom," Taylor said. "So it could be an adventure."

Tom turned to him. "You didn't go to your prom?"

"People wouldn't have been quite as accepting in 1989," he said.

"You could have gone with a girl. Didn't you and Gen know each other back then?"

Taylor shrugged. "She had a boyfriend. It wouldn't have been right. It's not a big deal."

Tom shook his head, not letting him dismiss it so easily. "Of course it's a big deal. It's a rite of passage."

"Did you go?"

Tom nodded. "I took my friend Holly. We had a nice evening along with a couple other couples."

Taylor didn't say anything, so Wayne spoke up. "What do you think?"

"I think you should go," Tom said. "You're just as entitled to go as anyone else."

"With Eric?" Wayne asked.

"Yes, with Eric. Have you asked him yet?"

"I mentioned it a couple weeks ago. He didn't really say yes or no."

Tom handed the sheet back to Wayne. "Well, be prepared that he may not feel comfortable attending a dance with all straight couples."

Wayne nodded. "We wouldn't be the only one, though, if you and Taylor are there. Will you go?"

Tom looked at Taylor, who had remained quiet. Taylor realized they were waiting on him and he looked up, nodding. "Of course we'll go. You know that. But, you're responsible for coordinating a babysitter, got it?"

"Got it!" Wayne said, jumping up. "I'm going to go call Eric now!"

Taylor smiled. "Just be quiet. Taylor's asleep. Why don't you check on the other two and make sure everything is okay?"

"Will do. Thanks, guys," Wayne said and wambled up the stairs, a little more quietly than his usual storming self.

Tom turned to Taylor. "What?"

"I didn't say anything," Taylor said, looking out the window.

"You've got the look on your face," Tom said, turning to face Taylor directly.

"I do not have a look on my face," Taylor said.

Tom rolled his eyes. "You're jealous, aren't you?"

"Tom, just let it go."

He repressed a smile as he took Taylor's hand. Taylor tried to pull his hand back, but Tom held fast. "Tay, it was just a few friends going out *as friends*. Nothing happened."

"I didn't say anything."

Tom smiled. "You didn't have to. I know you, remember?"

Taylor wrinkled his nose and turned away. Tom leaned forward and put his arms around him, kissing his cheek. "Remember, I chose you."

"I never got to go to my prom."

Tom smiled, still holding him close. "Then this is your prom, too."

"Do we get to go out after?"

"It wouldn't be prom if we didn't."

Taylor smiled, nodding. "In that case, I'll go to the prom with you."

Tom kissed him again. "You mean all I had to do to get a hot date like you was be cheap and easy?"

Taylor laughed, wrapping his arms around Tom. "Honey, you are anything but cheap."

"Don't you forget it," Tom said. Beside him, the phone rang in its cradle on the table.

"Who could that be?" Taylor asked and Tom reached to answer it.

"Beats me. It's our line, though, so it's probably not Eric." He pressed the talk button and answered. "Mom? Hi. What's up? We're fine. Yeah, the kids are fine, too."

Tom and Taylor exchanged glances. "Uh, help doing what, Mom?" Tom asked. "Now? Well, yeah, I mean it's been tough lately because we've all been so busy, but we're adjusting. You do? You are. Oh." Taylor watched him and Tom looked back as his mom spoke into the phone. "Okay, hang on. Let me see what Taylor thinks."

Taylor waited and Tom took the phone away from his mouth. "They want to come out for a few weeks to help us with the kids while the school year is wrapping up."

"Did you tell them about the college?"

Tom shook his head. "Not yet. I wanted you to be the first person I told."

"Romantic," Taylor said, smiling again. "We could use the help," he agreed.

Tom held the phone back up to his ear. "What? Yeah, I did. Just this afternoon. I was just telling Taylor when you called. Yeah, I'm pretty excited about it, too." He looked at Taylor and rolled his eyes. It was not unusual for his mom's phone calls to go on for quite some time.

Wayne bounded back down the stairs with Wendy in his arms.

"Who's on the phone?" he asked Taylor.

"Tom's mom."

"Oh, cool. Hey, I left a message for Eric, but I know he'll want to go. You guys are good to go, right?" Wendy squirmed in his arms, playing with his hair and giggling.

Taylor nodded. "I'm sure Tom will let them know tomorrow."

"This is going to be a lot of fun, you know?" Wayne said, happy as ever.

"Yes, it is," Taylor agreed. "What's Chad doing?" he asked, changing the subject.

"He's going to take a nap before dinner. Wendy asked if we could go for a walk, so I'm going to take her out."

Taylor nodded. "Okay, let's plan on dinner at six."

"We'll be here," Wayne said and made his exit out the front door, with Wendy walking under her own power and holding his hand.

"Wedding? I suppose it's going well," Tom said, giving Taylor the "huh?" look. "Yeah, we picked up our tuxes the other day. Gen doesn't want a bachelorette party, since half her people are guys, so we're just taking her to dinner."

Taylor started to get up, realizing it might be a good idea to use the respite of the kids being otherwise occupied to get their own meal started.

"Then which wedding are you talking about?" Tom asked, still on the phone. He reached out and took Taylor's hand, pulling himself up to follow him. "Our wedding? Well, Mom, with all the stuff we've had going on, it kind of got tabled."

Taylor glanced back at Tom, who took a seat at the table, while he pulled hamburger patties from the freezer. Gone were the days of veal, chicken, lamb, and the like. Kids did not eat such fancy food and it was too expensive to throw away. So, they had discovered the wonder of hamburgers, various dishes that fell under the heading of "stroganoff," and other things that did not involve vegetables. They were working with the kids to broaden their dietary horizons, but they also had to remember they *were* kids and couldn't be expected to eat like a couple thirty something gay men. Taylor smiled—he always qualified the statement as "gay men," pointing out if they were thirty something straight men, their diet would almost certainly have beer in place of wine. Tom would have been quick to point out only one of them was thirty something, but what he didn't know…

"I didn't think dad was that comfortable with it," Tom was saying. His conversation with his mother had long since taken on a life of its own, omitting Taylor's presence as he stared at the floor. Taylor smiled—in their three years together, he had gotten used to the calls and the closeness of Tom and his family. Taylor's parents had called about two weeks before to let them know they would be out of the country for a month. Seemed a client of theirs was insistent that his new home contain *only* materials and objects from Florence. So, Taylor's dad, the architect, had gone to research available construction materials while his mom, the decorator, went to find art. He was sure they wouldn't have called at all, except Bryce reminded them it might be nice for them to tell Taylor directly, rather than have it come up in his regular email correspondence with his brother.

"Of course we still want to get married. I mean, we can't get 'married,' but we thought the ceremony was a good idea. The timing is just off. The kids take so much of our time, Wayne is getting ready to graduate, Gen's wedding is coming up. We're only two people, you know," Tom said. He looked up to catch Taylor's eye, a pleading expression on his face. Taylor smiled and blew him a kiss, Tom held his hand to his heart.

"I don't know, Mom. Yes, we can discuss it when you get here. Yes, Taylor said he'd be glad for the help, too. No, he doesn't think you're imposing. Mom says hello and she loves you," Tom said, the last directly to Taylor.

"Hello and love back," he said, arranging the patties on a plate to grill when the kids got up. He went about collecting the rest of the necessary food.

"This weekend? Sure. There is? No, I didn't know that." He looked at Taylor. "Did you know there's a campground about ten miles from here?"

"Never needed one," Taylor said. "I only go camping with you and we just need a tent and a sleeping bag." Tom smiled at the memory as his mom's tinny voice continued to sound in his ear. Taylor grabbed a basket from one of the cupboards and lined it with a couple linen napkins. They didn't have to be complete heathens after all. He filled it with enough hamburger buns to match the number of patties, then set it aside to continue preparing the meal.

"Okay, we'll see you then. Yeah, love you too. Okay. Bye," Tom said. He clicked the phone off and set it on the table. "Sorry, Tay."

Taylor smiled. "It's okay, I'm just pulling dinner together. So, they're coming here?"

Tom nodded. "For at least a month or two. They usually spend a lot of the summer traveling. Now that they're both retired, they don't have to meet any particular schedule. They're bringing that big travel trailer and they're going to stay at the campground. Mom knew we didn't have any room with all the kids."

"Their timing is actually good. With Wayne's prom and graduation coming up, the extra hands will be a big help."

"It'll probably let Wayne off the hook for coordinating a babysitter, too," Tom agreed, helping set the table.

"I promised him you'd make sure we were setup to be chaperones tomorrow."

Tom nodded. "Will do."

Taylor stopped, facing Tom, head cocked. "So, what do chaperones wear to a prom?" he asked, smiling.

The next night, Taylor sat in much the same place as he had the night before, with many of the same thoughts running through his head. Wayne had an exam that day, so Tom had gotten up to handle the baking in order to give him a little extra time to sleep, meaning Taylor had more or less been awake at the same time. As their schedule had come closer and closer to something that might be defined as "normal," Taylor found it more distracting when he had to sleep alone. Even as the weather got warmer, he enjoyed the comfort of having Tom beside him. Without him, Taylor would sleep in fits and starts before finally giving up and getting up with the sun. He rubbed his tired eyes.

The back door closed with a slam, catching his attention. All three kids were napping upstairs, so whoever was coming in needed to be a little more quiet. To his surprise, it was Wayne who came barreling through the kitchen door, his face red with anger. He slammed his backpack on the table as he stormed into the living room.

"What unbelievable *bullshit!*" he exclaimed, throwing himself into one of the chairs, arms crossed over his chest, brow a deep furrow and his hair matted to his forehead. Taylor wasn't sure, but he thought his lip might be quivering.

"Afternoon, Wayne," Taylor greeted. "Something on your mind?" He chose to hold his reprimand on the door in favor of finding out what had Wayne so worked up. In all the time Taylor had known him, he'd only heard him curse a handful of times.

"They wouldn't sell me a *ticket,*" Wayne said. His bottom lip was definitely quivering.

"'They' who?"

"The *school*," Wayne said. "I tried to buy tickets today and they asked who would be accompanying me, so I told them Eric Driskell. They said two boys can't come to the dance together. So, I said, *fine*, I'd like two individual tickets. Then they told me only students of the school are allowed to buy tickets unless they're accompanied by a student. And *no*, I can't accompany him, either." He looked up, a light mist of water on his bottom lids. "How can they do that? It's not right!"

"No, it's not," Taylor agreed. "Where's Tom?"

"He was in with the principal when I left. I just ran home. I needed to be on my own for a while." He stared at the floor, still breathing heavily.

The back door slammed again and Taylor turned to see Tom come through the kitchen door and drop his briefcase on the table much as Wayne had when he came in.

"What a load of horse shit!" Tom exclaimed, seeing Taylor on the couch. "You're not going to believe this!"

"With the amount of swearing you two are doing, I'd probably believe anything," Taylor said. Tom caught sight of Wayne and immediately went to sit down in the chair next to him.

"Are you okay?" he asked.

"Yeah," Wayne said. He rubbed at the corners of his eyes, but said nothing more.

"Anybody care to explain?" Taylor asked, sitting up to face his two friends.

Tom leaned forward, facing Taylor. "Apparently, a couple people running the prom ticket sale decided Wayne couldn't buy tickets for himself and Eric."

Taylor nodded. "I got that part so far."

"So I went to have a word with the principal. Seems his daughter was one of the little gems who gave Wayne a hard time."

"What did Hargreaves have to say?"

Tom took a breath, clearly collecting his own thoughts. "He said the decisions about the dance are generally left up to the students. But it gets better."

"Yes?" Taylor prompted.

"I told him you and I wanted to volunteer to chaperone. He said, under the circumstances, 'he wasn't sure that would be appropriate.' He was afraid our presence could offer a 'disruptive influence.'"

"Really?" Taylor asked.

Tom nodded. "He said he didn't want to seem like he was unsupportive, but that he had to take into account the feelings of all the students who would be attending."

"What did his daughter say?" Taylor asked, looking at Wayne.

Wayne took an uncertain breath. "She said it wasn't natural, it wasn't right for two boys to go to a dance together. She said dances are for 'normal' people." He nearly choked on the last part as he said it.

Taylor nodded, keeping cool in the face of his friends' strong emotions. "Were there any other people there?"

"Yeah," Wayne said with a nod.

"What did they say?"

"A couple of them told Crissy to just sell me the tickets and leave me alone. Emmy kind of got into it with her and that's when the principal came over."

"Did anyone say anything negative toward you?" Taylor asked.

Wayne looked up, confused. "No, I don't think so. Everybody seemed about as surprised as me. I mean, it's not like it's a secret anymore. Crissy is just mean. She's like that to everybody she doesn't like."

"Who makes the decisions about the chaperones?" Taylor asked Tom.

Tom shook his head. "I don't know. The teacher in charge of this class is Sally Jenkins. I haven't talked to her about it yet, but she's a friend of mine at the school, so I can't imagine it will be a problem."

Taylor nodded, thinking. He reached over and picked up the phone. "Do you have your district phone book around here?" he asked Tom.

"It's in the drawer," Tom said. "Who are you calling?"

Taylor retrieved the book and stood. "You guys just wait here. I'll be back in a couple minutes."

"Taylor..." Tom said.

"Trust me," he replied, then went into the kitchen. Sitting at the dining room table, he scanned the book for a particular phone number, found it, and dialed.

"Hello?"

"Is this Joel Weiss?" Taylor asked.

"Yes?"

"Hi, Joel. This is Taylor Connolly. We met a few months ago over the incident with Wayne McInerney."

There was a pause, then the voice on the other end continued. "Oh, of course. I remember you now, Taylor. What can I do for you?"

Taylor set the book down and leaned back in the chair, putting his feet up on the chair across from him. "I just had a conversation with Wayne and Tom McEwan," he began.

Again, there was a pause, then Joel answered, "I thought I might hear something about that."

"Then you're aware of the situation?" Taylor asked.

"I have some knowledge of it. I know there was an incident at the high school today and Tom had a conversation with Dr. Hargreaves. I don't have all the specifics, but I have a general idea," Weiss said.

Taylor nodded. It was much as he'd expected. "Joel, can I talk to you off the record for a minute?"

Another pause at the other end told him Weiss was not completely comfortable with their discussion or the course it was taking, but Taylor had an idea of the kind of person he was from the last time they had spoken about Wayne's situation. He hoped he was right.

"I'll tell you what I can," Weiss said, more quietly.

"What kind of person is Hargreaves?" Taylor asked.

"How do you mean?"

"From the discussion I just had, my understanding is it was Hargreaves' daughter who started the altercation with the students. When Tom confronted him about it, he then told Tom that he didn't think it was a good idea for Tom and me to be at the prom because we could be a 'disruptive influence.' I'm trying to understand the kind of person we're dealing with here. Is he generally a good person who just isn't thinking clearly, or does he have a personal agenda that is being forced into the light?"

Weiss sighed. "I'll be honest with you, Taylor, I don't know the man that well. Obviously, I can't go into specifics about cases in the district, but my impression is he's not hateful, just a little old fashioned. Since his daughter was involved, I don't know what other factors may be in play."

"So you're of the opinion that we're not dealing with a situation where he's attempting to use his influence because he doesn't like homosexuality?"

"I don't think that's the case," Weiss said. "Again, I'll be honest and tell you I have nothing to base that on but my own opinion. Hargreaves tends to take the more cautious route when faced with a potentially problematic situation. He probably honestly thinks what he said was in the best interests of both you, Tom, and Wayne."

"What do you think?" Taylor asked.

Weiss gave a small chuckle. "I can't really say, Taylor. I *am* counsel for the district, after all."

Taylor returned the chuckle. "Right," he said. "I guess I'm just asking your opinion as a person—do you think Wayne has a right to bring the date of his choice to the prom?"

"Off the record and just as me personally, and not a representative of the school district?"

"Just you."

Weiss sighed. "Yeah, I think he should be able to go."

"Thanks, Joel," Taylor said. "I'm calling Hargreaves next. Do you need to be on that call?"

"Not unless one of you asks me to be. Our discussion was off the record. My advice to both of you is not to get any attorneys involved unless you have to."

Taylor smiled. "That's always good advice. Thanks, Joel. Have a good night."

"You, too. Bye, Taylor."

Taylor hung up, then walked back into the dining room. Both Tom and Wayne looked at him expectantly, but he just held up a finger and said, "One more minute." He fished through the small stack of mail sitting on the hutch and found what he was looking for. He went back into the kitchen and dialed Hargreaves' number.

"Hello?" a young female voice answered the phone.

"This is Taylor Connolly calling. Is Dr. Hargreaves available?"

"We're just sitting down to dinner," the voice on the other end of the phone said bluntly.

"Is this Crissy?" Taylor asked, taking a shot in the dark.

"Yes." Her response was clipped and condescending.

"Hi, Crissy," Taylor said, choosing to treat her with more respect than she was offering him. "I'm sorry to disturb you during the dinner hour, but this won't take a minute. Would you let your dad know I'm calling, please?"

He heard her muffled statement to her father and his snapped response. Taylor couldn't make out the words, but he knew she had been rude and her father had chastised her for it. That said something for him, at least.

"Mayor Connolly? I apologize for my daughter. I don't think she understood who was calling," Hargreaves said quickly. "I'm sure I know what you're calling about, don't I, Mayor?"

"I'm sure you do," Taylor said, then pressed on before he could speak. "I wanted to thank you for the invitation to the school's annual prom. I received it in the mail this week. For once, my schedule will finally allow me to accept and attend."

Silence greeted him from the other end of the phone. Taylor was very confident that whatever the principal had been expecting, that wasn't it.

"That's, uh, that's wonderful, Mayor. We'll be honored to have you, of course..."

"Thank you, Dr. Hargreaves," Taylor said, his voice still jovial and conversational. "Tom and I have been looking forward to attending for the last few days. Tom mentioned something last night about needing additional chaperones for the dance. We are, of course, perfectly willing to offer ourselves as public servants of the town. Did Tom have a chance to discuss that with you today?"

"He, uh, um, we did discuss it, yes," Hargreaves stammered. "Really though, Mr. Mayor, the school would not want to impose on you or Mr. McEwan."

Taylor smiled. "Oh, it's no imposition at all. After all, we'll want to make sure Wayne doesn't get into any mischief while he's there, since he's in our care. You know, he's really looking forward to this event. The support he's received from you and the rest of the school has meant so much to him."

The other end of the phone was silent. Taylor waited a few extra seconds to let Hargreaves sweat it out, then said, "Dr. Hargreaves? Are you there?"

Hargreaves cleared his throat. "Uh, yes, sorry Mr. Mayor. We are, uh, of course, looking forward to seeing Wayne there as well."

"Good," Taylor said. "His boyfriend will be in from Ohio that weekend, so a party sounds just about perfect. I'm just thankful we're in a district as progressive as this one. You can be proud, Dr. Hargreaves, in knowing that you look out for the best interests of all the people under your care at the high school."

"I, uh, thank you, Mr. Mayor. That's very kind."

"Don't mention it, Dr. Hargreaves," Taylor said. "Now, I don't want to keep you from your dinner and your family any longer. You have a very nice evening and I'll see you in a couple of weeks."

"Yes, uh, you have a nice evening, too, Mayor Connolly. See you then."

Taylor hung up the phone and turned to the door. He jumped as he saw two pairs of eyes staring back at him from where the door was just slightly ajar. He broke into a smile and both Tom and Wayne rushed into the room.

"You did it?" Wayne asked excitedly.

Taylor smiled. "I don't think you should have any problem getting your tickets tomorrow," he said simply.

"Thank you!" Wayne said as he kissed Taylor on the cheek and hugged him tight.

"How?" Tom asked.

Taylor held out the invitation for Tom to read. He looked up, a broad smile on his face. "You're incredible," he said, kissing Taylor and joining in on Wayne's hug. Taylor held them both, smiling himself. For once, they had won.

Chapter Fifteen

Prom

Taylor stood in front of his closet, arms crossed over his bare chest, a scowl on his face. What to wear? It was a gay man's nightmare—prom night, but no idea whether to go with the tux for the whole night or take a change of clothes for later. Well, that wasn't precisely true—he knew their plans for the latter part of the evening and the general look that would be acceptable. But it was kind of fun to dress up in a time when he didn't get to do that much anymore.

He sighed, looking at his reflection. How times had changed—a few short years ago, it was one event after another, always some reason to be in full black-tie attire. Tom had been amazed to learn Taylor had not one, not two, but *four* tuxedos. They had decided that, since they were going as a couple, they should have matching tuxes in their own right. Twenty-five hundred dollars later, they each had a perfectly tailored matching tuxedo that would be sure to be out of style in a year. Taylor had insisted on a three-quarter length jacket, giving it a more eastern flair.

"Oh, will you stop?" Tom lamented as he came out of the bathroom. "Why is getting dressed always such an ordeal for you?" He asked, reaching into the closet to extract his own clothes. "We've only had these things for the last month. Now get dressed before we wind up late."

Taylor snapped out of his reverie, looking at Tom's reflection in the mirror. His hair was still askew from the shower, and he wore only his boxers, just like Taylor, who couldn't help but smile as he watched him fiddle with his shirt on the hangar.

Tom caught his eye and grudgingly returned the smile. He returned to the closet and handed Taylor his own tux package. "Here. Shirt, socks, pants, jacket. It's that easy."

Taylor reached out to him and Tom couldn't resist. They held each other in the relative quiet of the house for a few moments, but were interrupted by a knock on the door.

"Taylor? Tom?" It was Wayne's voice.

Pulling on his shirt, Taylor opened the door. "What's up?"

"Do you know how to do one of these?" Wayne asked, holding an untied bow tie in front of him.

"Sure," Taylor said. "Come here." They stood in front of the mirrored doors and Taylor placed the fabric around Wayne's neck, then carefully tied it. "Let me know if it's too tight," he said.

"It's supposed to be too tight, isn't it?" Wayne asked.

Taylor smiled. "Tight enough to look snazzy, but you don't want to pass out on the dance floor."

"The dance floor?" Wayne said.

Taylor watched him in the mirror. "You are planning to dance, aren't you?"

"I didn't figure we should push our luck," Wayne said. His tie tied, he turned to Taylor. "Crissy has still been pretty miserable."

"You push your luck," Tom said from behind Taylor. "We'll be there if Crissy needs to have her priorities changed."

Wayne smiled and pulled them both into a hug. "I love you guys."

"We love you," Taylor said. "Now, get downstairs. Eric should be here any time."

Wayne frowned. "Yeah, where did he go?"

"I asked him to take care of something for me," Tom said.

"Oh. Okay." Wayne left and Taylor closed the door behind him. He turned to find Tom holding out his socks. "Socks, pants, jacket. You're almost there."

Taylor gave him a look and he broke into a smile. "Come on, big guy," he said. "We're going to have a lot of fun tonight."

"Is that so?"

"Promise," Tom said. He tucked in his shirt, then adjusted his belt. Their tuxes hadn't required bow ties, a point they both agreed was ideal. By sticking with a belt, they could take off their jackets and wind up with a more casual formal look that would still impress.

As Taylor closed his own belt, he slid his feet into the patent leather shoes a tux demanded and he groaned as he did it.

"Fashion before comfort," Tom reminded. "Rule twenty-six."

"If my feet had their way, I'd go straight," Taylor said.

"Fortunately, the rest of you is firmly gay." Taylor turned sharply and Tom laughed.

"What do you think?" Taylor asked, holding his arms out in front of him and judging his appearance in the mirror.

"I'd do ya," Tom said, buttoning his last button on his jacket.

Taylor looked at him, mouth agape. "Who flipped your switch tonight?"

Tom grinned broadly. "Oh, come on. This is high school—we're conservative compared to them."

"Good point," Taylor said. He led the way as they went downstairs, meeting Wayne in the living room. He had his back to the window, so he didn't see Eric had returned until he was at the door. Tom let him in and he smiled as he saw Wayne. Like Tom and Taylor, they had opted for identical tuxes, but of a more traditional style with white shirts and dark navy blue ties.

Eric held out a flower for Wayne's lapel. "May I?"

Wayne picked up a corresponding flower from the table. "Please do," he said, reaching to pin his flower on Eric's lapel.

"Look at our boys, they're all grown up," Tom said.

"Somebody should be," Taylor said quietly. Tom elbowed him in the ribs as Wayne and Eric turned to face them.

"It's all set," Eric said.

"Thanks," Tom said with a nod.

"What's going on?" Wayne asked, realizing something must be up.

"We wanted to make sure you got to travel in style," Taylor said. He held out a hand in the direction of the door. Wayne swung the door open, then stopped cold.

"You're kidding."

"Nope," Tom said. "It's all yours."

As they walked outside, Tom's parents met them in the driveway, the three kids in tow, his dad snapping picture after picture, capturing the sheer surprise on his face. Gen and Miguel had joined them and for once, even Miguel was smiling broadly. In front of them, topped by a giant red bow, was a brand new black Jeep, with all the bells and whistles, gleaming in the evening sun.

"You can't...this can't...I can't..." Wayne stammered, running a hand over the smooth fender. "Mine?" he asked, an expression of sheer shock and joy on his face.

"Yours," Taylor said.

"We wanted to do something really special for you," Tom said. "You're going to need to be able to get to school and back next year."

"But this is too much," Wayne objected.

Taylor shook his head. "Not for family."

Wayne hugged them both tightly, then turned back to his Jeep. "Do you think it's okay to drive it there tonight? I don't want anything to happen to it."

Taylor nodded. "I have it on good authority that the Chief plans to come by and will have somebody on duty the whole night. He's even got a couple designated spots for VIP's."

"God, Taylor, this is incredible."

"Can we go for a ride?" Chad asked, breaking away from Tom's mom.

"Yeah! Just a quick one," Wendy said.

Donna pulled the children back over to her. "Another time," she said. "Wayne and Eric have somewhere to be."

Wayne turned to her. "It's okay, Mrs. McEwan," he said. "Just a quick trip," he said to the kids.

"Car seats," Tom objected.

"End of the block and back, slowly," Taylor said, a hand on Tom's shoulder.

The kids cheered and clamored into the vehicle with the help of their adopted "brothers." Eric jumped in the passenger seat as Wayne took the bow off and put it in the back. He jumped in, then took the keys Eric still had and started the Jeep. Gently backing it out of the driveway, he headed toward town, moving no more than fifteen miles per hour.

Taylor Thomas lay with his head on Gen's shoulder, awake, but just barely, a pacifier in his mouth. As the adults watched, the Jeep turned around and slowly made its way back in their direction.

"We can't thank you guys enough for looking after the kids tonight," Tom said to his parents and Gen and Miguel.

"It's our pleasure," Gen said. "You guys just make sure to have fun tonight."

"You can count on it," Taylor said. Wayne pulled back in and put the Jeep in park, then helped the two children out of the back.

"That was *fun!*" Chad said, running up to Taylor.

"Can we go again?" Wendy asked, wrapping her arms around Tom's leg.

"Later, kids," Tom said. "For now, we want you to be good for Grandma and Grandpa and Aunt Gen and Uncle Miguel. We'll see you in the morning, okay?"

"Okay," Wendy said, decidedly more subdued. They kissed both kids on the cheek, then waved as the audience all moved back to Gen's yard, where they had been playing.

Tom walked around the back of the house and pulled the Jag forward, freshly cleaned and detailed for the evening. Taylor waved to Wayne and Eric and watched as they took off down the road in the direction of the school. As he got in the passenger side, he noticed a large duffel bag in the back seat and looked at Tom expectantly.

"I knew I could never get you back in a tux in the morning," he explained.

Taylor smiled and they pulled out, waving to their family, then turning to follow the black Jeep toward the school.

Inside the gymnasium, the room was awash in dark tuxedos and satin dresses. It was a chance for the young people of the town to show off and be shown. According to Tom, the class was about one hundred twenty students—large enough to be a good party, small enough that they all knew each other. The theme, like so many other proms for so many decades, was the sea, so various sea related things were strewn about and hung from the ceiling to give the "illusion" of being under water. Taylor smiled to himself—at least they'd tried.

As expected, the town Chief had greeted them when they pulled up and offered them one of two reserved parking spots next to his own car. Sure enough, Wayne's car was in the other spot. A number of other cars were parked nearby, so as not to seem too obvious, but Tom had mentioned they were all staff.

Wayne had been planning to take the Jag and pick up Emmy and Dan, but the Jeep hadn't forced too much of a change of plan—except Eric wound up having to ride in the back with Dan rather than force Emmy to try to navigate her way to the back in her satin dress. On Wayne's advice, she had chosen a stunning dark green dress that went well with her eyes and complexion. As Wayne had explained to her, having a gay best friend had to have some kind of perks.

Inside, Principal Hargreaves greeted everyone as they came in. Taylor smiled as he made a special point of greeting Tom and him, noting that he seemed a little embarrassed over the flap a few weeks before. The day after Taylor's phone call, Tom reported Hargreaves had stopped in to his classroom just long enough to offer an apology and say he would be honored to have the Mayor and his "partner" attend. Taylor had laughed at Tom's description of him stumbling over what to call Taylor, but had appreciated the effort all the same.

Off to one side, just outside of the gym, a table had been setup to vote for a number of honors that would be bestowed by the prom king and queen. Though the "royal" voting had already occurred, the court would be elected that night, including best dressed, best couple, best hair, and a number of other "bests" designed to let the cheerleaders and football players show off.

Taylor shook his head. Some things never changed. Though he had not attended his own prom, he remembered vividly the pomp and circumstance surrounding it. Though by no means counting himself as a member of the "popular" crowd, he'd had enough friends who were to remember the backstabbing and infighting that had gone on for "key" positions. The last he'd heard, the prom queen had three kids and was living in Iowa somewhere.

"Tom! Taylor!"

They turned to see Emmy bustling toward them, trailed by her entourage of men. Her sandy blonde hair was arranged in ringlets held up at the back by an antique turquoise clip and allowed to fall down around her ears and brow. Just behind and beside her, Dan kept pace, wearing a dark tux similar in style to Wayne's and Eric's, except with a green tie and vest to match Emmy's dress.

"Wow, Em!" Tom exclaimed, giving her a hug. "Who knew under all that flour there was a princess!"

"I could say the same thing about you," she quipped. Ever since Tom had come out, she had been very comfortable with sparring with him about his sexuality. When Wayne had come out, she'd been in heaven, proclaiming they could all go boy watching together.

"If only my king was as handsome," Tom said, shaking hands with Dan.

Taylor took the verbal jab in silence, but Eric was there to back him up. "That's okay, Taylor, when I saw Emmy, I told her she was almost enough to make me go straight," he said, earning a jab from Wayne.

"And what's with this 'almost' stuff?" Emmy asked, her hands on her hips.

Taylor glanced up to see Crissy Hargreaves walking in their direction. She was trailed by her own entourage of satin-clad chatty-cats, their claws extended and teeth bared at any who happened upon them.

"Ladies," she said quietly, just loud enough for Tom and Taylor to catch. Tom started to turn, but Taylor put an arm over his shoulder. "Not now," he said quietly.

"What did she say?" Wayne asked.

"I think she was asking why a bunch of cools cats like us haven't made it to the dance floor yet," Taylor said more loudly. In the gym, a few people had already started to dance, while the rest milled outside, still waiting for friends to show up.

"Good question," Emmy said, taking Dan by the hand.

"I agree," Eric said, reaching for Wayne's hand. Wayne's eyes got a little wide at the prospect of Eric taking his hand. What was okay for their time alone or with their gay friends was a little different in a public setting.

"You know, I think it's about time for you to shake your grooooove thang, too, mister," Tom said, taking Taylor's arm. As they started to walk away, he saw Eric just put his arm around Wayne's shoulders. Tom smiled, knowing some things would take time. Fortunately for Wayne, Eric was incredibly good at being patient.

Shortly after their first dance, Dan reminded them that they might want to get their pictures taken before everyone got hot. Dan and Emmy went first, making a beautiful couple. Dan was only an inch or so taller than Emmy to begin with, but with her heels, he came off shorter. Emmy apparently realized the problem and slipped out of her shoes before the picture. He wrapped his arms around her and they both looked picture perfect as the computer displayed their digital image for convenient immediate review.

Tom had watched Wayne's reaction and noticed how he had been withdrawing all night. So, when their turn came up, he volunteered for him and Taylor to go next, telling the photographer, "we want one just like that."

Fortunately, Taylor had a couple inches on Tom anyway and their shoes were basically identical, so they just looked their usual magnetic selves naturally. Taylor had gelled his blond hair into a more pronounced style, while Tom kept his darker hair its usual casual simplicity. Their picture, to Tom's delight, came out every bit as good as Dan and Emmy's.

"There you go, now you have a prom photo," Tom announced proudly to Taylor.

"And we don't look a day over nineteen," Taylor said.

"Maybe nineteen hundred," Crissy said as she pushed past them. "Can you take us next?" she asked the photographer. "I'm going to need to be on stage shortly, so I wanted to be sure the picture of Brian and me was ready."

Tom started to say something, but felt Taylor's hand on his arm. "Let it go, hon," he said in Tom's ear as Crissy and her charge took their positions.

"She can't keep treating people like that," Tom objected.

"She won't," Taylor said, "Trust me."

Tom glanced at him, but saw something in his eyes that caused him to be quiet. The light flashed and Crissy's moment of glory was past. She pushed past them again, her pink satin making "swish-swish" sounds as she walked. Taylor had to give "Brian" credit—he'd worn a matching pink tie and cumberbund.

It was once again Wayne and Eric's turn and Eric pointed to a pose he wanted for them. Wayne frowned, not able to see what had been selected. Tom could tell he was nervous, so while the photographer set up the shot, he leaned over to Wayne.

"Hey, are you having fun?"

"Yeah."

"Why don't you look like it?"

Wayne glanced from side to side. "People keep looking at us."

Tom smiled. "They're looking at everybody, not just you."

"But they keep expecting us to do something."

Tom shrugged. "So, why not give 'em what they're expecting. We did." Wayne just glared at him, still very uptight. Tom continued. "You're leaving here in a couple weeks. Would you rather look back and smile about enjoying yourself or wish you'd taken the opportunity while you had it?"

"Okay, we're ready here," the photographer said.

When Wayne looked over, he saw Eric sitting on a block, his arms out to him. Wayne looked as though fire would shoot from his eyes as he saw what Eric had done. Then, with one last glance at Tom, he started laughing and ran over and took his place on Eric's lap, wrapping his arms around him and holding him cheek to cheek. Eric grinned broadly at the break in Wayne's mood and they both posed for the camera, Wayne even throwing up one leg.

As the flash dimmed, Wayne leaned in and kissed Eric on the lips, then hopped up. Behind them, a crowd had amassed and they all broke into applause as the two looked over. For his part, Wayne just beamed, but Eric turned a little red. Wayne took a bow, then took Eric's hand and led them to the computer, where their picture easily put the two other couples' to shame.

Crissy watched them from the sidelines, her own expression acidic. She turned and walked toward the gym.

"I'll be right back," Taylor said.

"Tay? Where are you going?" Tom asked.

"Trust me," he said again.

Just inside the gym, Taylor caught up with Crissy and took her by the elbow.

"Hey!" she said, pulling her arm away. "What are you doing?"

"I want to talk to you for just a minute," Taylor said, speaking just loud enough to be heard over the music.

"Why would I want to talk to you?"

Taylor watched her in the dim light. He realized for all her bravado, her greatest fear was that no one would notice her. She craved the attention and used her abrasive personality to gain more of it.

"You can talk to me now or you can talk to me after I talk to your father," Taylor said simply.

"What can you tell him?"

"I saw your boyfriend sneak around back when we got here."

Crissy maintained her persona, but he saw the fear at the back of her eyes. "So?"

"They weren't drinking Gatorade," Taylor said.

"You don't know anything," she objected. Taylor said nothing, his face stoic, just watching her. "You can't prove anything," she said. "How can you prove it? You can't. So why don't you just go back to your little girlfriends and leave me the hell alone."

"You're right," Taylor said. "Short of an immediate sobriety check, it would be difficult to prove what they did. And I know you have a limo tonight, so I'm not particularly worried about it."

"Then *why are we here?*" she insisted.

Taylor nodded. "Two things. First, you will go and tell them to dump whatever is left, immediately. If I catch even a hint of drunkenness, I go to your dad. Second, you take your miss-bitch attitude and stow it. If I see you so much as glance the wrong way at anyone else here tonight, I go to your dad. You got me?"

"If you think—" Crissy began.

"Save it," Taylor said. "This is not negotiable. Those are my terms and I'm not kidding for a minute. Are you in or out?"

Crissy watched him, hatred seething from every pore of her being, then slowly smiled, as best she knew how. "Of course, Mr. Mayor. Thank you for bringing this to my attention. I'll take care of Brian at once."

"Tread lightly, Crissy. This had better be the last time."

She smiled and nodded. "Of course, sir. I apologize for the trouble we've caused you. Have a nice evening, Mr. Mayor."

Taylor watched her go and shook his head. As she left, the rest of his party walked in, looking for him.

"Everything okay?" Tom asked.

"Everything's fine," Taylor said.

Tom looked in the direction of the departing Crissy. "What did you tell her?"

Taylor smiled. "I just showed her there are still some leagues she's not big enough to play in." He looked at the other young people standing in front of him. "All right, you guys, enough loafing around. This is a dance, not a tennis match. I want to see some footwork."

An hour or so later, they all had beads of sweat on their foreheads and the guys had long since dumped their tux jackets. Dancing was fun, but it was also more exercise than any of them tended to get on a regular basis. Tom and Taylor occasionally had to make the rounds as chaperones, but Emmy was in her element, surrounded continuously by three guys, all of whom had reasonable dancing skills.

To his credit, Dan was not the least bit intimidated by sharing his evening with a gay couple. At one point, Emmy insisted on sharing a dance with Wayne as Madonna's "Crazy for You" filled the room. Eric started to leave the floor.

"Where are you going?" Dan asked, catching his arm.

"It's a slow dance," Eric pointed out.

"What, I'm not good enough for you 'cause I'm straight?"

Eric broke into a broad grin and wrapped an arm around Dan's waist as he took the offered hand. Wayne and Emmy laughed and pointed, but Dan managed to keep a perfectly straight face as he watched his girlfriend and her best friend. Tom and Taylor joined them, eyebrows raised in surprise as they saw the revised couples.

As the song came to an end, Wayne walked over and tapped Dan on the shoulder. "Can I have my boyfriend back, please?"

"I don't know," Dan said. Emmy turned his head and kissed him. "Right. Okay," he said and they all laughed.

Instead of another song, the audio system squeaked as a mic came to life and Dr. Hargreaves stood before all of them. "And now, the time you've all been waiting for," he began and Tom turned to Taylor.

"Want something to drink?" he asked.

"Yeah," Taylor answered, "Diet something would be great."

"I'll be right back," he said. As he turned to go, Wayne took drink orders from the rest of the group and followed him.

"And now, the Prom King for this year's class," Hargreaves said, "Wayne McInerney...?" His voice trailed off as though he could scarcely believe it himself.

Tom and Wayne froze as the spotlight found him near the door. Everyone clapped and a couple people came and led him to the stage. Wayne's face was pale and he looked like he might be in shock. Emmy rushed over and handed him his jacket just before they slid the crown on his head.

"Oh no," Taylor said, a sudden burst of insight in his mind.

"And this year's prom queen," Hargreaves continued, "Miss Christina Hargreaves!"

She strode forward, every bit playing the part and kissed her father lightly on the cheek. As she turned, Taylor made sure he was the first person she saw and her eyes lingered on him ever so briefly before turning on Wayne. For his part, he looked like he was ready to die on the spot, but she plastered a smile on her face and held out her hand for him to lead her to the dance floor. They danced to some tune Taylor didn't recognize then returned to the stage as Crissy's father read the other names.

"And last, best couple goes to...Wayne McInerney and Eric Driskell," Hargreaves said. His voice squeaked at the end, but he held it together. Crissy's date, Brian, had been nominated for best dressed man, so at least it wasn't as bad when she went to dance with him and Wayne went to dance with Eric.

After all the hoopla was over, the friends all milled back into their own groups and Tom and Taylor brought drinks to everyone.

"Congratulations, Wayne," Taylor said, handing him a glass.

"Thanks," Wayne said, again non-plussed.

"Oh, come on," Eric chided him. "It's not every day I get to dance with the prom king, or even get elected best couple."

"You didn't have to dance with Crissy Hargreaves," Wayne said.

"No, but I got to dance with you," Eric answered, batting his eyes.

Emmy stood with her arm around Dan. "Awww, that deserves a kiss," she said. Wayne shot her a glance, but then turned and gave Eric a quick peck.

"See, a kiss makes it all better," Dan said. The crowd had started thinning as people made their way out and off to various parties.

"So what's your plan?" Tom asked, turning to Wayne.

"We rented a couple rooms at the Marriott downtown so we could just hang out and then crash whenever we feel like it."

"Yeah, I know that part," Tom said. "Remember, we're on that plan, too. We just made them put us on a different floor."

"Thank God," Taylor added. "You guys are too rowdy."

"You ain't seen nothin' yet," Dan said. "You should have heard what Eric was talking about when we were dancing!"

"How much longer are you staying?" Tom asked, returning them to the topic.

"I don't know, how much longer will you be here?" Wayne asked.

Taylor shrugged. "We can pretty much leave anytime. They only asked the parent chaperones to stay as long as the ceremony and maybe a half hour after, since most people leave anyway."

Wayne nodded. "Okay. One more dance?" he asked, turning to his friends.

"One more dance," Emmy confirmed

Together, the three couples walked onto the dance floor and fast danced until the next slow song started up, then broke into pairs. Above, someone had actually installed an old mirrored disco ball and it swirled simulated stars around them to the sound of Celine Dion's "My Heart Will Go On."

"So, how was your prom?" Tom asked Taylor.

Taylor smiled. "Perfect."

Tom nodded, leaning his head into Taylor's shoulder. "I have to tell you, this was a lot more fun than my high school prom."

"Maybe it's because we're old enough to actually appreciate it now," Taylor observed.

"Maybe," Tom agreed. "Or, maybe it's just the better company."

Taylor leaned his head over on Tom's. "I've gotta tell you, it was worth the wait. I can't think of anyone I'd rather be here with."

"Me, either," Tom said. They danced on in silence, simply enjoying each others' embrace. As the song came to a close, the lights brightened a bit and a fast song replaced the more soothing melody.

"I guess that's it," Taylor said. Hand in hand with Tom, they headed for the door.

"Mayor Connolly?"

As one, they turned to find Crissy waiting for them, her prom queen attire still perfect. She smiled, but instead of the plastic, hate-filled smile she'd worn all evening, this one seemed more genuine.

"Crissy?" Taylor acknowledged.

"I just wanted to say thank you, you know, for not wrecking the evening."

Taylor nodded. "Same to you," he said.

She smiled, more ruefully. "Well, I guess we're all going off to the Holiday Inn for a little party," she said.

"Have a good time and be careful," Taylor replied, reverting to his more parental role.

"You too," she said, then walked away.

"What was that all about?" Wayne asked, filling the space she had vacated.

Taylor sighed. "Later," he said. "You guys ready to go?"

"Sure are," Wayne said.

"Okay. Here's the deal—we'll follow you as far as the hotel. The rooms are all paid for. Once you're there, you're on your own. Stay out of trouble."

"The rooms are paid for?" Eric asked.

Tom nodded beside Taylor. "Yes, both of them. Call it a little thank you gift from Downey's to Wayne and Emmy."

"Wow," Dan said. "Thanks, guys."

"You're the best," Emmy said, kissing each of them. They all traded hugs and then went to their respective cars.

"Everything okay in there, Mayor," Police Chief Embry asked, still sitting in his car outside the school.

Taylor nodded. "Just like you said it would be, Chief."

He smiled. "Yep, I saw the limo drive off a couple minutes ago. Kids looked okay."

"You know your stuff, Chief," Taylor agreed.

"Oh, I've been around the block a couple times," he said with a smile. "You kids drive safe yourselves, okay?"

"Will do, sir," Taylor said. "See you soon."

"That you will, Mayor. That you will."

Taylor got in the car next to Tom and they headed off. Tom followed the black Jeep just close enough to keep its taillights in view, but far enough that they wouldn't cramp the kids' style—or let the kids cramp theirs. Finally, a night on their own again. Taking Taylor's hand, he smiled and drove into the night.

Chapter Sixteen

Endings

Taylor pulled into the parking lot, heading directly for the spot the Chief had promised he'd save. For once, Taylor was very glad he was the Mayor of the town.

As he'd expected, business had picked up more as his reputation and the reputation of the firm grew. He, Pete, and their new attorney Samantha had barely been able to keep up with the cases and Taylor had begun personally arguing in court again. As Pete and Sam had pointed out, he was the best orator they had.

It wasn't until the week before that it had dawned on him he had to be in court on the day of Wayne's graduation. Fortunately, Tom's parents had been a godsend. They spent most of their day either watching after Wendy and Mini-Tay or helping keep an eye on the store. Taylor hated the idea of them deciding it was finally time to go home. He suspected that might take a little longer, though, since Mandy had announced she wanted to come spend a few weeks with everyone for the summer. She already knew Eric and Wayne, and had heard good things about Emmy and Dan. The idea of being around her niece and nephews was more than she could pass up.

At any rate, Taylor knew the judge well enough to ask for an early recess for the day, especially given the circumstances. All was well until he tried to get out of the city and found himself in bumper to bumper traffic with the freeway shut down from four lanes to two. It had added a good twenty minutes to his trip and prompted a call to Chief Embry for help. As he'd expected, the man was more than congenial, telling him he'd planned to attend anyway. That was another thing about a small town—virtually any occasion brought out everyone to attend.

Putting the car in park, Taylor pulled the roaring cat key from the ignition and folded the end into the remote. Tom's parents had taken their newly purchased sport utility vehicle to transport the little ones and Tom had just ridden to school with Wayne, knowing he could come home with Taylor. So, for once in a very long time, Taylor got to drive the Jag again. He smiled to himself—not the Jag guy anymore.

"Thanks again, Chief," Taylor said, rushing from the car.

"Always a pleasure, Mr. Mayor," Embry replied. "There's something you ought to know about," he said, pointing in the direction of the building. There, leaning against the wall in the late afternoon sun, was a man Taylor had thought not to see again.

"You've gotta be kidding," Taylor moaned.

Embry nodded. "Already talked to him, Mayor," he said, his Wilfred Brimley accent thick as ever. "He's not going to cause any trouble."

"Thanks, Chief," Taylor said. "Think I should say anything?"

The chief shrugged. "Wouldn't hurt to say hello. He's a might more humble than he used to be."

"Okay," Taylor said, then headed toward the man. He double-checked his watch. Ten minutes.

As he walked up, the man straightened his shirt and adjusted his tie. It was clear from his attire he wasn't used to formal occasions, but Taylor had to at least give him credit for making the effort.

"Mayor Connolly," he said, holding out his hand.

"Mr. McInerney," Taylor acknowledged, shaking the hand briefly.

McInerney held up his hands, no doubt anticipating Taylor's thoughts and comments. "I don't wanna cause any trouble here, Mr. Mayor," he said. "That's why I'm just waiting back here. Only the Chief even recognized me."

Taylor nodded. "He told me you were here."

McInerney smiled thinly, more an expression of embarrassment and discomfort than of pleasure. "I just wanted to see my boy graduate. He'll be the first boy in our family to do that, you know. My other boy, Teddy, dropped out of school when he was sixteen…followed after his old man, I'm 'fraid."

Taylor said nothing, just watching him and letting him speak.

"My son," he said, "Is he a good boy?"

Taylor nodded and smiled with pride over his adopted "little brother." "He's an amazing person, Mr. McInerney, one of the best people I've ever known. You can be very proud of him."

McInerney nodded. "I am, you know that? I am. I was hard on him, probably harder than I shoulda been, but I wanted him to grow up right, to be strong. He was always so quiet, I's afraid people'd take advantage of him. I mighta been wrong in my methods, but I'm glad for the result."

"He's a good person," Taylor agreed, not seeing a point in condemning McInerney's actions further.

"I saw him pull up with that other fella, Tom. What'chu call him?"

"My spouse," Taylor said simply.

"Right," McInerney said, still obviously confused. "Does my son…does Wayne…have a…?"

Taylor nodded. "Wayne has a boyfriend, someone he met a few months ago. They've been doing very well."

"So he's happy?" McInerney asked.

"Yes."

"Good," McInerney asserted. "His brother ain't amounted to much. I want Wayne to find a better life for himself—better than the one I was gonna be able to give him."

Taylor smiled, feeling compassion for the mixed up man before him. His treatment of Wayne was unforgivable, but somehow Taylor knew there were explanations—not excuses, but reasons—for how McInerney had behaved. And whatever the case, he'd gone to a lot of trouble to make his way back in time to see Wayne graduate.

"He's going to college in the fall," Taylor said. "He wants to be a teacher, like Tom, and a writer. He gets straight A's in Journalism."

"A writer? How 'bout that?" McInerney said.

Taylor checked his watch and realized things were about to begin. As if on cue, his phone rang with Tom's number. He excused himself and flipped it open.

"Hi, I'm right outside."

"What are you doing?"

"Wayne's dad is here. We were just talking for a minute."

"*What?* Where's the Chief?"

"It's okay, honey, don't worry. I've gotta let you go."

"Okay. Just get in here."

"I'll be right there." Taylor closed the phone and turned back to McInerney. "Mr. McInerney, I need to go. They're ready to start."

"Thanks for talkin' to me, Mayor," he said. "And thanks for lookin' after my boy so good. You and your…spouse…is real good people."

Taylor shook his hand again. "Mr. McInerney, would you like to come in and sit down?"

He shook his head. "No, that's okay, Mr. Mayor. I can see just fine from here. I just want to see him get that piece of paper and I'll be off."

"Don't you want to at least say hello?"

Again, he shook his head. "No, sir. I don't want to cause him any more pain, not on a day like today. This is his day to shine. You just tell him please, one day somewhere down the road, that his old man was here. Please?"

"You can count on it," Taylor said. He turned and walked through the gate to the outdoor stadium where they had setup the ceremony. Tom, Dr. Hargreaves, and the superintendent all waited on the stage. At the base, two people helped Taylor into a black robe and collar bearing the colors of his alma mater, where he'd gotten his law degree. Dr. Hargreaves gestured for him to take a seat next to Tom.

"You took your sweet time," Tom hissed, giving him a sidelong glance.

"Traffic. I got here ten minutes ago."

"Any problem with McInerney?" Hargreaves rose and walked to the podium to begin the presentation.

"No, everything was fine. Don't say anything to Wayne. I'll fill you in later."

"Got it," Tom acknowledged as Hargreaves began to speak.

Aside for starting two minutes late for reasons no one ever fully understood, the ceremony went off without a hitch. The graduating class included all but one of its seniors, an unfortunate situation where a girl got pregnant during the previous semester and was unable to finish school. The downside to a small town was everyone knew exactly who was absent.

Tom had been tapped to read the names of the graduates while Hargreaves handed out the diplomas and Superintendent Caffery, and Taylor shook their hands and offered congratulations. Taylor just laughed when Emmy pulled him into a big hug, her mascara running just a bit as she smiled, but he could barely contain his surprise when Dan did the same thing, saying, "Any friend of Emmy's…"

Taylor did fine until he saw Wayne come up the stairs. He didn't even remember the person or two in front of Wayne, as his eyes never left him. Wayne shook Hargreaves' hand and accepted the piece of paper he was given. Where everyone else had simply kept moving, he stopped to briefly hug Tom from behind, where he stood reading names at the podium. He then came over and shook hands with Caffery, then pulled Taylor into a tight hug like he would never let him go. For his part, Taylor wasn't letting go either and the school, who had voted Wayne their prom king, broke into applause.

At last they let go and Wayne wiped the tears from his eyes as Taylor did the same, and made his way down the stairs. Tom's eyes met Taylor's for just an instant and he gave a small smile and a nod, then turned back to the rest of the graduates. Wayne never saw his father, standing just to the side of the bleachers, nor did he see the cheer he gave, easily the loudest in the place, as his son took his diploma. And he didn't see the single tear that made its way down his own face as Wayne clutched at Taylor for those few seconds on the stage.

That evening, Tom and Taylor took the whole family, including their extended friends Emmy and Dan's families, and filled Alberto's. For his part, their old friend had positively beamed when Tom asked him if they could rent the restaurant that evening. Alberto had even tried to offer it for free, but neither Tom nor Taylor would hear of that. The food was, as always, extraordinary, and the kids were all but inseparable, insisting that their "prom dates" Tom and Taylor share a table with them. Rounding out their table were Wendy and Chad, who clung to Wayne and Eric as they usually did when they could.

Though Taylor had kept an eye out for McInerney, he didn't see him again and, as good as his word, he didn't say anything to Wayne. For once, Wayne seemed perfectly satisfied that he *was* with his family and showed none of the usual symptoms that he was missing his blood relatives. He'd commented in passing that his mother hadn't even bothered to call, but that was all he'd said, spending most of his free time with the younger kids or Eric.

Beside Taylor, Tom sat with his chair close, his arm over the back of Taylor's chair, his thumb gently caressing Taylor's shoulder. It was a virtually unconscious gesture as he sat talking to Emmy, but Taylor liked it. Chad sat next to him, drawing on the back of his placemat with the crayons Alberto kept on hand just for him, alternately showing his work to Wayne and Taylor. When he wasn't entertaining Chad, Wayne was discussing some of the classes he and Dan were taking together in the fall. Like Wayne, Dan was a Journalism major and both of them had applied for positions on the school paper.

Wendy kept Eric occupied, telling him various adventures her dollies had shared during the day while they rode around with grandma getting things for Wayne's graduation party. As much as Tom and Taylor had wanted to do everything themselves, the offer of help from Tom's mom was simply more than they could pass up. They had made the plans together, along with Gen, to use both backyards for the festivities, but Tom's mom had done most of the shopping to collect what they needed.

Taylor smiled. For as hectic as the year had been, the outcome was better than he ever could have dreamed. He missed John and Sandy terribly, even then, but the joy their children had brought to their lives was immeasurable and he would always be grateful for the good that had come from the tragedy. Their extended family continued to grow, both in blood relatives and others who they had more recently met. Emmy and Wayne had always been friends, but they had really bonded as she helped him overcome his family strife and deal with his coming out. In the three years Taylor had known her, he'd come to respect her innate wisdom and understanding of the people around her. As he glanced at the next table, he saw another young woman who shared those qualities and he knew what an amazing friend she had been to him.

Casually and quietly, he laid his hand on Tom's leg and gave it a little squeeze under the table. Tom never even broke stride in his conversation, but reached down to take Taylor's hand in his, resting them gently on the table, for all to see. In the subdued light of the restaurant, their identical platinum Tiffany bands glinted together, the only sign they truly needed of the inseparable bond between them. Taylor smiled to himself and nodded, knowing his life was truly whole.

The next morning, Taylor pushed open the door to the bakery, a tiny bell announcing his presence. The sun was just over the horizon, its rays beginning to warm the cool store. By the time the first customers showed up, the summer heat would already be invading, but the air conditioners helped keep it at bay. One thing both Tom and Taylor agreed on was the door had to be open in the summer. As the Downey's had originally, they kept the tradition of only an old screen door during business hours to keep out the bugs.

Inside, Emmy was loading one of the display cases with the first round of donuts. Saturday morning was one of their busy days—people got up early to get a jump on the day and there was no better way to do that than with fresh baked goods. Taylor watched as she adeptly handled the trays, sliding them in like the expert she was.

The entire team had decided to stay on part time during the coming year, while training a new team to cover days when they couldn't be there. Tom had been very pleasantly surprised when Emmy and Wayne had come to him and offered to stay on part of the time. The bakery was simply too good a job for them to pass up while they were in school. The fact that all of them were very close friends no doubt further aided the decision.

"Mornin', Taylor," Emmy greeted.

Taylor thought back to that fateful morning, over three years before, when he first stopped at Downey's. Only Tom had been working and Taylor had been the only customer, giving them a chance to chat, if only briefly. It wasn't until his second visit that he met Emmy. In later times, she admitted to him she'd suspected something was up between them from the moment she saw how he looked at Tom and how Tom looked back. She'd even tried to get info on him from Tom, but Tom wouldn't budge until the morning after their first Spring Dance. When he admitted what had happened that night, Emmy, then only fifteen, had switched into protective mode and not allowed anyone but Gen to talk to him. In her own way, she helped to bring them together, a fact neither of them ever forgot.

"Hi, Em. How's it going?"

She smiled. "Just great. Hard to believe this is it, huh? Last day." She stopped her stocking and leaned against the case as Taylor rounded the cabinets and joined her behind them.

"You're off, then Wayne, then Tom, then everybody's back to school," Taylor remembered, knowing the new summer schedule like the back of his hand.

"Are you ready for us to all be students again?"

He laughed. "Not a bit. But somehow I'll manage."

"You could go back, too," she suggested.

Taylor shook his head. "Not a chance. I got my law degree and that's enough for me. Besides, I think Pete would kill me."

Emmy smiled. "At least this time, there are enough people to keep everything going."

"You have no idea how true that is," Taylor agreed, sliding past her. Emmy turned to continue stocking the last of the shelves while he walked to the baking room. Inside, Tom and Wayne worked like a well-oiled machine, staying out of each other's way while being there when the other needed an extra hand.

Wayne's development and recovery had continued to the point where there were very few obvious signs of his former life. He smiled constantly and always had a caring word or positive observation to offer. People brightened when they talked to him, much as they did with Tom, as though sensing the honesty of his soul.

It was several moments before either baker noticed Taylor's presence, when Tom caught him out of the corner of his eye. He turned, his ever-present Taylor Smile on his face as he walked over.

"I'm covered in flour," he cautioned.

"It's never stopped us before," Taylor said, giving him a kiss. "How's everything going?"

"Great," Tom said. "The night team had everything going before we got here. Wayne and I agree they're ready to be on their own."

Taylor nodded. "Good thing, since Emmy is gone next week."

"They're on their own starting Tuesday," Tom said. "Of course, I'll be around if they need anything, but mainly we're in the store next week."

"I wouldn't say that too loudly," Emmy said, pushing the now empty rack into the room. "They'll be fine." She took a rack of bagels and headed back out front.

"You're helping Em today?" Wayne asked.

"At least for the morning rush," Taylor said. Out front, the bell sounded again.

"Sounds like it's starting now," Wayne observed.

Before Taylor could walk back to the door, Eric appeared. He'd cut his hair the week before, deciding the longer style wasn't working in the heat of summer, but it still caused Taylor to do a double take.

"Where's my honeybun?" Eric asked as he entered the room.

Wayne held out a hot crossed bun. "Here you go."

Eric smiled. "That's not the one I'm looking for," he said and kissed Wayne.

"See, the flour doesn't stop him, either," Taylor observed to Tom.

Eric turned to Taylor. "Hey, would you let the landlord know the bulb is out at the top of the stairs?"

Taylor nodded. "Storage closet, top shelf," he said.

"Thanks," Eric said. "We about killed ourselves carrying stuff up there last night."

Tom turned to him. "Everything situated okay?"

"Just about. Thanks for all the furniture—it really makes a big difference. We decided to each take a room so we can study without disturbing each other if we need to."

Tom nodded. "Good plan. Your parents were okay with everything?"

Eric shrugged. "I won't say they were thrilled, but they understand our need to be together and the design program at the university does have a pretty good reputation. It's only a half hour drive to the city, so it sure beats four hours each way on the weekend. And they like Wayne," he said, glancing to the flour covered baker with a smile.

The bell sounded again out front and this time Taylor heard voices talking to Emmy.

"Are you working today?" he asked Eric, noticing he was wearing a maroon Downey McEwan's T-shirt and khaki shorts. Tom had decided they should all have T-shirts, so he bought them in a variety of colors. Taylor had taken a simple athletic gray that he could wear when he went running in the afternoon, and Wayne had opted for a bright green that "brought out the color in his eyes." Tom still teased him about it.

"I was planning on it," Eric replied.

"See you out front, then," Taylor said, then made his way back to the store.

Taylor passed the bag over the counter to a smiling Mrs. Jenkins. As she did each and every Saturday, she appeared promptly at eight AM, just like clockwork, and her bag of fresh, warm baked goods was waiting for her.

"You're such a dear, Taylor," she said, accepting the bag. "You boys take such good care of me."

Taylor smiled. "You're our best customer, Mrs. J," he said.

She made a dismissive motion with her hand. "Oh, I don't know about that. How's Tommy?"

"Tommy's good, Mrs. J," Tom answered, appearing from the hall with a fresh tray of bagels in his hands. He dropped them into a waiting basket with effortless efficiency, just like he always did, then set the empty tray on a waiting rack, turning to stand with Taylor. "How's your granddaughter doing?" he asked.

"Oh, she's fine, she's fine," Mrs. Jenkins answered. "She met a lovely young lady a few months ago. Do you know, they come out to see me every Sunday afternoon? Sometimes, they insist on bringing food to cook for me. Isn't that sweet?"

"You're a lucky lady, ma'am," Tom said.

Mrs. Jenkins smiled, an action that involved her entire face. Her curls were teased into a white cloud of perfection around her head and she was wearing one of her many pink cardigan sweaters over a white blouse and light slacks. Taylor had observed once she was like a grandmother to the entire town and she positively beamed.

"Well, I won't keep you boys. I know how busy it is here. You should be proud—it was never this busy before you took over. You're absolutely wonderful here."

"Thank you, Mrs. J," Taylor said. "You have a wonderful morning and we'll see you next week."

"That you will," she said, walking to the door. "That you will." At the door, she stopped as another person stood and held it open for her. "Why thank you, dear," she said.

"Anytime, Mrs. Jenkins," Gen said. Outside, Molly stood with her tail wagging, eager to greet the lady as she passed down the sidewalk.

"Mornin', Pussycat," Tom greeted, holding out her chocolate croissant and milk. To Taylor's knowledge, Tom remained the one person in all the universe who was allowed to call Gen by her old high school nickname. Few others even knew of its existence, and those who did were threatened with bodily harm should they utter it.

"Hi, Tommy, how are you?"

"Great, thanks," he said. "Keeping busy?"

Gen smiled. "Oh, you know. Ever since the wedding, Miguel thinks he should have a say in how things are done."

"Silly boy," Taylor said. "He clearly missed a memo."

"For sure, honey," Gen said, seating herself at a table. Tom and Taylor each took a croissant for themselves and joined her, sharing a glass of milk between them. Emmy and Eric continued to hustle behind the counter, preparing for the next wave of customers.

"How is Miguel?" Taylor asked.

Gen smiled, her Miguel Smile. "He's great. I tell you, that vacation was exactly what we needed." On her finger, a small gold band complimented the enormous diamond Miguel had bought her as an engagement gift. "You guys are taking off in a couple weeks, right?"

Tom nodded. "Everything's set. A couple nights in the islands, a cruise, then a few more nights in the islands. Just the two of us, no kids, no jobs, no distractions."

"What ever will you do?" Gen asked, her dark eyes sparkling with mischief.

"Sleep," Taylor said simply, biting into his croissant.

"Sometimes," Tom agreed, eyeing him with a subdued smile.

The screen door slammed open and two small bodies burst into the store. "Dad! Dad!" Chad and Wendy cried, rushing to their two dads. There had been some dilemma when they first moved to live with Tom and Taylor about what to call them. For a while, they had called them by their first names. Finally, one night after they had rescued Chad from a "monster," he'd asked if it was okay if he called them both Dad. He wanted to make sure his dad, John, wouldn't mind. Tom had told him he thought his dad would be glad to know Chad thought of them as dads. Wendy had naturally followed her brother's suit and little Taylor would never know the difference.

Tom scooped up Wendy while Taylor took Chad. "Where's Grandma?" he asked.

"She's coming," Chad said. Outside, Tom's mom had parked their car in front of the bakery and had Mini-Tay in her arms. She came in, a broad smile on her face to greet them.

"The kids wanted a donut on their way to the park," she explained. Little Taylor rested with his head on her shoulder, a pacifier in his mouth. When he saw Tom, he reached out. Tom lowered Wendy to stand on the floor and took the baby.

"You can each have one donut," Tom said. "Go ask Aunt Emmy or Uncle Eric for whatever kind you'd like and be sure to tell them thank you."

Chad jumped down and ran to the case with his sister. They both stood surveying their options, but unlike most of the children in town, didn't touch the glass. Tom had pointed out to them that if they touched it, someone was going to have to clean it. When that someone turned out to be them, they decided maybe it was easier to leave well enough alone.

"Hi, Mom," Tom greeted, giving her a kiss on the cheek. She took the other seat at the table as Taylor returned with a croissant for her, too. He handed her the plate and gave her a peck on the other cheek.

"You guys are off to the park today?" he asked.

"For a little while, until it gets too hot," Donna said. "Then we're going to get Grandpa and go look at houses."

"So you're definitely moving here?" Gen asked.

Donna nodded, smiling. "Now that we're retired, there's really no reason to be there. Mandy doesn't live at home anymore and the boys can use the help. We like this area and it'll be nice to have family around again."

"Where are you looking?"

"There are some nice homes with property about five miles from here. Don has been wanting to get a couple horses and there are a couple that have good barns on a few acres of land."

"Horseys!" Wendy cheered, crawling up into Tom's lap. "Grandpa's gonna buy horseys!"

"Thanks, Mom," Tom said. "I'm sure you won't mind when they want to spend the weekends at your place…"

Donna shrugged biting into her croissant. "What are grandparents for?"

Gen rose and handed her tray across the counter to Eric. She dusted a couple crumbs from her shirt, facing the table.

"Will I be seeing all of you at the dance this evening?"

Donna shook her head, sipping her iced tea. "Not us," she said. "Don isn't a big dancer, so we're just going to stay home and look after the kids so the boys can all go."

"We'll be there, though," Tom confirmed, his hand resting lightly on Taylor's arm.

Gen smiled. "Good, see you then."

Epilogue

Taylor stood in front of his closet, arms crossed over his bare chest, a smile on his face. What to wear? It was his usual dilemma, and after three plus years with Tom, it was just funny. Instead of rows of clothes, a simple linen shirt, shorts, and sandals faced him—Tom had set out the clothes ahead of time. He shook his head, laughing to himself. There was no doubt that Tom was the organizer of the family. Even after all they'd been through together, it impressed Taylor to watch him juggle their schedules so well.

Reaching into the closet, he took the shirt and slid it on, watching his own reflection in the mirror. He could scarcely believe he was the same person who had come to this town a little over three years ago, his life apparently in pieces around him. In a matter of days, he'd met Tom and everything came together. Somehow, it was always the littlest things that helped remind him.

"Oh good, you found the clothes. I figured I'd save you the drama," Tom said. He had chosen a similar, but not identical, outfit for himself, with a slightly darker shirt and boat shoes. "Mom and Dad are situated with the kids. They're going to take them out to dinner and then go see that new fish movie everybody is talking about. They're just going to keep them overnight."

"Really?" Taylor asked, tucking his shirt and adjusting the belt on his shorts. He slid his feet into the sandals and was ready to go.

"Yeah," Tom confirmed. "They don't want to stay up late and they didn't want us to have to come in early."

"And Wayne and Eric have the apartment," Taylor continued.

Tom smiled the Smile. "Yeah, tough night, huh?" Taylor took his hand and they made their way down to the car, careful to step over the sleeping cat at the door.

The dance was, like all the rest, at the town park. And it was, like all the rest, crowded with members of the town. Gen and Miguel had driven separately, but followed them in. Wayne and Eric met them in the parking lot, having just walked down from the apartment they were sharing over the bakery. They had each opted for simple T-shirts with cargo shorts, comfortably casual.

"You look nice," Eric said, observing Gen's trademark flowered dress. She laughed and gestured to his clothes.

"You look like you're ready to party."

Eric nodded. "Imagine that."

Together, the six of them made their way toward the music, while Tom, Miguel, and Wayne went to get them something to drink. Rob and Mel spotted them and made their way over.

"Evenin', Mr. Mayor, Gen," Rob greeted, a hint of a drawl in his speech. "Nice to see you here tonight." He turned to Eric. "I'm not sure we've met."

Eric held out a hand, smiling. "I'm Eric Driskell, Wayne's boyfriend."

Rob shook his hand and nodded. "Oh, right. I guess we did meet before didn't we? But your hair was longer."

Eric nodded. "Got it cut last week for the summer."

"Got it," Rob said. He turned to Taylor. "See you at the game on Sunday?"

Taylor nodded. "Wouldn't miss it. Tom's just itching to go after that team from Springfield."

"We all are," Rob agreed. "See you on the dance floor."

Mel gave Taylor a wink, then followed her husband toward the crowd. Tom and Wayne returned, carbonated cola beverages in hand for their significant others.

"Hey, Gen, Miguel ran into somebody he knows back at the beer tent. He said he'll be right over."

"Okay, thanks," Gen said. "I'll go track him down."

She headed off and the foursome stood, sipping their drinks. Across the sea of people, Emmy spotted them and waved. Dan followed her gaze, saw them, and waved too. They started to make their way over.

"This is fun," Wayne said. "We missed the spring one. The only other dance I've ever been to is Prom."

"In that case, we need to get you dancing," Tom said, leading the way. Emmy and Dan saw their destination and headed toward them.

As they approached the dance floor, lights pushed back the approaching darkness, flashing a variety of colors on the participants. It was a warm night and everyone was already damp from sweat, but no one seemed to care. As they reached the edge of the crowd, Taylor moved to step around someone.

"Excuse me," he said.

"Taylor?"

He looked back, then stopped cold.

"Faith."

She smiled, albeit self-consciously, and held out a hand. "It's good to see you again," she said. "How have you been?"

Taylor shook her hand briefly, then let it go as Tom came up to stand beside him.

"Good, good," he said. "You?"

"Great, thanks," she nodded. "Hi, Tom."

"Faith." Tom was civil, but none of his characteristic warmth came through. Though Faith's actions had driven the two of them together, he still felt uncomfortable around her.

"Enjoying the evening?" Faith asked.

Taylor nodded. "Yes, it's good. We're just meeting some friends. Are you here with anyone?" He froze as he realized what he'd said. Tom's hand discreetly took his and gave it a very firm squeeze.

Faith nodded. "Yes, I'm here with my fiancé. We're getting married next month."

Tom's grip loosened and Taylor smiled. "Really? That's wonderful. Congratulations."

"Thanks, Taylor," Faith said.

"Well, we really should get out there. Best of luck to you," Taylor said and Tom took his cue to move away.

"You, too," Faith said.

They met Wayne and Eric, who had met Emmy and Dan, on the dance floor. They all started moving to the beat as Emmy came up to Taylor.

"What did *she* want?"

Taylor smiled at Emmy's ever-present protectiveness. "Just to say hello."

"Humph," Emmy said.

The music went on for a few more fast songs, then slowed to something the couples could dance to. They each paired off, swaying together to the music. Tom and Taylor held each other, shoulder to shoulder, cheek to cheek.

"This *is* fun," Tom said, referencing Wayne's earlier comment.

"Makes the chaos of the rest of the time bearable, huh?" Taylor said.

"Always."

Taylor leaned back, looking into Tom's eyes. "So, still the luckiest man in the world?" he asked.

The Taylor Smile appeared and Tom nodded. "Without a doubt," he said, then kissed Taylor.

The music played on and Taylor watched their friends, all gathered around them. Wayne and Eric held each other tightly, moving softly to the music while Emmy and Dan stared into each other's eyes and laughed, their shared good humor too much for either of them. Gen and Miguel and Pete and Anita appeared and nodded to them. Taylor was again forced to reflect on how lucky he was, on how lucky he and Tom were, to have found a place so warm and accepting of them.

They had truly found their peace.

Afterword

"May you live in interesting times."

It's an old quote that can alternately be a blessing or a curse, depending on the intent of he who says it. As *Finding Peace* goes to press, the issues faced by its characters have been receiving national and international attention.

The Supreme Court of the United States has just given what may be one of the most important rulings in its history. On its face, *Lawrence v. Texas* protects the right of two consenting adults to be intimate, without bias toward the nature of the act or the gender of the participants. But, far more importantly, *Lawrence* validates the idea that citizens of the United States have the same rights, regardless of their sexual orientation. *Lawrence v. Texas* is one case—the first of many, no doubt—and hopefully, the catalyst that starts an avalanche that ultimately leads to validation and recognition so that others, like Tom and Taylor, can realize their dream of public union.

Even now, individual states are following the lead set by Vermont in allowing same-sex or non-traditional couples to enjoy protections similar to those of married couples. The week before the U.S. Supreme Court decision, the Canadian government announced it will not appeal a decision by provincial courts that held banning same-sex marriage is unconstitutional. How long will it be before our own government recognizes that marriage is marriage, regardless of the gender of the participants? How long before we can take these deplorable "Defense of Marriage" acts and flush them back to the depths from which they came?

This was also the year of same-sex couples at high school proms. Even as *Lawrence* was being argued before the Court, courageous young people throughout the nation were doing their part by shrugging off the roles society had assigned to them in order to be who they are—and who they want to be. An indication of the changing times, the news created little stir—the kids went, had a good time, and the life continued.

Freedom for glbt individuals is about far more than the right to live their lives. It's about the right of every American to live a life free of discrimination, free from persecution and derision, happy and safe in his or her home. Throughout history, the activists may have changed, but the goal remains the same—women's suffrage, civil rights, gay rights—it's not about "creating" special rights for a given group, but about offering that group the same rights and freedoms as any other. When we extend freedom to a new class, we enhance the collective freedom of us all.

Life is never dull for Taylor and Tom, but they learned, as we all do, to take life one day at a time and to enjoy each day, for it will never come again. In *Finding Faith*, they learned to be true to themselves. In *Finding Peace*, they learned to be true to each other, with a bond and a commitment that not even lack of societal endorsement could break, and to share that strength with others when they needed it. They learned it's both our individual and collective strength that will carry us forward, through these interesting times, into the adventure that lies ahead.

I hope you've enjoyed *Finding Peace*. It has been my singular joy and honor to hear from so many readers from around the world, and to read of their experiences. To all my readers, old and new, I'd love to hear from you. As always, you can reach me by email at *andrew@andrewbarriger.com*, and you can stay up to date on what I'm up to by visiting my website, *www.andrewbarriger.com*.

And yes, there are still more stories to tell—keep an eye out for *Finding Hope*.

May you live in interesting times!

Andrew Barriger
June 2003

0-595-28823-5